Ace Books by Jeanne C. Stein

THE BECOMING
BLOOD DRIVE
THE WATCHER
LEGACY

continued . . .

THE BECOMING

"This is a really, really good book. Anna is a great character, Stein's plotting is adventurous and original, and I think most of my readers would have a great time with *The Becoming*." —Charlaine Harris, *New York Times* bestselling author of *From Dead to Worse*

"*The Becoming* is a cross between MaryJanice Davidson's Undead series, starring Betsy Taylor, and Laurell K. Hamilton's Anita Blake series. [Anna's] a kick-butt bounty hunter—but vampires are a complete surprise to her. Full of interesting twists and turns that will leave readers guessing. *The Becoming* is a great addition to the TBR pile." —*Romance Reviews Today*

"With plot twists, engaging characters and smart writing, this first installment in a new supernatural series has all the marks of a hit. Anna Strong lives up to her name: equally tenacious and vulnerable, she's a heroine with the charm, savvy and intelligence that fans of Laurell K. Hamilton and Kim Harrison will be happy to root for . . . If this debut novel is any indication, Stein has a fine career ahead of her." —*Publishers Weekly*

"In an almost Hitchcockian way, this story keeps you guessing, with new twists and turns coming almost every page. Anna is well named, strong in ways she does not even know. There is a strong element of surprise to it . . . Even if you don't like vampire novels, you ought to give this one a shot." —*Huntress Book Reviews*

"A wonderful new vampire book . . . that will keep you on the edge of your seat." —*Fallen Angel Reviews*

LEGACY

JEANNE C. STEIN

ACE BOOKS, NEW YORK

THE BERKLEY PUBLISHING GROUP
Published by the Penguin Group
Penguin Group (USA) Inc.
375 Hudson Street, New York, New York 10014, USA
Penguin Group (Canada), 90 Eglinton Avenue East, Suite 700, Toronto, Ontario M4P 2Y3, Canada
(a division of Pearson Penguin Canada Inc.)
Penguin Books Ltd., 80 Strand, London WC2R 0RL, England
Penguin Group Ireland, 25 St. Stephen's Green, Dublin 2, Ireland (a division of Penguin Books Ltd.)
Penguin Group (Australia), 250 Camberwell Road, Camberwell, Victoria 3124, Australia
(a division of Pearson Australia Group Pty. Ltd.)
Penguin Books India Pvt. Ltd., 11 Community Centre, Panchsheel Park, New Delhi—110 017, India
Penguin Group (NZ), 67 Apollo Drive, Rosedale, North Shore 0632, New Zealand
(a division of Pearson New Zealand Ltd.)
Penguin Books (South Africa) (Pty.) Ltd., 24 Sturdee Avenue, Rosebank, Johannesburg 2196,
South Africa

Penguin Books Ltd., Registered Offices: 80 Strand, London WC2R 0RL, England

This is a work of fiction. Names, characters, places, and incidents either are the product of the author's imagination or are used fictitiously, and any resemblance to actual persons, living or dead, business establishments, events, or locales is entirely coincidental. The publisher does not have any control over and does not assume any responsibility for author or third-party websites or their content.

LEGACY

An Ace Book / published by arrangement with the author

PRINTING HISTORY
Ace mass-market edition / September 2008

Copyright © 2008 by Jeanne C. Stein.
Cover art by Cliff Nielsen.
Cover design by Judith Lagerman.
Interior text design by Kristin del Rosario.

ISBN: 978-0-441-01626-6

ACE
Ace Books are published by The Berkley Publishing Group,
a division of Penguin Group (USA) Inc.,
375 Hudson Street, New York, New York 10014.
ACE and the "A" design are trademarks belonging to Penguin Group (USA) Inc.

PRINTED IN THE UNITED STATES OF AMERICA

10 9 8 7 6 5 4 3 2

To my first writing partner and good friend, Miyoko Hensley, slaying her own demons with style and grace

To family, those related by blood and those related by the heart

To the writing community, critiquers, publishers, booksellers

And to readers, those who attend conference panels and those who write to say they love my books and those who simply buy the books and remain anonymous—

Anna and I thank you.

I 'VE BEEN A VAMPIRE FOR SIX MONTHS.
During that time I've gotten used to drinking human blood, experienced the exquisite *pleasure* of the blood drive, the union of blood and sex.

That's the good part.

In that same six months, my home was burned to the ground and my best friend and business partner kidnapped and almost killed by a vampire who said that he would show me the way. Avery said that he loved me.

He lied.

I learned I had a thirteen-year-old niece from the woman who pimped her out to men for money—her mother. Then found out that *she* had lied.

About everything.

Trish is not my niece, yet I perpetuated the lie so my parents could become the kid's guardian. A gift to them when I can be their child no longer.

I lost my human lover, Max, because he learned what I

am in the worst possible way—he saw me in action. Saw me turn and kill as a vampire.

Recently, I separated myself from my vampire mentor and the Watchers, an organization that teaches supernaturals how to survive in today's world. Part of my job was to terminate rogue vamps. It's not that I didn't like the work. I liked it too well.

I'm determined to live as human. Sometimes it's hell. Sometimes, like today, it seems easy.

CHAPTER 1

WHEN I WAS HUMAN, I HATED THE HOLIDAYS. Hated the inescapable dirge of mindless Christmas songs. Hated being force-fed hope and joy. Hated the contrived joviality. To me, Christmas was a stark reminder that in a few days, my brother would be dead yet another year, killed in a senseless accident a few days after "the haphappiest time of the year."

Yet here I am this mid-December afternoon fourteen years later, a big dumb grin on my face, enduring a crush of smelly humanity for the chance to help my niece pick out a gift for my mother.

My niece.

I can say that now without the mental quotation marks around "niece."

In a couple of months, Trish has become as much a member of my family as I am. Maybe more so since she's human and I'm not.

I'm a vampire.

Another thing I have come to be able to admit (only to

myself, naturally) without an internal shudder of disgust or shame.

I'm a vampire.

I accept it, like being blond or having green eyes. I wasn't born a vampire. I was made one. I've adapted to the reality of the situation, and truth be told, can forget about it for, oh, minutes at a time.

"Aunt Anna?"

I love the sound of that. I can't help myself. I respond by giving the beautiful, healthy thirteen-year-old girl at my side a hug.

She pulls away, but she's grinning. "What was that for?"

"No reason. Did you decide?"

We're in Horton Plaza, at Tiffany's, a selection of earrings spread on a velvet mat in front of us. I am standing to the left of Trish, out of mirror range, since casting no reflection is one of the drawbacks of being a vampire who lives among mortals. I can also watch Trish unobserved and marvel at how far she's come in the last three months.

When I first met her, Trish Delaney was a runaway. Her mother, Carolyn, showed up at my parents' house one night and announced that Trish was their grandchild. Carolyn, whom we hadn't seen since my brother died, concocted an elaborate story about not finding out she was pregnant until after my brother's death and being too scared to approach my parents for fear they would react the same way hers had—demand she have an abortion. She came to us then because she was afraid Trish was in real trouble—involved in drugs and murder—and had nowhere else to turn. She also came because she knew what I did for a living. I'm a bounty hunter by trade and expert at finding people.

And we bought it.

Turns out, most of the story was a lie. Carolyn was the one who turned Trish over to her abusers, for money. She's dead now, and the dirtbag directly responsible for what happened to Trish is dead, too. Three others are awaiting trial. We're hoping they'll plead out so Trish won't have to relive the horror. Trish understands that they may not.

But for now, here she is—a long-legged thirteen-year-old teetering on the verge of womanhood who can smile and laugh and feel secure in the knowledge she has finally found a family that she does not have to fear. If the worst happens and she has to testify at a trial, she knows we'll be right there with her. In the meantime, we're going to enjoy the holidays.

As a family.

Trish has an earring in each hand. "It's between these two. Which do you like better?"

One is a knot of gold, the size of a dime. The other, a delicate filigree hoop.

"The hoops. Mom likes hoops."

Trish holds the chosen one up to her own ear and checks the mirror. "I like these, too." She hands the earrings over to the salesperson. "We'll take these, please."

The saleswoman is a thirtysomething sleek-haired brunette wearing a shade of red lipstick that would brand me as a tart. On her, it looks regal. She smiles and slips the tray with our discarded choices behind the counter and nods to me.

I properly interpret the nod but defer to Trish with a shrug. "My niece is buying."

One carefully shaped eyebrow lifts the tiniest fraction. "And how would you like to pay, miss?" she asks Trish.

Trish returns the smile. "Cash."

The saleswoman nods and turns to ring up the purchase.

"Are you sure you have enough cash?" I whisper to Trish. "Because I can—"

Trish's face glows. "I want to do this myself," she says.

"Without Grandma and Grandpa Strong, I don't know where I'd be right now. I want to show them how much I appreciate everything they've done for me."

I give her shoulder a squeeze. Unfortunately, I do know where she'd be. Either with a truly miserable bitch, her real grandmother, or in a foster home. Hard to say which of those alternatives would have been worse.

Which is why I made the decision I did. Neither Trish nor my parents know that she is not really my brother's child. DNA tests confirmed it, tests that I've buried. I'll never be sure if Carolyn knew the truth or not. It doesn't matter. Trish is where she belongs and if I have any say in the matter, where she'll stay.

The saleswoman is back. "That will be $297.80," she tells Trish.

Trish grins at me, pulls three one-hundred-dollar bills out of her wallet and hands them over. About the only good thing Carolyn Delaney did in her last months on earth was to take out an insurance policy naming Trish as beneficiary. Maybe she sensed that the mess she'd gotten them in would not end well. Maybe it was a pathetic attempt to tell Trish she was sorry when that end came. In any case, most of the money went into a college fund, but my parents thought Trish should use some of it on herself.

What Trish has done is use most of it on gifts for her new family.

The only thing nicer than Trish looking so happy that she can pay for the earrings herself is the expression on her face when the saleswoman comes back with one of those delicious blue Tiffany signature boxes. She slips the box into a matching bag and hands it to Trish along with her change.

Trish is beaming.

I feel like I must be beaming, too. At least until we ease our way back into the throng circling Horton Plaza. The

shoppers have the look of hungry wolves. More desperation than inspiration on these less-than-happy faces. You'd
think there were only two shopping days left before the big
day instead of two weeks.

This many pulsing jugulars makes my own anxiety start
to peak. The hair prickles on the back of my neck.

Time for a break. "I would kill for a cup of coffee," I tell
Trish, when in fact what I'm feeling is I'll kill if I don't get
a cup of coffee.

"Starbucks?" Trish asks. "Or do you want to try the coffee bar at that new restaurant?"

Since that new restaurant belongs to someone I'd give
up drinking coffee to avoid—my business partner's ex-
girlfriend Gloria—it takes me a millisecond to respond.
"Starbucks."

Definitely, Starbucks.

We reverse directions and head toward Broadway.

Usually, my senses are on high alert when I'm in a
crowd. It's natural and instinctive. The animal side of my
nature scans the air like bug antennae for any sign of danger, for any vibration of impending doom.

This time, the internal radar fails miserably.

My breath catches in my throat.

It's suddenly right in front of us.

As if conjured up from my worst nightmare, she's slipped
like a cockroach right past all my defenses.

I clutch Trish's shoulders, ready to propel her in the opposite direction.

Too late.

A hand reaches out and stops me with a firm grip.

Trish is smiling, unaware of the peril.

"Hey, Gloria," she says. "David didn't tell us you were
back in town."

CHAPTER 2

I STARE. GLORIA IS NOT SUPPOSED TO BE IN TOWN. She's supposed to be in Los Angeles or New York, doing whatever the hell supermodels do.

Shit.

Gloria aims her thousand-watt smile at Trish. "He doesn't know yet," she says. Then she puts a finger over her lips. "I want to surprise him so if you see him first, don't spoil it, okay?"

Trish nods that the secret is safe. "We were going for coffee. Want to join us?"

Shit. Shit. Shit.

With all the obnoxious, rude teenagers in the world, my family has to end up with a nice, polite one. My insides curl into a ball.

I'm saved by a shake of Gloria's auburn mane. "I can't, honey. I do need a word with your aunt. Do you mind?"

Trish nods again. When Gloria doesn't immediately launch into whatever it is she needs to tell me, Trish accepts that it's one of those adult things and moves off to look at some decorations in a nearby store window.

I watch Trish, then turn reluctantly to fix my attention on my least favorite person, human or otherwise, in the entire world.

Gloria Estrella is a model and an actress. A well-known model and actress. Now, as we stand here in Horton Plaza, life seems to shift into slow motion as those passing around us cast one look at her and falter in their steps. Even though half-obscured behind oversize sunglasses, women recognize the heart-shaped face, the huge almond eyes, the artfully tussled mane of shoulder-length hair. Men recognize the tits and long legs. She has on jeans and a cashmere sweater and three-inch Ferragamo pumps, but men know what's underneath. They see the Victoria's Secret model prancing on TV ads in thong underwear and a push-up bra every damned day.

I hate her.

She hates me right back. Usually, we avoid each other like I avoid garlic. She's noxious to my system.

Which makes her desire to talk to me that much more puzzling. As far as I know, we have nothing to talk about. Gloria used to date my partner, David. Used to, being the operative phrase. Gloria hasn't seen David in two months. I had begun to believe I'd never have to see her again. It was a wonderful, liberating fantasy.

I shift from one foot to the other. "How did you know I was here?"

Gloria slips the glasses off her face. "I saw you in Tiffany's."

Terrific. Remind me never to shop in Horton Plaza again. "What do you want? Can't be about David. Last I heard you'd broken up."

She tilts her head. "Why would you think that?"

"Why? Maybe because David was shot and you didn't bother to call to see how he was doing."

She drops her eyes. "Oh, that."

Oh, that? David was laid up for two fucking months. He had been shot by a psycho hit man who held us responsible because we got his guy into custody before he could make good on a contract. Gloria didn't call or come by once during David's convalescence. I know. I took care of him myself.

"I have to talk to David. In fact, I planned to go by your office this afternoon. I can explain it to him. I can make it up to him."

Her faltering tone implies she's not as confident as she pretends. Good.

I narrow my eyes at her. "I wouldn't bother if I were you. David hasn't mentioned you once. I think he's over you. Finally. For good."

She bristles at that and the bitch shines through. "Don't kid yourself, Anna. David still loves me. He's left me dozens of messages. Got one this morning, in fact. Do you want to know what he said?"

I'm shocked at this bit of news. So shocked my traitorous body reacts with an involuntary start. David never tried to contact Gloria when I was around. I can't believe he went behind my back. A flush of anger creeps up my neck.

Gloria catches the reaction and smiles.

Damn her. "Whatever you have to say, make it fast. Trish and I have more shopping to do."

She looks over at Trish. "She's a beautiful girl. Do you think she'd be interested in modeling?"

After what Trish has been through, the last thing my family wants is to have her exposed yet again. There are two reasons I don't jump down Gloria's throat right now for suggesting it. Trish really *is* beautiful enough to be a model, and Gloria doesn't know what happened to her. Hopefully, she never will.

It takes effort, but I moderate my anger and reply gruffly, "She's only a freshman in high school. She's too young to be subjected to that kind of life."

My tone clearly implies that what I mean by "that kind of life" is nothing good and that it's directed at Gloria, but surprisingly, she doesn't bite. In fact, she doesn't pursue the subject or the insult.

The muscles at the base of my neck tighten. This is not Gloria. I study her more closely. For the first time, I notice frown lines at the corners of her mouth and faint dark circles under her eyes. Through the makeup, her perfect face is shadowed by what? Worry? Grief?

I stifle the urge to clap my hands and do a happy dance.

However, doing that would imply I care. The truth is, if it wasn't for what she said, that David has been in touch with her, I'd be out of here in a heartbeat. As much as I dislike her, I care for David more. He finds something in Gloria that touches him. I can't see it but evidently, he's not over her the way I'd thought.

"You didn't stop me to talk about Trish. What do you want?"

Her gaze pulls away from Trish. "I need your help."

"With what? Your Christmas shopping? If you think I'm going to waste my time helping you get back in David's good graces, you'd better think again. I have more important things to do."

Gloria doesn't respond. She shifts uneasily from one foot to the other, her hands in fists at her sides, her eyes darting over the crowd like a rabbit ready to bolt at the approach of a fox. When she looks at me again, there's no mistaking the emotion clouding her eyes.

"I may be in trouble," she says finally. "Big trouble."

In that instant, I know what she says is true. Her irritation and anger are gone, swept away by a more powerful emotion. An emotion my vampire nature can pick out of the air like a bad smell.

Fear.

CHAPTER 3

FEAR UNLEASHES THE SAME REACTIONS IN A VAM-
pire that it does in humans. Flight or fight. Only in
vampires, those reactions are exaggerated. Right now, the
vibe rolling off Gloria makes me want to get as far away
from her as I can. I haven't heard Gloria's story. I don't
know or care what her problem is. From what I'm picking
up, my instincts are screaming that to be standing with her
in this public place is dangerous.

Not for me.

For Trish, one of the humans I care about more than my
own life.

I listen to my instincts.

I hold up a hand. "I won't do this with Trish here. I'm
taking her home. I'll be back in an hour. You want to meet
at the office? Or at David's?"

She shakes her head. "I have to go to the restaurant.
Will you meet me there?"

"Should I call David?" It galls me to ask, but David just

recovered from one bad situation. If there's another brewing, he damn well should know.

"No." The answer is abrupt. "I need to talk to you alone first."

If I'd been alone, I would have grilled her about that. I'm not alone. Without another word, I turn away from her and beckon to Trish.

Trish raises an eyebrow when I explain that I'll have to take her home. Still, she doesn't argue or complain. Not the way a "normal" teenager would react to disappointment. Trish's life has been far from normal, and the therapist she's been seeing says it will be a while before she can express any negative feelings. She's still too afraid we'll send her away.

It makes me incredibly sad.

On the ride back to my parents, I let her prattle on with a steady stream of excited, cheerful banter about the coming holidays. I join in, but my mind is on Gloria. I've never seen her like that—subdued, solemn, scared.

Whatever's going on with her must be big.

Trish leaves her packages with me and starts up the steps to the house. My mom is at the door to let her in before she reaches it. Mom's dressed in sweats, her hair pulled back, a flour-stained apron tucked around her slender frame. She waves a jaunty hand and gestures for me to come in.

For a moment, I'm plunged into the depths of a memory. My brother and I coming back from a shopping trip and finding Mom in the kitchen, wearing a holiday apron decorated with another smear of flour, the sweet aroma of sugar cookies filling the house.

I suddenly want more than anything to join them. An ache in the middle of my chest, a visceral, physical longing, is strong enough to make me reconsider my promise to Gloria. What kind of trouble could she be in?

The kind of trouble that brought her to her worst enemy to ask for help.

Reluctantly, I roll down the passenger-side window and explain that I can't join them because I have an appointment. I see them in the rearview mirror, Mom and Trish, their arms entwined as I pull away.

To deny me this time with my family makes my resentment of Gloria grow. If her life wasn't in serious danger before, it is now.

"Glory's" is the too cute name Gloria and her business partner, Rory O'Sullivan, came up with for the restaurant. By the time I arrive, it's five in the afternoon. Too early for the dinner crowd, but not the TGIFers. The bar is hopping. The restaurant is at the Broadway end of Horton Plaza. It attracts clientele from nearby retail stores as well as lawyers and judges from the two courthouse facilities a couple of blocks away and bureaucrats from federal and city offices next door. In my jeans, blazer and Nikes, I'm the only non-suit in sight.

It draws attention. I don't know what men think when they look at me, but I know how they act. As I push through the happy-hour crowd, more than one restraining hand and questioning smile is directed my way. Under different circumstances, I might pursue it, an opportunity for a night of unencumbered fun and games. Being a vampire is liberating in that sense. But not tonight. Tonight I'm here for a reason. For Gloria's sake, it had better be a good one.

I ignore the smiles and invitations for drinks and head for the door at the back of the bar. I knock once and push it open.

Gloria is seated behind a desk, staring out the window at the caterpillar of lights on Broadway heading down toward the waterfront. She doesn't turn at the sound of the door opening. I don't think she knows I'm in the room.

"Gloria?"

She jumps, nearly out of the chair, and whirls to face me.

The look on her face, as if I'd done something wrong by coming in, makes me want to turn around and march out. "You told me to meet you here, remember? What the hell is wrong with you?"

Her expression loses its edge, becomes apologetic. "Sorry."

Gloria apologizing to me? It's the end of the world as we know it.

I park my butt on the corner of the desk. "I'm here. You have two minutes to tell me why I should stay."

Gloria's eyes cloud. "I'm in trouble."

"I heard that the first time. What kind of trouble?"

I've known Gloria for five years. Never has she looked at me the way she's looking at me now, with something other than condescension or malice in her expression. I wish she'd stop. I'm much more comfortable with the old hate/hate relationship. She looks scared and it's unnerving. "Well? You're down to ninety seconds and counting."

Suddenly she starts to cry.

Cry.

I jump up. Then I remember. She's an actress.

But those are real tears running down her cheeks, and there's real snot running out of that five-thousand-dollar nose job. Her face is red and blotchy.

This is not theatrical crying. This is for real.

I'm so stunned, I don't know how to react. In spite of the sobs shaking her shoulders, I can't bring myself to put a consoling arm around her. This is Gloria, my arch nemesis, after all. I do the only other thing I can think of. I grab a box of tissues from the credenza under the window and shove it at her.

"Here," I command gruffly. "Clean yourself up. Tears are murder on cashmere."

She pulls a couple of tissues from the box and dabs ineffectually at her face, leaving a trail of mascara and eye-liner to mark the path of her tears. Now she looks like a deranged raccoon.

It takes great effort on my part not to mention it.

I wait for Gloria to compose herself. I'm only going to ask what's wrong once more. If I don't get an answer, I'm out of here.

"If this is about smoothing things over between you and David, you can't believe how wrong you were to come to me. I've been deliriously happy to think he'd dumped you. You've done nothing but try to undermine our business relationship for as long as I've known you. Don't think for one minute I'd plead your case—"

I'm getting warmed up when Gloria throws me another of those unfathomable looks. A plea? For what? It stops me cold.

She pushes back from the desk and stands up. "You know who my business partner is?"

I could be living in a cave and I'd know who Gloria's business partner is. Rory O'Sullivan is second only to Donald Trump in notoriety. He's a billionaire. A collector of high-end real estate, art and classic cars. He inherited a modest fortune and parlayed it into a megafortune. I think he's listed as the fifth or sixth richest man in America.

All this flashes through my head in the time it takes me to say, "Yes, I know who your business partner is. What about him?"

Gloria has crossed to the wall opposite the windows. She studies her reflection in a huge gilt mirror. I take a careful step out of mirror shot as she wets a tissue with the tip of her tongue and carefully wipes away the ruined makeup.

Only when she's finished does she square her shoulders and walk back to the desk. "Please sit, Anna. I need to tell you something."

That sounds more like the Gloria I know and hate. The

"please" is uttered as a formality. It's an order from the queen. Still, she has piqued my curiosity. I don't take a seat but lean against the far wall, crossing my arms and nodding at her to go ahead.

"What I'm about to tell you has to stay in this room," she begins. She doesn't wait for me to agree or disagree. As usual, she assumes her word is the world's command. "Rory and I went into business together to start this restaurant. It was simply another business deal for him. For me, it was much more. It was a chance to ease my way out of the beauty business and into something different."

She flashes a deprecating smile. "You have no idea how stressful the life of a celebrity can be. You see only the glamour and the clothes and the prestige . . ."

She lets her voice drop as if waiting for me to confirm. Truth is, the only thing I see when I look at Gloria is arrogance and conceit and ego. The trifecta of the self-indulgent bimbo. I shrug at her to get on with it.

She misinterprets the gesture as concurrence but does continue, which is, after all, what I want.

"Rory seemed the perfect partner. He had experience in the restaurant industry and the clout to attract a top chef. He oversaw all the details from furnishing the place to stocking the bar to hiring the help. We invested equal amounts of money, but really what he wanted from me was image and contacts. Show up here when I'm in town and get my show business friends to patronize the place when they are."

She stops, breathless from the exertion of telling the story. She glances back at me, her lips trembling. She's about to start crying again.

"Gloria, this is old news. What's your point?"

She pinches the bridge of her nose between a thumb and forefinger as if to stop the renewed threat of tears. She draws a deep breath. I wait, counting. If she hasn't picked up the narrative by the time I get to ten—

"Yes, there is a point."

She made it under the wire. I was up to eight.

"Rory is blackmailing me."

The obvious questions spring to my lips. "Why? What did you do?"

This time the old Gloria flashes through. "How like you. To assume I did something. Why is it so hard for you to see me as a victim?"

At least she didn't say "innocent" victim. I lean toward her. "There aren't enough hours in the day to answer that."

She frowns, and for a minute, I think she's going to lash out. Once again, she surprises me by backing down. "I understand why you might feel that way, but you have to believe me; I'm not to blame for this."

Her tone is sincere, she's not fidgeting, her eyes don't slither away from my gaze. Could she actually be telling the truth?

I try a different tack. "Rory O'Sullivan is a prominent man. If he's ready to risk jail by blackmailing you, he must have a powerful reason. He's not doing it for money. What does he want?"

"What do you think?" Gloria's tone is peevish, the tone of a spoiled child, the tone of one who thinks the answer to that question should be obvious.

It's not obvious to me.

"I'm not going to play twenty questions with you, Gloria. What does he want?"

She heaves a long, deep sigh. "He wants me to sleep with him."

A pause. This time the eyes do slide away.

"Again."

CHAPTER 4

"HE WANTS YOU TO WHAT? OH MY GOD! ARE YOU fucking kidding me?" I'm screeching like a scalded cat. I can't help it. Neither can I help lunging toward Gloria. It takes great effort not to bare my fangs and howl. My fist connects with a crystal hunk on the top of the desk, and it flies across the room and crashes into the wall.

"You pulled me away from a wonderful afternoon with my niece because of this bullshit?"

Gloria looks stunned at my reaction. "That paperweight was a gift from David. You broke it."

I snatch up another crystal knickknack and heft it. For two cents, I'd hurl it at her cheating head.

She raises both hands in front of her face and takes a step back. "Anna, please. This is serious. Rory won't take no for an answer. He keeps pushing and pushing. He's threatening to go to David. To tell him that we've slept together. You know how David will react."

"I know how I hope he'll react."

She pays no attention. "It will kill him. He may do something foolish."

I'm shaking I'm so angry. I hold the crystal whatever-it-is like a weapon and advance on her. "I have an idea. I'll save O'Sullivan the trouble. I'll tell David. It will give me great pleasure."

Gloria is smart enough not to argue, to remain quiet for a minute before offering a subdued rebuttal. "I know you don't like me," she says softly. "But think about how this will affect David. He still adores me."

I glare down at her. "I don't know that. In fact, I only have your word that he wants to get back together with you."

She leans over and picks up her purse. She opens it and pulls out a cell phone. Without a word, she scrolls until she finds what she's looking for, queues up a message and holds it out to me when it begins to play.

"Gloria. It's David. Again. I miss you. Please call me. I don't know what I did to make you angry, but whatever it is, I want a chance to make up for it. Please, baby. I love you."

She lets the message indicator play, too. The time of the message was ten fifteen, December 14. This morning.

She lays the phone on the desk, waiting for my reaction. Her expression is carefully neutral. It's a good thing. One smile of smug satisfaction and I would hurl this knick-knack at her.

As it is, I pass a hand over my face, take a deep breath and ask, "What possessed you to come to me with this? You must have known how I'd react."

"It's simple. I love David. I know you love him, too. You don't want him to get hurt."

Her reply surprises me. Or maybe it's the way she says it. She actually sounds as if she means it, but there's something else. A thrill of apprehension touches my spine.

"Has Rory threatened to do more than *speak* to David?"

She looks away.

I reach over and grab her chin with my hand, forcing her to face me. "Has he?"

She flinches and draws a quick breath. "I don't think he'd really do anything to him. If you'd talk to Rory. Tell him you'll go to the authorities, or the press, if he doesn't leave me alone. Tell him you have connections in the police force. Tell him you'll have him arrested for harassment or something if he doesn't stop. He'll listen to you. I know he will because you'll make him."

It bubbles out of her in a torrent. When she finally runs down, I step back from the desk, afraid if I don't put some distance between us, I'll give in to the impulse to bitch slap her across the room.

I shift the thing in my hand and see it's a crystal clock. I toss it from one hand to the other, thinking. I've seen pictures of O'Sullivan. I can't tell from a picture how big he is, but my partner is an ex–football player and I *know* how big David is. I also know he can take care of himself.

But thinking about the picture makes another image skitter through my head like a rat released from a trap. "O'Sullivan is married. He was here with his wife and kid for the opening of this place."

She lowers her eyes. "That's why I thought sleeping with him the one time would be harmless." She emphasizes "the one time" as if the qualifier makes it excusable.

"Unbelievable. Only you would call adultery harmless. So turn the tables on him. Tell him you'll go to his wife. Or the press. He has as much to lose as you do. More since this is a community-property state."

She shakes her head. "I tried that. He doesn't care. He says he and his wife have an open marriage and the publicity might actually be good. For both of us. He likes the idea of being seen as a philanderer. Improves his bad-boy image, and if we're seen as a couple, that won't do the restaurant business any harm, either. Anna, he's not normal."

"And you are? Christ. You betray David, and now you want my help to keep it from him. Why should I?"

Gloria pauses, then her face brightens as if my asking that question is a good thing. "I know what you're thinking, how this looks." Her tone glimmers with hope. "The night it happened, David and I had a fight. A bad one. I was vulnerable and Rory took advantage of it."

Gloria vulnerable? Beyond belief. I have an easier time picturing a rhinoceros being victimized by a flea. "When did this happen?"

"A couple of months ago. You were off doing—whatever it is you do when you disappear."

She cuts herself off with a sharp intake of breath.

Too late.

"You're saying the fight was about me? That this was my fault?" She doesn't have to answer. It's there on her face. "Oh, Gloria, you are dumber than a sack of hair if you think I'd help you."

There's a long, tense silence while we stare at each other. I don't know why I don't walk out. I don't know why I'm not pulling her hair out and screaming. I don't understand any of it until it hits. The flash of inspiration. It must have been simmering in the back of my mind from the moment Gloria mentioned the word "blackmail."

This could be the opportunity I've been waiting for.

I smile. "You know what, Gloria. I've changed my mind. I will talk to Rory."

Relief softens the lines around her mouth until she realizes I'm not quite finished.

"In return, you are going to do something for me."

The frown comes back.

I wish I could tell her she was going to disappear out of David's life forever, but that isn't my call. What I can do is see that she's out of mine.

"If you and David do work things out, you are never going to denigrate me to him again. You will never disparage our partnership or try to convince him to find someone else to work with. You are going to become my biggest fan."

Gloria's mouth opens in protest, but promptly closes again. I see the wheels turning in her rattrap of a brain. She's trying to figure how long this deal would have to stand.

"Forever, Gloria."

"And if I don't agree?"

"Then you'll have two people blackmailing you."

It's her turn to stare at me. I'm patient. I'm immortal. I stare back until she comes to the only conclusion she can.

"All right. I agree."

"Great. Where can I find Rory?"

She releases a long sigh. "He'll be here tonight. Around midnight. Can you be here then?"

Good. I want to get this over with. I smile a toothy smile at Gloria. "One thing you need to understand. This is a onetime deal. You fuck around on David again . . ."

Gloria folds her arms in a weary gesture across her chest. "You may not believe this," she says. "But I really do love him."

I toss the clock to her and she almost trips over her own feet to catch it.

She's right.

I don't believe it.

CHAPTER 5

I'M SO KEYED UP WHEN I LEAVE GLORIA, I CAN hardly stand it. My skin feels too tight, my nerves tingle like exposed electrical wire. There's only one sure thing that relieves pressure for a vampire. Well, two things, actually. Unfortunately, I don't have a sex partner right now and Gloria has made me so angry I don't trust myself with an unsuspecting human male. I have to do the next best thing. Feed.

Needing human blood to subsist has its problems. It's not like you can walk into a hospital and ask for a transfusion. Even if you could, it would be of no use to the vampire. Blood that's been pushed through tubes and refrigerated loses its essence.

Hunting on your own can lead to unfortunate consequences. While the existence of vampires is a secret well kept from most of society, there is a faction that not only knows we exist, but makes it a mission to exterminate us. Leaving hysterical victims or desiccated corpses is a sure way to attract unwanted attention.

What's a vampire who needs fresh, warm, straight-from-the-donor blood to do?

Luckily, I know.

It's a little after six, and I have plenty of time. Beso de la Muerte is a Mexican "ghost town" not on any map. It's about an hour from San Diego, depending on traffic and the backup at the border. My need is great and my car is fast. I make it in forty-five minutes.

As I pull into town, if that's what you can call a dirt road lined with decrepit wooden buildings, I'm amazed to see three dozen motorcycles lined up in front of the saloon. I've been coming here since the beginning of my vampire existence, and usually there's a car once in a while. But I've never seen anything like this.

I have to park a good block from where I want to go, and walk. The bikes, all Harleys, gleam under a half-moon like jewels. Softails. Fat Boys. Big V-Twins: Flatheads and Knuckleheads. Custom and vintage bikes that set their owners back serious money.

The throbbing beat of a heavy-metal band pierces the desert quiet. I know the owner of the place, Culebra, and this is not his type of music. He prefers the shrill cheerful wailings of Mexican corrido music. If he's agreed to play what I'm hearing now, it can only be because the patrons inside are spending a shitload of money.

I send out a mental probe—testing to see if I can determine who or what is inside. I get nothing back. No vibrations that indicate otherworldly beings. A raging libido jumps into overdrive along with my salivary glands. Humans who come here do so for two reasons: they are willing to allow vampires to feed from them and/or they have been granted Culebra's protection for one reason or the other. In either case, if the bikes belong to humans, I'm sure to get what I need.

I'm sifting possibilities through my head as I approach

the door. Humans agree to be donors not only for the money they are paid, but because it is an erotic, extremely pleasurable experience. If you are a vampire, combining feeding with sex is pleasure amplified a thousandfold. It's taken me a while to get over the hang-up of indiscriminate sex/feeding with a stranger. I've come to accept it as one of nature's ironies. Take procreation away from the vampire, but make the act so agonizingly pleasurable that the vampire craves sex as much as he craves blood.

Still, I'm not ready to do what most of my vamp pals have—establish a monogamous relationship. "Marry" a human to have both a partner and host. Not that I have that option. At the moment, I don't have a human boyfriend.

Which is where Beso de la Muerte comes in.

I push through the swinging doors. The place smells of pot and patchouli. I'm glad I don't breathe anymore. Two deep breaths, and I'd be high.

No one pays the least bit of attention to me as I make my way through the crowd. It's largely female. Amazon women dressed head to toe in leather, sporting jackets with an insignia I've never seen before—a wolf superimposed against a full moon. They're loud. Brittle laughter and shrill voices compete with the throb of the music.

I look around for my friend, Culebra. He's a shape-shifter and the owner of this supernatural safe house. He's not behind the bar. His mortal employee and a woman I don't recognize are bartending. I send out a mental greeting.

Culebra? Are you here?

At first, there's no response. Then I detect a ripple in the karmic fabric that feels a lot like alarm. I'm about to follow the path of the transmission when Culebra bursts from the back room.

What are you doing here, Anna?

Not exactly welcoming.

Nice to see you, too.

His distress at my presence blazes forth like an astral flare. His thoughts radiate a peculiar vibe I can't read and he's shut down the conduit between us that would allow me to understand what's provoking his reaction. It's a cerebral roadblock that ratchets my frustration up another notch.

What's the problem? I had a stressful day. I want to feed. I make a sweeping gesture with my hand. *Plenty of humans in here.*

He steps close and the lines around his mouth tighten. *There are no donors here for you. You should go. Now. Come back tomorrow.*

No donors? The place is full of them.

No, Anna. You won't want to feed from anyone here. Trust me.

I don't. It doesn't make sense. *You'd better explain. I'm not picking up any mental vibes. No shape-shifters. No vamps, either, that I can detect.* I stop and reconsider, "tasting" the air like a dog sniffs for a scent. Something is coming through that I hadn't picked up on earlier. *Okay. There is one vamp. In the back. She's feeding. Why can't I?*

Culebra has a face that Sergio Leone would have cast as a villain in one of his spaghetti westerns. Craggy, world-weary, expressive.

Right now, the expression is embarrassment—a strange emotion coming from one who has been nothing but a good friend to me. What could possibly be causing this kind of reaction?

Unless he's trying to protect me from something—or someone.

Who's in the back?

No answer. But I know I've hit on something. He's exerting such great effort to shield that information from me mentally that he doesn't detect the physical movement behind him.

A vamp walks into the room, a tall, willowy redhead with

a sprinkling of freckles across the bridge of her nose and green eyes shining with contentment. She acknowledges me, a fellow vamp, with a subtle nod of her head. She doesn't shield her thoughts. Why should she? She detects no threat. She's fed and she's had sex. She's content. She's holding the arm of the donor whose expression mirrors her own. He's a big man, walking with a slight limp. When he looks up and sees me, his eyes flicker, his face goes blank.

For an instant.

Then he smiles. A cold, impersonal smile.

"Hello, Anna."

The vamp looks from one of us to the other, a spark of interest quirks one perfectly shaped eyebrow. *You two know each other?*

Oh, yes. It takes a minute for me to recover from the shock. Another to acknowledge her question with a nod. Oh, yes, we know each other.

"Hello, Max."

·

CHAPTER 6

M Y VOICE ECHOES IN MY HEAD, COLD, SHARP AS the crack of ice on a frozen pond.

Max and I stare at each other.

"This is getting to be a bad habit." The bitterness in his voice is as obvious as the vamp on his arm.

I don't respond. I don't need to. I know exactly what he means. This isn't the first time we've run into each other unexpectedly here in Beso de la Muerte. He's a DEA agent, or at least he was the last time I saw him. He and Culebra have worked together. Neither has ever explained how or why, and I haven't pushed.

Tonight, though, is different. These circumstances are different.

I'm struck dumb by what I see in front of me. I can't take my eyes off the man who, until a few months ago, was my boyfriend and lover. Max and I have had an on-and-off relationship for the last few years. The off times have always been my fault; I accept that. When he walked out of my life for good, he did it because he found out what I was. He saw me turn. He saw me kill. The circumstances warranted it. Still, I assumed he couldn't come to terms with a girlfriend who needed to suck more than the obvious every few weeks.

To find him here, and know that he and this vampire shared what he didn't want to share with me, provokes hurt and confusion. I don't deal well with those emotions. When I was human, I tended to wield them like a double-edged sword against whoever had the bad fortune to injure me. That hasn't changed. Instead of beating my breast and asking him why, I revert to the familiar. I attack.

"Well, well. This is interesting. You decide getting fucked by a strange vampire is better than getting fucked by one you know?"

The vamp with Max takes a step back. *Whoa,* she says. *I didn't know he belonged to someone. He showed up and offered himself.*

At the same time she's conveying that message to me telepathically, Max is throwing me a puzzled frown. "How did you know we had sex?"

I feel my face split into a sour smile. "I smell it on you. Was it good, Max? It must have been to overcome your sensibilities about screwing a vampire. Which is why I assumed you left me."

His expression hardens, confusion into anger. "Don't lay that on me, Anna. You hid what you were from me for months. You would never have told me at all if I hadn't been there to see it."

He's right. Hiding what I've become from the mortals I want to stay close to has been the hardest adjustment to this vampiric experience. "I was right to hide it, wasn't I? You walked out on me. Didn't bother to say good-bye, and yet here you are. When did you decide to become a donor? Was it when you realized how great the sex is? Not so easy to get off with mere mortals when you've experienced the ultimate, is it?"

"You should know." There is a resentful edge to his voice. "You hadn't gotten off with me until that last time. It's what made it so great, wasn't it? You fed from me. It was the only time I'd satisfied you since you turned into . . ." His voice breaks off. "This."

He reaches behind him and grabs the arm of the vamp. She is not expecting it, caught up in the exchange between Max and me. She recovers in an instant. She puts her head down, snarls and bites down on his hand hard enough to draw blood.

I don't come to his defense. I would have reacted the same way to being manhandled.

He snatches his hand away and looks down at the ragged wound. "This is what you are, Anna. An animal. I come here to remind myself why I can't love you anymore."

Culebra interposes himself between us. "Take this outside," he says. "You're making the natives restless."

For the first time, I'm aware that, except for the pulse of the music, it has grown quiet in the bar. A half dozen women have separated from the others and are creeping toward us. They seem to be sniffing the air, mouths open, eyes narrowed.

I raise a questioning eyebrow to Culebra.

It's the blood. Take Max outside and heal the wound. Quickly.

But the redhead steps forward. *He's with me. I'll do it.* She looks up at Max and says quietly. "You need to come with me. Now. You've made the pack nervous."

He has his eyes on me, but he follows her outside without arguing. He's seen what a vampire can do when provoked. When the doors swing closed behind them, the six who were creeping up on us turn as one toward someone behind them. Though I don't detect movement of any kind, they must get some kind of signal. They slink back to their places at the bar.

I skewer Culebra with a look. *The pack? What are they?*

He doesn't answer right away. He's watching the crowd at the bar, waiting for the tension to drain from the room. When the decibel level rises to its former ear-splitting pitch, anxiety still clouds his eyes, and I can tell he's far from relieved.

Culebra, I ask again. *What are they?*

His eyes flick back to me. *Werewolves.*

Werewolves? I repeat stupidly. I look around. There are at least forty of the creatures in the bar. A shudder of revulsion runs down my spine. The fact that they look and act human is not a comfort. I look and act human, too. Most of the time. *All of them?*

Culebra follows my gaze as it sweeps the room. *Yes.*

Explains the emblem on the jackets. I know how strong I am and how powerful Culebra is, but still, these are not good odds. *Are we safe?*

He takes my arm and steers me toward the door at the back of the bar. If that's his answer, it's not reassuring. But neither is going through the same door Max and his new girlfriend exited earlier. I smell Max. His sex, his blood. It's distracting enough to make me ask, *When did Max start coming here?*

Six weeks ago.

Not long after we escaped from Mexico. Where Max found out my secret.

Culebra is watching my face. He's not prying into my thoughts. Maybe he doesn't want to feel the emptiness. He says, "You asked me if we were safe from them." He gestures toward the bar.

Perhaps he does feel it. "Nice change of subject."

He nods and waves me into a chair. "We are safe. In theory. Weres are only dangerous in their animal form. Still, they are a pack. Bloodlust can bring the animal to the surface. There have been documented cases of a pack in human form tearing apart a large animal for sport. Especially when drugs or alcohol are involved."

I glare at him. "So you let them into your bar to drink and smoke pot? Doesn't sound so smart to me."

"I know the leader of this pack. She promised me there would be no trouble. They are on their way across the border. She asked to stay the night. I agreed. They are paying well for the privilege."

This still does not sound like something Culebra would agree to. He shrugs, divining my thought.

I had no idea you would show up tonight. You fed only a week ago. The weres are moving on in the morning. The camp is otherwise empty. I saw no harm in granting the request. As for Max . . .

He pauses, eyes on me while he lets himself into my head. I don't try to stop him. It's easier than trying to explain what I'm feeling. Anger toward Gloria and her ridiculous situation, and now hurt and disappointment because of Max.

The problem with Gloria can be easily fixed. You may be able to settle it tonight when you see this business partner. I am sorry seeing Max upset you. I didn't realize you had come in until it was too late.

Is that supposed to make me feel better? I come to this place as much for refuge from the irritations of the mortal world as for sustenance. Should I call ahead from now on to make a reservation?

Culebra lifts an eyebrow.

I know I'm overreacting. Max has as much right to come here as I do. Maybe more, since he and Culebra were friends long before I came into the picture. Still, the thought that I might run into him again on the arm of another vamp sends a stab of resentment through my gut.

Culebra's expression softens from irritation to sympathetic acknowledgment, but he says nothing. What can he say? This is my problem.

I turn away abruptly. I can't think of any reason to stay here. I can't think of any clever parting remarks. Maybe I'll go back to Glory's and wait for O'Sullivan to show up. Then, after I take care of him, I'll pick up one of those eager yuppies and bring him home with me. Fuck his brains out and send him on his way.

I feel Culebra's disapproval. It hums through the air like radio waves, but he can't help and he can't stop me.

He doesn't try.

Just as I don't bother to say good-bye.

CHAPTER 7

I'M ALMOST AT THE DOOR WHEN ONE OF THE FE-male weres steps in front of me. It's not an accident. She looks at me and rumbles a growl, challenging, threatening. A growl rises in my own throat, and a rush of adrenaline burns through my veins. The vampire springs into defensive mode.

The bar is suddenly quiet.

"What do you want?" My voice is harsh, my muscles tense.

The woman stares at me. "Are you Anna Strong?"

She knows my name?

Startled, I take a step back to get a better look. Do I know her? She's as tall as I am. Brown, close-cropped hair. Dark eyes in a face that would be pleasant if not for the hatred in her expression. She's wearing a pair of skin-tight jeans and a worn leather jacket zipped to her neck. She makes an elaborate show of stripping off her jacket and letting it fall to the floor. She's wearing a tank top that reveals a right arm decorated with an elaborate multicolored tattoo, something with an eagle and a waving flag. It also reveals well-muscled shoulders and rock-hard biceps that she flexes like a prize-fighter.

I'm damned sure now that I don't know her, but I can't help it, the posturing makes me smile. I feel like I'm back in junior high facing a school-yard bully. Swallowing back the urge to laugh, I ask, "Are you calling me out, sunshine?"

It's not the reaction she's expecting. A frown tightens the thin lips. "You think this is funny?"

Culebra is suddenly between us. "Stop it."

Two words, but his tone cuts like a whip. He faces the were. "You are a guest here. Have you forgotten?" He turns toward the crowd at the bar. "Sandra, you gave your word there would be no trouble. Are you abusing my hospitality?"

The were takes a step back and turns toward the bar. I turn, too, though at first I can't tell who he's addressing. Then there's movement as the crowd parts to let someone through. A woman. She separates from the rest. She doesn't say anything; she looks. At me.

My pulse starts racing. I can't move. I can't look away. I don't want to.

She is stunning. More than beautiful. Tall, lean, dressed in black form-fitting leather. Her dark hair is cut to frame her face, a showcase for eyes that flash blue green in the light of the bar and generously curved, slightly parted lips. Her smooth skin glows with pale undertones, as if even inside, she's bathed in moonlight.

The effect is at once devastating and unnerving. Every eye in the room is riveted on that perfect face. I've never felt anything like it—a sexual vibe so strong it transcends gender and species. I can't believe I didn't notice her before.

Only Culebra seems immune. He puts a hand on my arm, tightening his grip to keep me at his side.

"Well?" he barks. "Do I need to ask you to leave, Sandra? Or will you honor your word?"

A smile touches the perfect mouth, lifts the corners of her eyes. "Tamara," she says in a soft, throaty whisper. "Apologize to the lady."

The muscle-bound creature in front of me wilts in disappointment, but she doesn't argue. "Sorry," she says in a tone that implies she clearly isn't. She picks up her jacket and moves to stand by the woman at the bar.

Sandra places an arm across Tamara's shoulders in a gesture as much possessive as defensive. Her eyes are not on Tamara or Culebra, however. They are focused on me.

I shift uneasily. Heat ripples my skin. I'm aroused, physically, embarrassingly, in a way I haven't been in months.

By a woman. Is it a spell?

Culebra is tugging at my arm, forcing me to turn away from those hypnotic eyes. He's pulling me toward the door. Dumbly, reluctantly, I allow myself to be led outside.

Only then is the link broken. I round on him. *What the hell was that?*

His smile is grim. *She likes you.*

Likes me? We were mind fucking—or didn't you notice? What kind of magic does she work?

He shrugs. *Werewolves emit a powerful sexual energy. It's what attracts humans. It's the way they propagate. Human reproduction is not available to them.*

Propagate? Hello, I'm not human. Another insignificant detail? We both happen to be women.

She may not know that you are vampire. They do not have psychic abilities except with other pack members. As for sex, werewolves are like vampires in that respect.

It's all he says. It's enough. Werewolves must *make* other werewolves as vampires do, with an exchange of blood.

What in the hell were you thinking letting a pack of werewolves camp out in your bar?

"There wasn't any trouble until you showed up. Come to think of it, most of the time there isn't any trouble until you show up," he says sharply. He jabs a thumb toward the door. "I think you're missing an important point. Sandra doesn't act like that around everyone. It's as if she was waiting for you. For you. Her pack mate knew your name. Aren't you the least bit curious why?"

Indignation at the charge that I am to blame for what happened inside suddenly morphs into a pool of uncertainty and rampant curiosity. I realize with a jolt that what Culebra said is true.

I turn to go back in. This time, if that muscle-bound Tamara tries to stop me, she's in for a surprise.

Sandra is inside. It's Sandra I need to see. I *feel* her tugging at the corners of my mind.

Culebra stops me by grabbing my arm. "Not tonight," he says. "I don't want trouble."

I pause, reading Culebra's concern. He fears for my— for *our*—safety. There are two of us and at least forty of them. He's right. If things go badly, the odds are not in our favor.

"I'll see what I can find out from the weres and get back to you tomorrow," he says.

I sigh. There is the matter of Gloria's indiscretion to take care of. If I'm lucky, maybe Rory O'Sullivan will try something and I can work off some of my aggression by slapping him around.

Culebra is in my head. He frowns, clucking his tongue. "You must find a way to curb your impulses," he says. "Bully someone like Rory O'Sullivan, and you can be sure he'll bully right back. Better to follow your first impulse and take a human sex partner. Do it before you meet O'Sullivan, please, not after. Lose your temper with him, and you risk exposure."

He sounds like a priest. Irritation slithers up and coils in the pit of my stomach. Diffusing that anger in a proper manner was the reason I showed up here.

Culebra releases a long sigh. *I know. I am sorry to disappoint you. You put yourself in this position, Anna, over and over. There is an alternative. You know it. Take one partner to satisfy your appetites safely. Settle down. There's nothing wrong with that. It's the prudent thing to do.*

Yadda, yadda, yadda. I've heard it before. This time when I stomp down the dusty boardwalk toward my car, no one tries to stop me.

CHAPTER 8

THE ENTIRE DEBACLE AT CULEBRA'S LASTED ONLY an hour. It felt like much longer. The drive through tourist traffic making its slow way back to San Diego gives me time to sort through conflicting emotions.

The first being shock and anger at Max. For obvious reasons. But also a tinge of regret at the way I reacted. In spite of knowing that it never would have worked out between Max and me, seeing him tonight hurt.

Then there's Sandra. I can't believe she affected me in such a potent sexual way. A response maybe to seeing Max? To knowing he'd just had sex with someone else?

Confusion. Why in hell would one of her werewolf buddies want to pick a fight with me? As far as I know, I've never come in contact with any member of the were family, so I can't have insulted or harmed one. Not intentionally anyway. My experience with the supernatural community has had its ups and downs, but the only time I've killed was in defense of myself or of the human community. I'm certain I've never killed a were.

By the time I get back to town, it's after nine and my head spins from trying to sort it all out. I need a drink, so even though it's too early to meet Rory, I head for Glory's.

The bar is more crowded than before. All the tables and booths lining the back wall are occupied. I work my way through the crowd and ask the bartender if by chance Gloria or her partner is in the back. He says no. Gloria left a while ago, and Mr. O'Sullivan isn't due for another couple of hours. I order a vodka martini, extra dry, hold the olives.

A thirtysomething wearing Armani and a sleazy smile moves off a stool and motions for me to sit. I do. He has the oily good looks of a lawyer, with designer horn-rim glasses and delicate hands. Defense, probably. The suit is too expensive and the hands too soft to belong to a prosecutor. He's drinking something in a tall glass with a fancy swizzle. He's definitely a defense attorney. The prosecutors I know wouldn't be caught dead with a paper-umbrella drink.

Neither would I. It takes more than a raging libido to be tempted by a drink like that, or the type who would order one.

Caught dead. I smile at my own joke. When my drink comes, Umbrella Man flips a twenty onto the bar and steps closer, misinterpreting the smile as an invitation.

I figure one good growl should discourage him.

Careful, Anna. Don't give yourself away.

Great. The familiar voice is an unwelcome intrusion into my head. I look past Umbrella Man. Williams is sitting at a table in the back. He's smiling, too, but it's only lip service. His eyes are veiled and serious.

Williams. What are you doing here?

It's good to see you, too. What's it been? Two months? You don't write. You don't call.

Very funny. I elbow my way toward him, ignoring the yelp of protest from Umbrella Man when I shove the drink back at him. *If you'll recall, you asked me not to contact you. From what I've been reading in the newspapers, you're not completely out of trouble yet.*

Williams moves so I can slide next to him on the bench seat. He knows I'll want to have the same vantage point he does. Like good cops, or vampires, our backs to the wall, eyes on the crowd.

He's in civilian clothes, slacks and a polo shirt open at the collar. He's handsome in a fiftyish, lean, graying kind of way. The gray is an affectation. He's a vampire, an old vampire, who is also the police chief of the city of San Diego.

At least technically.

Two months ago he got in trouble because of a rather unconventional police sting operation. Unconventional because it involved a civilian—me—and because although a bad man was caught, a deputy was killed in the process. It wasn't Williams' fault but as chief of police, every good thing he'd done in the ten years of his tenure faded when compared to the harsh reality that he'd lost one of his own. He's on administrative leave now, defending his actions and his office to every civilian and police review board in existence. He has not yet been reinstated, and now here he is, sitting by himself in Glory's nursing a beer.

Coincidence?

I think not.

"Why are you here?"

He tips his own glass toward me. "That's what I like about you, Anna. There's no bullshit in you. Culebra called me. Told me where you were headed."

"I just left him. I have a cell phone. Why would he call you instead of me?"

He focuses on the beer in his hand with much more concentration than it merits. He's also closed off his thoughts. Culebra seemed annoyed when I left but not worried. Why would he send Williams to find me unless . . .

"If this is about getting back on the Watcher team, you

can forget it. I told you I don't want to be a part of that anymore. I'm living as a human now. I intend to as long as I'm able."

He leans his head close to mine. "Except for inconsequential things. Like drinking blood, right?"

I want to slap that sarcastic smirk off his face. Instead, I take his beer out of his hand and raise it to my own lips, swallowing the "fuck you" response with the beer. It galls me that Williams, who has a mortal wife and holds down a mortal job, is relentless in his attempt to persuade me to abandon *my* human roots to pursue what he mystifyingly calls "my destiny." A destiny he refuses to define or explain. What I do know, however, is that it involves distancing myself from my family, something I won't do.

We've been doing this dance as long as I've known him.

Someone has entered the bar, causing a ripple of excitement to run through the crowd. I look up in time to see Gloria make a grand entrance. She's stunning in a short dress of gold lamé, her hair piled on top of her head, all traces of this afternoon's crying jag erased from that radiant face.

She cruises through the crowd, bestowing the favor of her smile on one and all. When she disappears through the door to the office, I scoot to the end of the bench and prepare to follow her.

Williams stops me with a hand on my arm. "Wait. I have something to tell you."

I shrug it off.

He doesn't let me go. His grip tightens.

Furious, I whirl on him. "Take your hand off me."

He releases my arm and holds up both hands in a gesture of surrender. "I'm sorry. You have to hear this. The were Sandra at the bar tonight? She's looking for you. Culebra said she'll contact you tomorrow."

I remember her power and beauty and the control she exerted over her pack. I'm actually excited at the prospect of seeing her again until reason rears its ugly head. "Do you know why?"

"It's complicated," he says.

"Isn't everything? Look, if you know, tell me. Why is she coming to see me?"

His eyes flash in the dim light. "She says she's Avery's wife. She wants you to know she's coming to claim what's hers."

CHAPTER 9

I DON'T KNOW WHAT KIND OF REACTION WILLIAMS expects from me. His expression is comical in its intensity. He looks like he's afraid I'll throw or hit something.

All I'm feeling is surprise and relief. To be rid of the last vestiges of Avery's impact on my life is what I've dreamed of and fought for since the bastard insinuated himself in my life six months ago. Avery made me believe he loved me, that he wanted to help me adjust to life as a vampire. What he really wanted was control. He destroyed my house, kidnapped David and would have killed him if I hadn't found him in time. I have no doubt he would have gone after my family next. When I drove a stake into Avery's heart, I was not only protecting myself but all the humans I love. I've never regretted it.

Williams knows that.

I climb to my feet and turn to look down at him. "So. Avery had a wife. Good. Finally, I can be free. Be sure to thank her for me."

His eyes widen a fraction. Then a slow, tight smile

touches the corners of his lips. "Not so easy. Avery's possessions are yours by vampiric right. She knows this."

"I don't care about vampiric rights. Why do we keep having this conversation? She can have every fucking thing Avery left. I don't want anything. Tell her that. Have Culebra tell her that. If I have to sign something, tell her to send it over. I'll sign any bloody document she wants. I want to get it over with. I want to be left alone."

I don't realize how loud I'm talking until I catch Williams' look of warning and glance around. The bar has become suspiciously quiet and all eyes are locked on me.

Jesus. For the second time tonight, I'm the center of attention. Exactly what a vampire wants. Only this time, all the eyes and ears focused on me are human. Did they catch the vampiric rights thing, or was that early enough in the tirade to be missed?

Williams grabs my arm and pulls me back onto the bench. I let him, hoping to diffuse the tension with a meek smile and feeble hand wave to the room. "Sorry, folks. My bad. My father and I had a bit of a misunderstanding."

Williams' dark thoughts lash out. *Father?*

Would you prefer I said lover? All it would take is one of those lawyers at the bar to recognize you.

But I don't have a daughter.

You don't have a lover, either. At least not here, not now.

My gaze sweeps the room. People are turning back to their companions and partners, conversation resumes. No eyes linger on us. *Disaster averted. Relax.*

Relax? He's practically foaming at the mouth. *God, Anna. You are impossible. What the hell were you thinking?*

I don't answer. If I do, I'll only spark another tirade. Williams and I are never going to see eye to eye on proper vampire conduct. Mostly because I don't want to be a proper vampire. I slam the door on my thoughts and climb again to my feet.

"See you, Williams. If you won't help me with Sandra, I'll find a way to handle it myself. Either way, it will be over. I won't expect to hear from you again. Thanks for once again reminding me of all the things I don't want."

Williams' expression softens into the last I would have expected. Anger gives way to sadness. He shakes his head. "You'll never get what you want. No matter how hard you try. I know you don't believe that." He looks away, then back at me. "It isn't real, you know. At least it isn't your reality."

And in the next instant, he's replaying my shopping trip with Trish this afternoon. Like a projected image, I see my face, glowing, expectant, when I look at her.

There's only one way to accomplish such a thing. Fury threatens to choke me, but I force the words through gritted teeth. "You're following me?"

He shakes his head. "Not me."

"Then who?"

"It's not important. What is important is the role you are destined to play, Anna. Until you accept, fully accept, what you are, you will be under surveillance. It's not negotiable."

He flips a ten-dollar bill onto the table and stands up. "So, go, live as a mortal in the limited capacity open to you. Soon enough the futility of it will become clear. You'll come back to us, Anna, because you'll have nowhere else to go."

I stare at him as he walks away. He doesn't look back. He doesn't have to. His last words hang in the air. It makes me sick to admit that Williams is right. No matter how hard I fight it, playacting can't change the reality of what I am.

I shuffle myself away from the table and toward the door through which Gloria disappeared a few minutes before.

I never thought I'd prefer Gloria's presence to well, *anyone* else, but right now, I need to get that last conversation out of my head.

I pause outside Gloria's office door to compose myself. My insides are quivering with a combination of frustration, aggravation and rage. At Williams. At fate. At myself because I've put myself in this ridiculous position of agreeing to help Gloria. Why didn't I tell her to go to hell this afternoon? If I had, I could be with my folks and Trish right now, pretending to eat Christmas cookies and listening to them laugh. Give Williams' flunky something to think about. That's the reality I want.

I glance around the bar, not really expecting to identify my tail. If I didn't sense a presence before, I won't now.

I look back at the door. The sooner I get this over with, the better. I don't bother to knock. I grab the door handle and push.

Gloria is sitting in the same chair, in the same position as I found her this afternoon. This time, though, her eyes aren't turned toward the window. She's staring at a piece of paper clutched in a hand that's shaking.

"What's that, Gloria? Your cosmetics bill for the month?"

When her attention switches to me, the expression on her face changes from shock to fury. She jumps to her feet, lunges toward me.

"It's a note from Rory," she says, waving the paper at me. "That bastard is threatening to file suit against me. For fraud. He says he'll claim millions in missing profits."

Wow. I'm almost impressed with the ferocity of her wrath. "Looks like he's changed his mind about the pussy, huh?"

It's a crass, bitchy thing to say, but right now crass and bitchy is how I feel. Gloria is so mad at O'Sullivan, she lets my remark go unanswered.

I jab a thumb toward the door. "I guess you don't really need me to hang around anymore. Obviously, O'Sullivan won't be showing his face here. I doubt your business partner will want to dilute his claims against you by risking a countercharge of sexual harassment. Which means I don't need to mitigate anything with David—"

"Mitigate what with David?"

The voice from the doorway makes the words lodge somewhere in the back of my throat. Reluctantly, I turn around.

My partner, David, ex-boyfriend of Gloria, or so I thought, is standing in the doorway. His blue eyes are alive with a spark I haven't seen in weeks. When I look back at Gloria, she's smiling at him, and her eyes mirror the same excitement.

A sick hollowness settles in the pit of my stomach.

Fuck. I thought my day was bad before. It's getting worse.

CHAPTER 10

GLORIA AND DAVID ARE GENERATING AS MUCH heat as a nuclear reactor. I step away from them, out of meltdown range, in self-defense.

They are locked in each other's gaze. I never understood that phrase before this moment. I keep waiting for the orchestra to appear and the music to swell.

"Jesus. You're like a couple of dogs in heat."

Not even my sarcasm breaks the mood.

David clears his throat and steps into the room, shutting the door behind him. He's dressed in jeans and a T-shirt and a leather jacket. His hair is brushed straight back and still wet, as if he stepped out of the shower and didn't want to take the time to dry it. Since he lives in a loft about five minutes from here, it's probably exactly what happened. Gloria called and he rushed right over.

The jerk.

They stare at each other. Then he and Gloria come together, drawn as if by magnets, like two of those stupid bobblehead dolls, and fall into each other's arms. They ignore me, like I was invisible. They kiss long, hard and noisily.

I can only take so much.

"I'm going to throw up."

David comes up for air, throws me an indulgent, sappy smile. "I should be mad at you," he says. "You didn't let me know Gloria was back in town."

In what parallel universe was I ever likely to do that? I stare at him. Then I stare at Gloria. "You want to jump in here anytime?"

But Gloria is hugging David, her face buried in his shoulder, ignoring me.

In another instant, they're both ignoring me because they're sucking face again.

There's a knock on the door. Loud. Insistent.

I arch an eyebrow toward the lovers. Neither makes a move to pull back or disengage. "Don't worry," I snarl. "I'll get that."

If I'm lucky, the place will be on fire. Which I may or may not tell David and Gloria. A good dousing from a fire hose is what those two need.

I yank open the door. There's a man in a suit frowning at me. He's flanked by two cops in uniform. He flashes a badge and looks over my shoulder at the lovebirds.

"Gloria Estrella?"

His tone is belligerent and hostile. It startles Gloria into breaking the lip-lock. It surprises me, too. I didn't think anyone talked to her like that except me. Makes me take a closer look.

He's about five feet ten, all planes and angles. Square jaw, stubborn, arrogant face, boxy physique under a ready-to-wear suit of charcoal gray. His mouth has a cynical twist that is vaguely familiar. When he looks at Gloria, it's not the way guys usually look at her. There's no drool dripping off his chin and his eyes reflect no admiration or lust. He's sizing her up like a perp.

The same way he sized me up not too long ago.

"Detective Harris?"

For the first time his eyes disengage from Gloria and flick to me. It's lightning fast. A camera lens focusing on an image, processing the shot, moving on to another. He doesn't confirm or deny that he recognizes me.

Doesn't matter. I certainly recognize him. What's a homicide cop doing in Gloria's office?

He shoulders his way past me into the room. The two cops with him crowd the door but don't follow him in.

Gloria straightens and pulls back from David. She rounds on Harris, her eyes flashing. "How did you get back here? This area is not open to the public."

He holds up the badge. "I'm not the public. You *are* Gloria Estrella." Not a question, a statement.

"Yes."

"You know Rory O'Sullivan?"

"He's my business partner in this restaurant."

"Not anymore."

Gloria gives Harris a slow, brittle smile. "Who are you? Is this Rory's idea of a joke? How much is he paying you to annoy me?"

She moves back toward David. One hand rests on his chest, the other on his waist. For his part, David's expression is not so patronizing or self-assured. He's looking at Harris with a mixture of alarm and concern. "Wait a minute, Gloria," he says, stepping around the desk. "Anna called this guy 'Detective Harris.' You're a cop? How do you know Anna?"

I wait to see how he's going to answer—if he'll remember. When Trish's mother was killed, he was the detective on the scene. Asked me to identify the body. Williams took over the case, and I had no more contact with him.

Harris nods at David. "She was a witness in a homicide a few months ago. Not why I'm here." He takes a picture from the inside pocket of his jacket. "Ms. Estrella, is this your partner?"

I get a glimpse of the picture as it passes from his hand to Gloria's. A head shot of Rory. Not a glamour shot. The eyes are open, fixed, there's a blood smear on one cheek and more blood up around his hairline.

Gloria sucks in her breath. She barely glances at the photograph before pushing it back at Harris. "What's wrong with him? Has Rory been in an accident?"

"Not an accident. Mr. O'Sullivan was shot."

"Shot?" Gloria's face pales.

"Is he all right?" David asks.

"No." Harris says.

David looks at Gloria. "Who would want to kill O'Sullivan?"

A smile touches the corners of Harris' mouth. "Good question. That's what I'm here to find out."

David steps between Gloria and Detective Harris. "You're questioning Gloria about a homicide?"

Harris lets a heartbeat go by before he says, "Who says it's a homicide?"

David points to the picture. "He is dead, isn't he? You said it was no accident."

Harris slips the picture back into a jacket pocket. He moves around David. "Ms. Estrella, I need to ask you a few questions."

David counters as quickly. He's gone into defensive mode. Not unexpected where Gloria is concerned. He places his six feet six, 250-pound ex-football-player frame squarely between Gloria and the detective.

Harris has to step back to look up at him. A move he's not happy to make. His expression darkens, his shoulders tighten. "Who are you?"

"I'm David Ryan. What's your interest in Gloria?"

The color in Harris' face deepens from irritated cherry to infuriated purple. "Are you her lawyer?"

"I'm her friend. Does she need a lawyer?"

This whole exchange has me watching openmouthed in astonishment. I know firsthand how crazy David is about Gloria, but I've never seen him so rabid in his defense of her.

Maybe a voice of reason is needed here.

I put my hand on David's arm. "David? Detective Harris hasn't accused Gloria of anything. Rory was her business partner. It's reasonable for him to be here. Don't you think you're overreacting a bit?"

David's eyes don't flicker for an instant from Harris. "I know how cops work. He wouldn't be here if he didn't suspect something. Gloria is going to have her lawyer present before she answers any questions."

As far as David is concerned, that's that. I've known him long enough to recognize the signs. He's planted himself like a big, dumb rock in front of Gloria, and nothing short of a bulldozer will move him.

I look over at Harris. He's irritated. I half expect him to draw his gun and order David out. Instead, he throws up his hands. "Fine. Have it your way." He yanks a business card from a jacket pocket and tosses it on the desk. "Ms. Estrella, you and your lawyer at SDPD headquarters in thirty minutes." He looks up at David. "You're not invited. If you advise Ms. Estrella not to appear or if I see you anywhere in the building, I'll have you arrested for obstruction of justice."

This time, David is smart enough not to argue. Harris leaves the office. He slams the door behind him. He slams it so hard the pictures on the wall bounce and rattle.

"That went well," I say. "David, what the hell's the matter with you? You just made things worse for Gloria. All she had to do was answer the cop's questions, and it would have been over. She doesn't have anything to hide."

Suddenly I realize that Gloria hasn't said a word. Now that Harris has left, she should be reacting in her usual prima-donna way—ranting against Rory and the cops. Blaming Rory for getting himself killed and Harris for inconveniencing her with a trip to SDPD in the middle of the night.

Instead, she's not doing or saying anything.

I look, really look, at her, focusing my vampire radar at the pale, perfect face. She hadn't acted surprised to learn Rory had been killed. Hadn't acted shocked. Hadn't asked how or why.

She barely glanced at the photo.

No. As much as I hate this woman, it isn't possible.

Is it?

"Oh my god."

David and Gloria do a half turn toward me. David says, "What is it?"

Gloria simply looks at me. Waiting.

"You already knew O'Sullivan was dead. How, Gloria? Did you kill him?"

CHAPTER 11

THERE'S NO REACTION FROM GLORIA.

David, however, explodes. "Are you nuts?" he yells. "Why would Gloria kill O'Sullivan?"

Yells. Not at Gloria.

At me.

I swallow a few times to mollify my own temper. I really want to bounce his head off the wall. Instead, I count to ten before saying reasonably, "Think about it, David. She didn't ask how or when or where Rory was shot. She didn't so much as look at the picture. What is she doing now? Nothing. No temper tantrum, no tirade. Is that the Gloria you know?"

I shift my gaze to Gloria. Then there's the trivial matter of O'Sullivan blackmailing you this afternoon for sex and suing you tonight for fraud. You can jump in anytime here, sweetie.

Gloria lowers her head, as if acknowledging my thoughts. Then she says in a subdued voice, "Anna is right."

David sucks in a breath, and Gloria raises a hand as if to

ward off his protest. "It's true. I did know Rory was dead, but I swear, I didn't kill him."

She may as well have sucker punched him. He stares at her, uncertainty creeping like a shadow across his face. "How could you have known? When you called me, you said you'd just arrived in town. It didn't take me more than twenty minutes to get over here."

She looks at me, and there's an instant when I think she actually expects me to come up with an alibi for her. She's crazier than I thought. When the only response she gets is my staring back at her, she lifts her shoulders in a half shrug.

"I had a meeting with Rory early this evening. At his house. I know I shouldn't have gone. He sounded so angry on the phone. I thought if we met face-to-face I could—"

She stops suddenly, realizing that if she says any more, she might give away what Rory was demanding of her.

David asks the obvious. "Why would Rory be angry with you? Business is great. You're here whenever you're in town. What else did he want?"

"Yeah, Gloria," I chime in. "What else did he want?"

Gloria's eyes flash at me, but she focuses on David when she answers. "He didn't say on the phone. Only that it was important we meet. So I went over. The front door was open."

Gloria starts to pace, wringing her hands. "Unusual, the door open like that, but I rang the bell anyway. I expected the maid must be close by. When no one appeared after a minute or so, I went inside."

Gloria has graduated from hand-wringing to picking at the fabric of her dress. She's not looking at us, and her expression is tense, drawn. I have the fleeting thought that she might be making this up as she goes along. With Gloria, it's not easy to determine where truth stops and delusion begins.

She's an actress. I wish I could crawl into that pea brain of hers and divine the truth, but she's not a vampire or a shape-shifter, so I can't. I push skepticism aside to catch the rest of the story.

"I called out to Rory. I thought I heard a noise from the den. When I went back there, I saw him. He was slumped over his desk. There was blood everywhere. I panicked and ran out. I came straight here." Those big eyes fasten with fierce intensity on David. "I called you. I didn't know what else to do."

Sounds fishy to me, but when I glance over at David, his expression never waivers from anxious concern. He believes every word out of Gloria's mouth. He looks ready to scoop her into his arms.

If David weren't here, I'd ask her why she agreed to meet Rory, alone yet, considering what was going on between them. Instead, I ask the second obvious question. "Why didn't you call the police? Like any rational, normal person would have done?"

"I was scared." The words come quickly. She's answering my question, but her eyes never leave David's. She couldn't be holding his attention more fiercely than if he'd been hog-tied to the desk.

I don't know whether she's telling the truth or not, but I've had enough of the drama. Time to send David on his way so I can get some direct answers from Gloria.

"David, go home. Detective Harris expects Gloria and her lawyer downtown in half an hour. I'll stay here until he comes. Gloria, get your lawyer on the phone."

David takes an instinctive step toward Gloria. "I'm not leaving. I'm going with her."

I take a step, too, between them. "Did you not hear what Harris said before he left? He'll have you arrested. I don't think he was kidding. You pissed him off."

David grabs my shoulders. "Then promise me that you'll go with her. Make sure she's not tricked into saying something incriminating."

"Her *lawyer* will be there. That's his job."

"I don't care. If you won't go, I will."

I remove his hands from my shoulders. "You can't help. If you'd stayed out of it when Harris was here, we wouldn't be having this discussion. Gloria will call her lawyer, and he'll protect her interests. That's what she pays him for, right, Gloria?"

We both turn toward the spot where until a minute ago, Gloria was pacing the carpet. Only now, there's no Gloria. The office door is open. I don't know how she did it, but like the alley cat she is, Gloria has managed to slink away.

CHAPTER 12

"SHE LEFT?" DAVID'S VOICE RATCHETS UP TEN OC-
taves in astonishment. He takes two steps to the door,
looks out. "She's gone." He turns back to me, bewilderment settling like a thundercloud on his features. "Why
would she do that?"

I look from the open door to David. Good question, but
David is out the door before I can speculate. I'm right on
his heels when his cell phone rings. That brings him up
short. He looks at the number and snaps open the phone.

"Gloria? Why the hell did you—"

He stops, listening, frowning. After a minute, he shuts
the phone without saying another word. He looks at me.
"That was Gloria."

"No kidding. What did she say?"

"She's leaving town. She told me she'd be in touch
soon. To stay out of it."

He yanks out his wallet and starts rifling the contents.

"What are you doing?" I ask.

He doesn't answer until he finds what he's looking for.

He holds up a business card. "Gloria's lawyer. I'm going to call him."

"For Christ's sake, she said to stay out of it. Let Gloria call her lawyer. She's the one in trouble."

David isn't listening. He's already at the desk phone and punching in the digits. I listen to the one-sided conversation.

"Hal? This is David Ryan. Yeah, I know. Long time. I'm calling because Gloria's going to need you. Oh, you're not? You're in Florida? It's three hours later there than California? Sorry. Um, do me a favor. If Gloria calls, will you tell her to get in touch with me? Well, yes, it could be serious, but Gloria should be the one to tell you about it. I'm sure she'll be in touch. Thanks, Hal. Sorry, again, about the time thing. Yeah. See you."

David sets the receiver down. "He's not in town." He passes a hand over his face and slumps into Gloria's desk chair. "Why did she take off? And where is she going?"

The answer that springs to mind—to hell, probably—is not going to help David. Nor is pointing out that Gloria is not behaving like the innocent she proclaimed herself to be.

I take his arm, pull him to his feet and steer him toward the door. "Come on. No use hanging around here. Let's go back to your place. We can have a drink and wait for her to call. As soon as she calms down, you know she will."

David nods glumly. We're heading toward the bar and the exit when we hear the commotion. It's coming from the parking lot outside. It's loud enough that it doesn't take a genius to figure out what's going on.

The press has gotten wind that billionaire Rory O'Sullivan was found dead in his home and that his partner, Gloria, was here at the restaurant. There's a cacophony of shouted questions. At first, I think they must have waylaid Gloria on her way out.

Until a familiar voice calls for quiet. Detective Harris' voice.

David plunges ahead, almost shoving me out of the way in his haste to see what's going on.

Harris is standing outside the back door, his hand on Gloria's arm. Video cam lights turn the dim parking lot into day, casting harsh shadows on his face. He must have been waiting for her to come out. If she was alone, he probably intended to follow her or to convince her to accompany him to the station voluntarily. Two police cruisers block the entrances to the parking lot.

David makes a move to push through the crowd. I grab his arm. "You want to make things worse? You know how Harris feels about you. Stay here."

Surprisingly, he heeds my advice. He shifts from one foot to the other, though, like a racehorse ready to break from the starting gate. One crook from Gloria's little finger, and he'll mow down everything in his path to get to her.

Harris is taking questions from the press, mostly giving pat cop-speak answers that imply Gloria is simply coming to the station to answer questions. O'Sullivan was her business partner. She's not been implicated in any wrongdoing nor is she a "person of interest." This is all routine. The press will be kept informed of any breaks in the case. Now, good night.

Gloria stands beside him, mute, subdued. When she sees David and me standing at the back of the crowd, she looks away quickly, not meeting our eyes. I feel David tense beside me.

Harris ushers Gloria to one of the waiting patrol cars. She doesn't resist. Camera strobe lights break the midnight gloom like a hundred rising suns. David stands beside me, his rage burning nearly as hot.

"That bastard," he says. "He waited for her."

I wish I could say something to ease David's concern. In truth, what Harris did is exactly what I would have done. Exactly what David and I have done in pursuit of a bail jumper. Waited to catch Gloria alone. Waited to get her away from David, her human pit bull. I watch the car pull away, followed by a dozen media vans. I hope Gloria's smart enough now to lawyer up before she answers any of Harris' questions. I saw him in action. He's one savvy cop.

I've never seen David so distraught. I don't know what to do to help him. Part of me doesn't want to. A day ago, I thought he and Gloria were quits. It galls me to acknowledge he hid the fact that he'd been calling her and begging her to get in touch with him.

Should I tell him the reason she contacted me today? That she wanted me to act as go-between and convince Rory to stop blackmailing her for sex?

Which would mean telling David that Gloria had slept with Rory.

How bad could that be?

The look on David's face answers that question.

He's watching the departing cop car, too, his dejection so intense I feel it like an ache in my own heart. Tempting though it is, I'm not cruel enough to add to his misery.

At least not tonight.

"Go home, David. There's nothing more we can do. Gloria will show up on your doorstep as soon as she's released. You know she will. Where else would she go?"

Hearing that galvanizes him into action. The last glimpse I have of my partner is David in the front seat of his Hummer, pulling out of the parking lot, cell phone at his ear. There's no doubt in my mind that he's calling his own lawyer, ordering him to get his ass down to the police department to protect Gloria.

I turn to go back into the bar. When I arrived earlier, this lot had been full. I had to park my car in the street, on Broadway. Cutting through the bar is the shortest route.

It's been a hell of a long day. Both the blood drive that drove me to Culebra and the sex drive that brought me back here are gone—dissipated like rain on a parched desert floor. All I want to do now is go home and go to sleep.

Hey, good-looking. I've been waiting for you.

The intrusion of a strange vamp voice in my head brings me to a stop. The bar is still crowded, but the happy-hour martini mob is long gone. The crowd now is young and raucous. The smell of beer and pot is not as strong as it was in Beso de la Muerte, but it's there. If Detective Harris had the nose of a vampire, this place would have been slated for a raid by the vice squad.

I look around. *Where are you?*

Over here. In the corner.

I follow the direction of the voice. There's a man, a young man, standing by himself in the shadows. He has wavy brown hair, shoulder length, so soft looking and shiny my fingers itch to run themselves through it. I can't quite make out his face, but he's dressed in jeans and an open-neck polo, and I let my eyes drift from broad shoulders to a narrow waist. Farther south.

Every nerve in my body starts to vibrate.

Who are you? Are you working for Williams?

He smiles and steps into the light. The face of an angel.

Who's Williams? Culebra sent me. He thought you might need a—distraction tonight.

Whoa. Suddenly, fatigue and lethargy are gone. Blood starts pounding, sending such a strong current of desire through me, my knees go weak.

The angel senses my reaction. *Was Culebra right?*

God bless him, I respond. *Your place or mine?*

CHAPTER 13

MORNING AT THE COTTAGE IS MY FAVORITE time. Sipping a cup of fresh-brewed coffee on the deck outside my bedroom is my favorite way to pass the morning—even a dark winter's morning like this one. It helps, too, that I'm blissfully sated from a night of blood and sex. It could be storming outside and I'd still be purring.

I reluctantly sent Culebra's "distraction," Lance, on his way a few moments before. Turns out he's an underwear model for Jockey and has an early morning photo shoot up the coast in Malibu. Seeing him in and out of underwear last night answered one of life's biggest questions. Are those bulges in the magazine ads real? I'm happy to report that they are—at least Lance's is. No padded jock straps necessary for that guy.

Turns out, too, that Lance has a last name, Turner, and a brain as agile as that lean, athletic body. He made me laugh, and he made me sweat. I'd like to see him again.

I'll have to find some appropriate way to thank Culebra. Glowing from the infusion of healthy vamp blood, second only to a human's in restorative powers, and feeling comfortable in my skin for the first time since the fiasco with Gloria started, I sink into a deck chair and take in the view.

I live in Mission Beach, steps from the boardwalk. I was a sophomore in college when my grandmother died and left me her fifty-year-old cottage. I've lived here ever since, though I had the place rebuilt after the fire Avery set destroyed it a while back.

I love it here. Sometimes, in the summer, it's a bother to be interrupted by some half-drunk partier, leaning on the doorbell to ask to use the bathroom. When I was human, I'd threaten to call the cops. As a vampire, all I have to do is show my true face and I never have a repeat offender. Never.

In winter, however, it's different. I think it's odd that winter in San Diego is considered the off-season. True, there is the overcast and the fog, a blending of shades of gray that often makes it hard to determine where the sky ends and the ocean begins. But the air temperature seldom dips below sixty and while the water isn't warm, it attracts a better surfing crowd. Not the sun-worshipping, hard-drinking, noisy, young hordes of summer, but a mature, serious, respectful group who honor the ocean rather than attempting to beat it into submission with their boards.

Wow. I hold the warm cup in both hands and press it against my forehead. That was almost poetic. Must be a combination of the fog rolling in picturesque swirls off the water and the calm that comes from a satisfying night of sex.

I know this glow won't last long. Williams said the were Sandra was coming to see me. Then there's David and his angst. I don't want to think about what kind of mood he's going to be in. Hopefully, if he comes into the office, it won't be with Gloria in tow.

The telephone rings as I'm about to go back downstairs

for a second cup of coffee. It's my cell phone. I grab it up and keep going, glancing at the caller ID. I expect to see our office number or David's cell number, but instead it's one I don't recognize.

"Hello?"

There's a moment of silence before it's broken by a breathy, "Anna?"

Great. Gloria. I resist the urge to disconnect and turn off the phone. "What do you want?"

"I need to see you."

"I don't want to see you. We have nothing to talk about. Are you with David? Does he know you're calling me?"

Another silence. "I haven't spoken with David since I left you both at the restaurant."

"What do you mean? Don't you know how worried he is? I can't believe you didn't call him as soon as you were released last night."

This time, the quiet at the other end of the line stretches on so long, I start to think we've been cut off, but then I hear a sharp intake of breath followed by a sob. "Gloria? What's going on?"

A small, shaky voice whispers, "I wasn't released. I've been arrested."

I don't have to ask for what. "Jesus, Gloria. Did you talk with a lawyer yet?"

"Yes. David sent his lawyer last night, and he referred me to a criminal attorney. A Jamie Sutherland. We meet this morning."

"So, why call me? You should be talking to David. He's probably crazy with worry."

There's a short, brittle bark of mirthless laughter. "No. He won't want to talk with me. You haven't seen the morning paper, have you?"

I'm in the kitchen now, and my eyes go to the front door. I hadn't bothered to pick up the paper yet, but I do now. The rubber band breaks in my haste to get at the paper and flies up to smack my chin.

"Damn it."

Gloria starts to whimper. "I know. I know. I've been such a fool."

She thinks I'm cursing her. Good. I shake out the front page and hold it up, balancing the phone between my ear and shoulder.

"Oh, fuck."

This time I am cursing her. The headline blares: "Gloria Estrella Arrested for the Murder of Billionaire Partner."

In slightly smaller print, the headline continues: "Wife of Rory O'Sullivan Says the Motive Is Love Affair Gone Bad."

"Love affair, Gloria? I thought you said you slept with him one time."

This time, when she doesn't respond, it isn't such a big surprise.

CHAPTER 14

GLORIA IS SOBBING SOFTLY. I ROLL MY EYES BUT don't say anything. She sounds scared. For some inexplicable reason, I don't feel like rubbing it in. I toss the newspaper in the corner and lean against the counter. I'll give her a minute. Christ. I must be getting soft.

The minute passes. Gloria is still snuffling. Patience has its limits. I don't intend to spend my morning listening to her spit and sputter into a telephone receiver.

Against all better judgment, I ask, "Why did you want to see me?"

She sucks in a noisy breath. "You need to know what happened between Rory and me. It isn't what you think."

"Oh, no? Are you telling me you didn't have an affair with O'Sullivan?"

She hiccups. "Well, okay, it is what you think, but there were extenuating circumstances."

This is not getting us anywhere. "You know what? I don't care. You should be talking to a lawyer. Or a priest."

"I will talk to the lawyer. First I need to explain it to you. So you can explain it to David."

"Oh, no. I will not be a go-between. You made this mess, Gloria. You need to clean it up."

"I'll hire you."

"For what?"

"To find out who killed Rory." She lets a heartbeat go by before blurting, "You can do it. You know things. You have contacts. The police won't investigate the way you can. They have no reason to. They think I did it. Even Rory's wife thinks I did it." She laughs. No mirth in the sound, only bitterness. "She came to see me last night. All Rory's talk about an open marriage was evidently just that. Talk. As far as Mrs. O'Sullivan was concerned, Rory was an altar boy. She's going to do all she can to pin this on me. I need someone on my side."

Boy, she is desperate to think I'd be on her side. "So, let me get this straight, you want me to help David—"

"Not David," she interjects quickly. "You. David can't know what you're doing."

"And how do you think I can hide this from him? I see him every day, remember?"

Her voice drops. "I don't think you will."

"What is that supposed to mean?"

"David is gone."

"Gone?"

She makes another gulping sound before exhaling in a noisy rush. "He left town."

"I thought you said you hadn't talked to him."

"I haven't. He went to police headquarters this morning and left a note for me with a cop he knows. He saw the newspaper. He believes the story. He thinks I called him yesterday because I knew what would happen when the story broke."

The realization makes my spine stiffen. "You did, didn't

you? You wanted to make it look like you and David were still together. For the press. To refute the affair story."

She pauses. "Yes."

That admission is so unexpected, it catches me completely off guard. I don't know how to respond. This time the silence on the line is my doing, a result of my fevered brain trying to accept that Gloria is actually admitting she fucked up. A brand-new experience.

I feel my resolve start to soften. Not out of sympathy for Gloria, but for David. Poor shmuck. He's probably off somewhere nursing his wounds. First he thinks he has his girlfriend back, then he finds out she was using him to deflect suspicion if she found herself in this predicament.

Wait a minute.

Why would she think she needed suspicion deflected? Unless . . .

"I asked you this once before, Gloria. Now tell me again. *Did* you kill Rory?"

"Of course not."

No hesitation, no heated objection to my asking. An unequivocal denial. I release a breath. "Why drag David into it?"

This time there is a pause. "I told you. I called him because I knew he'd be on my side. Then, when the story broke, if David and I were together, no one would believe Rory and I had—"

"Had what? Been fucking around?"

My first impulse, to tell her what a bitch I think she is, is interrupted by a second possibility. Another flash of inspiration like the one yesterday that had Gloria promising not to talk trash about me to David. This one is even better. I can use Gloria's desperation to my advantage. I can get rid of her once and for all.

"Okay, Gloria. I'll come by the jail and see you this morning. If you want my help, there will be conditions."

"What are they?" The tone is muted, resigned, as if she already knows or suspects what I'm about to say.

"First, you cut David loose. For good. He deserves better."

"I know."

"I mean it. No calling him. No sneak visits. If he calls you, you hang up. You don't answer his messages. You don't send him a birthday card. He is out of your life."

"Okay." Tiny voice.

"Second, I expect to be paid for my services." I do some quick, mental arithmetic. How much could I soak her for? May as well make the aggravation worth my while. "Two hundred an hour, plus expenses. Starting now."

"Agreed."

So quickly? Shit. I should have asked for more. I shrug it off and continue, "Anybody as rich as O'Sullivan will have made enemies along the way. What can you tell me about him?"

"Nothing."

"What do you mean nothing? You invested a good chunk of change in that restaurant. You must have checked him out beforehand. Or at least had your lawyer check him out."

There's a few seconds of profound silence before that tiny voice comes back. "My lawyer only researched what was pertinent to our deal. I was interested in opening a restaurant, and Rory was there with the funding and the know-how to make it happen." A bit of a whine creeps into her tone when she adds, "I told you this before."

"What about when you two were together? What did you talk about?"

"Nothing, really. We'd discuss the restaurant. Furniture. Staff. Business stuff."

"I mean when you were *fucking*, Gloria. He ever let anything slip? Ever mention trouble with other business partners or at home?"

The whine morphs into irritation. "We didn't talk all that much."

This is getting us nowhere. I glance at my watch. It's almost eight. "I can be at the jail at ten. When do you see your lawyer?"

"In about fifteen minutes. He's going to try to set a bail hearing after the arraignment. I'll either be back here or at home by ten. I'll let you know."

We ring off. I place the phone on the kitchen counter and pick up the paper to finish reading the article about O'Sullivan's death. I need the distraction. My gut is screaming that I've made a huge mistake agreeing to help Gloria. At least, whatever the outcome, David will be rid of her once and for all. If I find nothing and Gloria has been lying and she really did kill O'Sullivan, David still comes out ahead. Gloria will be in jail.

I scan the article. O'Sullivan is portrayed as a sterling citizen, reputable businessman and loving husband and father. Gloria, on the other hand, is characterized as a spoiled home wrecker who killed O'Sullivan when he refused to leave his wife. No surprise there. That description is offered by the grieving widow who knew of her husband's affair—one she had been told was over. According to her, O'Sullivan had come back to the bosom of his family weeks ago only to be hounded by a scheming Gloria who would not leave him alone.

That's too much for me to swallow. I hate Gloria. I also know Gloria. She's too vain and self-centered to go begging after any man. Especially when she had a backup. She might have had a dalliance with O'Sullivan, but chase him? No. Not with David waiting in the wings.

David.

I snatch up the phone again and call David's cell. It goes right to voice mail. Then I try the office number and punch in the code to check messages. There's one.

From David.

"Left town. Don't know when I'll be back. Don't try to get in touch."

Ah, how like David. Short, sweet and completely devoid of any useful information.

I don't give up that easily. I know he has a cabin in the Cuyamaca Mountains. I also know the caretaker's telephone number.

The guy answers on the first ring. I tell him I'm David's mother and there is a family emergency. David has turned off his cell and would he be so kind as to walk over to the cabin so I could talk with him?

I've never met the person behind the gravelly voice but I thank him profusely when he agrees. There's about two minutes of silence while I picture the guy walking the hundred yards or so from the caretaker's house to David's cabin. No small talk. I like that.

Then I hear the knock on the door, his explanation of why he disturbed David, and in another few seconds, David is on the line.

"Mom? What's wrong?"

"Uh, sorry, David. It's me."

Silence.

"I wanted to be sure you were all right. Not like you to disappear."

"No, that's more your style."

His tone is clipped, hard. He's more upset than I thought. "Okay. I deserve that. I admit, I've disappeared off the radar a few times—"

"A few times? I've always respected your privacy. I thought you'd show me the same courtesy."

His voice is tremulous. With anger? With sadness? I wish I could see his face.

I wait a beat, then say, "I'm sorry about Gloria."

The bark that comes across the line holds more disbelief

than humor. "Right. You're sorry about Gloria because she's such a good friend of yours."

Okay. Now his attitude is beginning to piss me off. "It's hardly my fault that you didn't see before this what a conniving bitch Gloria is."

"Now that's the Anna I know and love. You should be happy. I *do* see Gloria for what she is. I've always seen Gloria for what she is. What you don't seem to understand is that it didn't matter. I love her."

He stops.

"I loved her. Past tense. It's over now."

"Then why did you leave?"

He doesn't answer for so long, I start to think he isn't going to. I'm about to ask if he's still on the line, when he says quietly, "Because I can't be around you right now."

"Around me? What the fuck does that mean?"

This time, there's no hesitation. "It means I don't want to see your smug face every time something about Gloria is on the news." He's biting off each word and spitting it at me. "You won't miss a chance to rub in what an idiot I've been. I can't take that right now."

His outburst stuns me into silence. Not that what he says isn't true. I have hated every minute he and Gloria have been together. I've also let him know that I've hated every minute of it. This is the first time he's acknowledged my antipathy. Always before he's ignored how I felt about Gloria or made excuses for her. I'd begun to think the stars in his eyes made him deaf, dumb and blind to any criticism of his egocentric girlfriend.

"Do you know," he says after a moment, "that I've asked her to move in with me a dozen times? She always had an excuse why she couldn't. A long-term modeling assignment. A new film. The restaurant. For the first time, I realize it was something quite different. She didn't want to be tied down to me. She wanted to be free to pursue other interests. Explains why she wasn't around when I was in the hospital, why she didn't come to see me when I was released. She was too busy with Rory."

He's probably right about that. At least the timing is right.

I don't know what to say to David to make the truth less painful. I'm almost sorry I tracked him down. For the first time in our association, I'm unsure how to proceed. I don't want to make him feel any worse than he already does and I don't want to antagonize him further. I'm sure as hell not going to tell him what I'll be doing for the next few days.

I clear my throat. "Um, David? I'm going to let you go. You take as much time as you need. Don't worry about the business. We don't have anything lined up. If a job comes up, I'll handle it. You do what you need to do."

The laugh that comes across the line this time is harsh with sarcasm. "What do you know?" he says. "Anna Strong, tongue-tied. Don't believe that's ever happened before. Well, I'm glad you've given me permission to take a leave of absence. Now, if you don't mind, I'm going to hang up. I'd appreciate it if you don't call here again. I don't want to talk to you. I don't want to see you. Is that clear enough?"

It's obviously a rhetorical question because before I can respond one way or the other, the line goes dead.

CHAPTER 15

WELL. I STARE AT THE PHONE IN MY HAND. I guess he's serious. There's a gnawing in the pit of my stomach that is as surprising as it is unexpected. That David would be angry and hurt at Gloria's manipulation is understandable. That he would be so pissed at me is unacceptable. I'd march myself right up to that damned cabin if I didn't have Gloria to take care of first. After that, regardless of what he said about not wanting to see me, he and I are going to have a talk.

The phone rings again. Once more, it's a number I don't recognize. When I open the connection a voice asks "Anna Strong?" before I have a chance to say hello.

The voice is a purr, soft, seductive. A tingle of excitement races up my spine. "Sandra?"

Her laugh is as melodious and sexually charged as the voice. "I'm flattered. You have been looking forward to my call."

My heart is pounding and my palms start to sweat. She doesn't say expecting my call, she says, "looking forward to." Truth is, I *was* looking forward to it. A thing that makes no sense and one I'm certainly not going to admit.

"Culebra said you'd be in touch." I hope my tone conveys nothing but casual indifference. Jesus, what kind of power does she possess to cast a spell over a telephone line? It has to be a spell. Nothing else can explain the wild physical reactions I'm experiencing. Heat rippling under my skin, a body aching to be touched.

"And you know why?"

Her words bring sanity rushing back. "Yes, you're Avery's widow. Listen, we have no quarrel. I am willing to relinquish his holdings. I don't want anything to do with his estate. If you've talked with Culebra, you know I've not set foot in his house nor have I made any attempt to claim his property. If you need me to sign something, I will. Have your lawyer send it over."

My words tumble out like debris on a flood-swollen river.

She laughs and says, "Please, Anna. Slow down. You are right. *We* have no quarrel. Still, we must meet. Are you free tonight?"

My thoughts flash on Gloria. I don't know where my investigation will take me, but surely I should be free for a few hours this evening.

A few hours? What am I thinking is going to happen when I meet Sandra? Will we need a few hours? To do what?

Get a damned grip. Once more, I slip into brusque mode. "I have work today. I can make some time tonight. Where shall we meet?" An echo of last night. Your place or mine?

"At Avery's."

It's not a suggestion. Immediately, my hackles go up. "No. Not there."

The laugh again, infectious, bright, but this time with a

sharp edge. "I'm afraid it must be Avery's, Anna. Shall we say nine o'clock?"

My heart is doing that wild tattoo thing against my ribs. Memories of what happened in Avery's house turn into a black serpent of despair that slithers up my spine. Still, I find myself saying, "All right. Nine o'clock."

"That's a good girl." The purr is back. "Have a good day, Anna."

She cuts the connection.

"That's a good girl"? I wouldn't take that condescending crap from a friend, let alone a stranger. I don't know what kind of magic this were-woman is working, but before we meet face-to-face, I'm damned sure going to find out.

I stare at the telephone, feeling like a boat loosed from its mooring. What did I agree to? And why in the hell did I? For six months I've resisted every effort on Williams' part to get me back into Avery's house and in two seconds, Sandra got me to agree to meet her there.

Shit. I have to go see Gloria. First, I have to see someone else. I'm pretty sure I'll catch him at home. He's a teacher and he doesn't drive. Where else would Daniel Frey be this early on a Saturday morning?

CHAPTER 16

DANIEL FREY LIVES IN MISSION VALLEY IN A large, upscale condo development overlooking the city. It's a gated community and I lean out the car window to ring his unit.

In a moment he answers with an abrupt, "Yes? Who is it?"

"What kind of greeting is that?"

"Anna?" A pause. "You're here to see me?"

"No. I'm here to see your neighbor. The cute old guy. Of course, I'm here to see you. Are you going to buzz me in or what?"

There's another pause.

"Frey, what's going on? Why aren't you buzzing me in?"

No answer. Another pause. Then, finally, the gate swings open.

I punch the accelerator and speed through before he changes his mind. What was that all about? I know I haven't seen him since we stopped a demon raising last Halloween, but we parted on good terms. I saved his life, for Christ's sake. Well, technically, an empath saved his life. I saved his ass, though, which allowed the empath to save his life, so that should count for something.

By the time I reach his door, I've worked myself into a pretty good sense of indignation. My finger is about to hit the doorbell when the front door swings open. Frey greets me with a frown and steps outside, pulling the door closed behind him.

"This really isn't a good time, Anna," he says.

For a minute, I'm too distracted by what he has on to be irritated by the less-than-hospitable greeting. He tries to pull a white terry robe closed, but he's not quick enough and the robe isn't big enough to keep me from seeing what he's wearing underneath.

Frey is a shape-shifter whose other form is panther. His human job is teaching, at my mother's high school, in fact. It's how we met. He's in his forties, tall, with salt-and-pepper hair and a face that reflects humor and intelligence. He's a conservative dresser, leaning toward slacks and open-neck polos. So to find him in a pair of baby blue pajamas with black cats stenciled all over them provokes an openmouthed gape.

His mouth forms a thin, rigid line. "What's wrong?"

Astonishment is giving way to an irresistible urge to laugh. Not the right reaction if I want his help. I swallow hard and struggle to erase the smile off my face.

The effort is not lost on Frey. His frown deepens. "Well?"

"I need to do some research. I figured your library would be the place to start."

"Research about what?"

"Your cousins."

"Cousins?"

"The were side of the family."

The brows draw together. "Shape-shifters are in no way related to weres. They are pack animals, dangerous in and out of their animal bodies." He looks at me and for the first time, something besides aggravation touches his expression. "Anna, you want nothing to do with weres. Hasn't Williams ever told you that?"

"No. He had his chance, too. I saw him last night. Anyway, I've got no choice in this. I need to know what magic they possess. What spells they can cast. I need the information before tonight."

He glares at me, a dark intensity shadowing his eyes. "What happens tonight?"

"I have to meet with a were. It's business."

"What business could you possibly have with a were?"

Frey and I used to be able to read each other's thoughts, the way I can with vamps. That changed when I stupidly bit him once, and fed from him, which broke that connection. I see in his expression that he wishes he could crawl into my head right now and pry the information out of me. I also see deep concern and a dawning realization that he may be able to do something to stop me.

"Frey," I say with a warning shake of my head. "You can't stop this. Don't try. No tricks. I know you think you would be protecting me, but believe me when I say if you do anything to try and prevent this, I'll be angry. More than angry. I'll be downright pissed. We both know that wouldn't be good."

He continues to stare at me, the internal debate obviously still raging. He, too, has the ability to cast spells. I have firsthand knowledge. He cast one on me a while back. Judging from that experience, though, I know he has to be present to invoke it and to keep the object of the spell under its control. Unless he plans to stay with me all day and night, I don't think he can really do anything to prevent my meeting with Sandra.

Still.

"If you want to help, let me use your books. Find out how to protect myself. Doesn't that make sense?"

The debate comes to an end. His expression is still anxious but he does swing open the door.

His sartorial taste isn't the only thing that's changed.

The last time I was in Frey's home, the decor was minimalist to say the least—the walls, the carpet, the furniture, all the same color—gray. There were no pictures on the walls, no knickknacks on the tables, not a single book on the smooth, marble block that serves as a coffee table.

That was then.

Today the walls are alive with colorful works of art—bold landscapes done in great slashing strokes of green and yellow and red. The furniture has been rearranged, not symmetrically, but clustered in front of the fireplace. Throw pillows tumble over each other and spill onto the floor. A stack of books and a fan of magazines battle for space with a huge bouquet of violet lilies on that same marble coffee table.

It takes me a minute to absorb it all.

"Wow," I say, turning to Frey, "when you redecorate, you don't fool around, do you?"

"But he does fool around with the decorator."

The voice comes from behind me, startling me into whirling around. I never heard her approach, never sensed the presence. She must have come from outside, the balcony. "What are you, a cat?"

She smiles. "Sorry. I should have made more noise."

Frey moves around me to stand beside the woman. She's tall, only an inch or two shorter than his six feet, and willowy thin. She has light brown hair drawn back from her face. Her eyes, blue, cool, are carefully hooded as she looks at me. She's pretty in an edgy way, velvet over steel.

She's dressed in a pair of pajamas that match Frey's—only hers are pink with little black cats—and, oh, a couple of other major differences: her top is low-cut, revealing a curve of breast, and her pants ride low on her hips, exposing a tanned stretch of trim abdomen. No robe for this one. She's immodesty personified.

Makes me see Frey in a new light. He and I had sex. Once. It was pretty damned good, too, but if this is Frey's girlfriend, he must have talents he hid from me.

She's watching me, a half smile playing on those full lips. It hits me then. She's reading my thoughts. Shit. She's a shape-shifter, too. She now knows everything that's gone through my head in the last few minutes. Too late now to close the conduit.

You might have let me know.

She laughs. *Why? This was so much more fun.*

Are you a panther, too?

No. She links her arm through Frey's. *A tiger.*

Figures. I knew she had to be some kind of cat.

Frey is looking from one of us to the other. "This isn't fair," he says. "I can only hear one side of the conversation."

She tilts her head up and gives Frey a kiss on the cheek. "Go tend to Anna's needs," she says. "I'm going to shower."

Color floods Frey's face as he watches her walk toward the bedroom. She must have thrown him a parting remark that I wasn't privy to.

"Care to share?" I ask.

"No." He straightens his shoulders and gestures toward the hall. "Let's go to the library."

I follow in his wake. "Does the sex kitten have a name?"

"She didn't tell you?"

"No. Would I be asking if she did?"

"Layla. Her name's Layla."

"Any last name?"

We're at the door to the library and he swings it open. He doesn't answer. He's never been secretive with me before and it's creeping me out.

"She said she's a decorator? Where does she work?"

No answer. Again. If he doesn't give me something to work with, how am I going to check this kitty out?

He's at the shelves, trailing a finger over a row of books. Frey's library is extensive, three walls of floor-to-ceiling bookcases. Each book has the name of a literary classic embossed on its spine.

The room smells of old paper and aged leather, like an antiquarian bookstore. Except that these books are not literary classics. They're books on magic. Cleverly disguised and protected by a spell.

Frey makes his decision with a grunt and a snap of his fingers. He pulls down a volume and turns to me, clutching the book against his chest.

"I'm still not sure I should do this," he says.

I hold out a hand for the book. "Look at it this way, if you don't and I walk into a were trap, will you ever forgive yourself?"

Again the grunt but this time, he puts the book in my hand. "Read the first three chapters. And chapter seventeen. They contain the relevant information."

The book lies heavy on my palm. The title says *Great Expectations*, and if I were human, what I'd see when I opened the book would be the Dickens text. What I see now upon opening the book is Old English calligraphy.

English?

I look up at Frey. "The last time I looked at one of these books, the text was some kind of hieroglyphic. Are they all different?"

He gives me a tight-lipped smile. "I wasn't sure about you then."

"You have the ability to change the text?"

"Oh, Anna, I have all sorts of abilities. You'd be amazed."

I stare at him. Having met Layla, he's probably right. As for the books, I knew they were spell protected. It appears Frey is the spellbinder. Impressive.

He takes my arm and steers me toward the door. "Promise me you'll be careful, Anna. And call me if you have any questions. In fact, call me after your meeting."

"You're that concerned about my meeting with the were?"

He looks grim again. "After you read those chapters, I'm hoping you'll reconsider the meeting. No business can be that important. Or if you must go, take someone with you for backup. Williams maybe. He seems to have some free time on his hands right now."

My thoughts are suddenly of Sandra. Irrational thoughts, like I don't want to share her with anyone. I shake my head to clear the cobwebs. That I would be thinking such a thing seems to make Frey's point.

I raise the book. "I will read this before I make any decisions. I promise."

He doesn't seem too impressed nor does he look relieved at my words. He opens his mouth to say something else when the bedroom door opens and a naked, wet Layla appears in the doorway.

"Oh," she says, making no attempt to cover herself or duck back into the room. "Anna, you're still here?"

Like I hadn't caught that probe she deliberately sent out a second before opening the door. Rolling my eyes at both of them, I head out the front door.

Layla is a piece of work, true, still I don't know why I'm feeling so agitated as I make my way back to the car. The last time we were together, Frey told me that he had a girlfriend. I didn't give it much thought. I would have expected her to be someone like himself. Dignified. Sedate. This tiger is clearly a man-eater. She'll gobble him up and spit him out in a New York minute if he isn't careful. Makes my spidey sense tingle. She's had a profound influence on someone I consider a friend—right down to taking over his living area.

I press the car lock on the remote and slip into the driver's seat. Layla will have to wait. I have plenty on my plate at the moment. Still, she's added to my to-do list.

Right after Gloria and David . . . and Sandra.

I have an hour or so before Gloria calls to let me know if I'm going to meet her at her home or in jail. Might as well get a jump on my "research." I settle the book on my lap.

It's as far as I get. My cell phone rings. I'm mighty popular this morning. The number on the display is a familiar one.

"Hi, Mom. What's up?"

"Oh, Anna." My mother sounds breathless and excited. "You are never going to guess what happened."

"You sound happy so it must be something good. Tell me."

"I'd rather do it in person. Can you come over now?"

Crap. I glance at my watch. I'd just make it to East County, where they live, and have to turn around and come back to meet Gloria. "I can't right this minute. Can't you tell me over the phone?"

She starts to laugh. "No. I have to see your face when you hear this."

"Can you give me a hint?"

"When can you get here?"

"Late this afternoon, maybe?"

"Excellent. Come for dinner. We'll be waiting. *À bientôt, ma chère fille.*"

She disconnects without waiting for me to respond.

Ma chère fille?

I close my phone and drop it back into my bag. What was that all about? My mom has always been a Francophile, but since when did she start talking to *me* in French?

CHAPTER 17

I CAN'T IMAGINE WHAT KIND OF SURPRISE AWAITS me this afternoon. Maybe she and Trish enrolled in a French-cooking class and they need a guinea pig to experiment on. Dad is not big on French cooking. Since I can't eat any kind of cooking, it may turn out to be a less-than-momentous occasion all around.

Oh well. May as well not waste good reading time. I settle back in the car seat and open the book to the first chapter. Unlike the first time I opened the book, it takes several seconds for the conventional text of *Great Expectations* to fade. Maybe once outside the confines of Frey's library, the book protects its secrets on its own. Does it hold off revealing the true text until it's sure the hands that hold it are no longer human? I must ask Frey how this works.

When the transformation is complete, it takes concentration on my part to interpret the actual text. Old English calligraphy is not the easiest to read. The language is flowery and antiquated. I flip to the front and understand why. The book is not dated. No author listed. No publishing information. No publisher, actually, since the pages seem to be handwritten. In ink. I'm surprised Frey would let me out of the house with such a valuable book. Knowing Frey, though, the book may be equipped with its own security system. If I tried to rip out a page or accidentally dropped it in the bathtub, my head would likely explode.

The first chapter is devoted to the history of lycanthropes, as the book refers to them (the word itself coming from the Greek—*lykos*, wolf, and *anthropos*, human). Roots that reach back into prehistory. It is believed that young warriors of many Indo-European civilizations went into the wilderness to live as wolves wearing animal skins and eating raw meat as a test of strength and courage. A closely related tradition was that of the "berserkers" or bear people, who fought with wild, unrestrained aggression in battle. Losing control of their animal aspects was often blamed for acts of horrifying violence.

Still, it was thought that a physical transformation of man into wolf or bear was impossible—that the human body of a werewolf would be at rest while the animal form prowled. Some medieval records dispute that and give accounts of werewolves being killed before a complete transformation. The creature might have human hands or feet covered with hair.

Not a pretty image. I wonder if it's true. I've only dealt with shape-shifters to this point. Does Sandra change completely or is she half beast, half woman?

The rest of the chapter explains the many theories of how a transformation takes place, though none of them involve the moon. Most have to do with charms and potions and belts of animal skins. Nothing that is of interest or could be of help to me if things go badly between Sandra and me tonight.

Nor is there anything that points to Sandra being particularly dangerous. Is Frey overreacting?

Maybe the next two chapters and chapter seventeen will be more to the point.

I glance at my watch the same instant my cell phone rings. It's after ten so this must be Gloria.

"How did the hearing go?"

"Can you come pick me up?"

She sounds tired. "I take it that means you made bail?"

"Yes. I had to relinquish my passport, though, and put two of my houses up for collateral. Barely covered the twenty million. With all that, the prosecutor still wasn't happy. Wanted me held without bail."

Imagine that. "You were charged with murder, Gloria."

"Thanks for reminding me, Anna. I'd forgotten why I'm in this shit hole."

Well, well. The bitch is back.

"I'll be there in about twenty minutes."

I disconnect before she can make another smart-ass remark. Maybe I'll get lost on my way to the jail and let her cool her heels for a while. I'm on the clock now, at two hundred an hour.

GLORIA IS WAITING ON THE STEPS OF POLICE PLAZA when I pull up. I don't blame her for waiting outside. I'd be outside, too. Jail stinks.

I start to honk my horn to get her attention when a young guy comes streaking around the corner and bounds up the stairs. Late for a court hearing, maybe?

Except that he doesn't head toward the door. He heads for Gloria. Straight for Gloria.

I slam the car in park and jump out. The expression on his face, desperation, anguish, stirs the hair on the back of my neck. I let the adrenaline kick in and race after him.

There's a long, sloping expanse of grass between the

curb and the stairs. Gloria is standing at the top. I open my mouth to shout a warning when she spies the kid and does something so completely unexpected it brings me to a dead stop.

She opens her arms.

The kid falls into them and starts to sob.

Gloria sees me at the bottom of the stairs. She straightens up and gently pushes the kid away. She's whispering something to him, right at his ear, something my vampiric hearing can't pick up. He turns and looks at me. Then as quickly as he bounded up the stairs, he's running back down. Like a jackrabbit avoiding a fox, he makes a wide arc around me. Before I can put out a hand to stop him, he darts away.

It only takes me a nanosecond to decide not to go after him. I've filed his image in my head. I've seen him before.

I join Gloria at the top of the stairs staring in the direction of the now departed young man.

"Who was that?"

When she fails to respond, I turn to look at her.

"Gloria? Who was that? Not a reporter. He's too young to be a reporter. He was upset. You hugged him. He's not another boyfriend, is he? Somebody else you've been cheating on David with?"

A thundercloud of anger sweeps across her face. "He's a kid, Anna. Barely fourteen. No, he's not a boyfriend."

"Then who is he?"

"He's a friend. That's all I'm going to say. Can you please get me the hell out of here? I want to go home. Take a long, hot shower. Then we can talk about what you're going to do to find Rory's killer."

She's already three steps ahead of me, running down the stairs in her haste to get to my car. Or to avoid answering any more questions about the mysterious young man. I'm not sure which. Not that it matters. I have a clear image of the kid's face in my memory. I know I've seen him before.

It's the only reason I didn't stop him or press her for answers. I'll get those on my own.

The kid can run, Gloria, but he can't hide.

Not for long. Not from me.

CHAPTER 18

WHEN WE'RE IN THE CAR, IT SUDDENLY OCCURS to me that there were no paparazzi at the courthouse. A bloody carcass doesn't attract vultures faster than a celebrity in trouble attracts the media. I half turn in the seat to look at Gloria.

"How'd you pull it off?"

I don't have to explain what I mean. She waves a hand. "My lawyer let it leak that I'd be arraigned at one this afternoon. Oops."

I have to admire his ingenuity though I pity the guy who walks out of the courthouse on a pandering charge and has a hundred flashbulbs go off in his face. I crank over the engine.

David's place has always been home to Gloria in San Diego. Since she knows better than to think I'd take her there, I ask, "Where are you staying?"

"I thought I'd stay with you."

The ten thousand reasons why *that* is not going to happen bubble to my lips like a geyser ready to spew. Luckily,

I stifle the eruption when I realize she's kidding. I know she's kidding because she's staring at me with a "gotcha" smirk on her face.

"I have a suite at the Four Seasons," she says.

"I should have guessed. Where else would you stay but the most expensive hotel in San Diego?"

She ignores the sarcasm, rests her head against the seat and closes her eyes. I accelerate away from the curb. At least she's riding in front with me. If she'd gotten into the backseat, I might have been tempted to kick her skinny ass right out of the car.

She's quiet on the ride to the hotel. I use the time to concentrate on that kid and where I've seen him before. It won't come. I'm not worried, though. I know I'll remember. Something will trip the memory and his identity will float to the surface of my subconscious like pond scum.

The Four Seasons is San Diego's newest and finest. We pull up to the front entrance and a valet is there to open my door before we've come to a complete stop. Another valet is at Gloria's door, gushing like an excited schoolboy when he recognizes her. He either doesn't know or doesn't care that she's coming from a night in jail. He rushes past us to open the door to the lobby. Gloria sweeps past him like the queen with her livery.

I follow after getting the valet ticket. No one rushes to open the door for me. I'm only her driver.

Gloria is at the front desk, collecting messages and her key. At least she waits for me to catch up before starting for the elevator. She goes straight to the elevator cordoned off with a red rope. A uniformed bellboy opens it for her and we pass into a car with only two stop buttons. PH1 and PH2. She inserts a key card and hits PH2.

The elevator whisks us up in perfumed silence and whispers to a stop. The door opens into the suite's marble foyer. It's a setup I've only seen in movies. There is a fountain, lots of greenery, and a carved, twelve-foot-high double door. She opens it with the same key card she used in the elevator and steps aside so I can go in first.

I've been in a lot of beautiful homes and hotel rooms, but nothing like this. The penthouse faces west with a view over the city, over Pacific Coast Highway, over a vast expanse of ocean. It's an unobstructed view, inside and out, both because we're twenty stories up and because the entire wall is made of glass. No structural beams or window frames. How they did it, I couldn't begin to guess. There is furniture on both sides of the glass, classical leather pieces on the inside, wicker chairs and lounges on a terrace outside. It's breathtaking.

It becomes more so when Gloria presses a button and the "wall" retracts. The salt-air smell of ocean wafts in.

Gloria takes a deep breath and lets it out slowly.

"God. I was afraid I'd never smell fresh air again." She tosses her key and the stack of messages on a small mahogany table near the couch. Not all of the messages, though. Before starting for a door to the right of the living room, she extracts three from the pile and palms them. She calls back to me, "I'm going to shower and change. There's coffee in the kitchen. Order room service if you're hungry. I can't stay in these clothes another minute."

She doesn't wait for a reply but disappears into what I assume is the bedroom, closing the door behind her. I wonder whose messages she so subtly removed. She obviously didn't want me to see who left them. Takes all the fun out of being nosy if the object of your snooping is on to you. I go through the ones she left behind anyway. Nothing but calls from print reporters representing everything from the *Enquirer* to the *Wall Street Journal*.

She took the interesting ones with her.

I wander in the opposite direction, finding the kitchen behind another of those carved doors. There's a cof-

feemaker already set up on the counter. I push the button
and beans grind, water filters and coffee drips into a cut-
glass decanter.

A coffeemaker with a crystal decanter. Why am I surprised?

There's something else on the counter. A copy of a
search warrant. The objects of the search include a gun and
a key card. Since there are no accompanying receipts, the
police left with nothing.

All the same, I open cupboards and look on my own.
What I find is everything the type of person who can afford
to stay here would need for spur of the moment entertaining . . . tins of foie gras and caviar, sleeves of toast points
and wafer-thin crackers, expensive chocolates. More ex-
ploring finds the wine cooler hidden behind cherry cabinet
doors, six bottles of wine and six bottles of champagne.
China, crystal, a silver service, gold-leaf flatware.

I sniff, letting vampire senses kick in. No residual smell
of blood means there were no bloody clothes stuffed in any
of these corners. No smell of cordite or oil. No gun, either.

A low, muted chime announces that the coffee is ready.
I grab a coffee cup and close the cupboards. I didn't really expect that there would be anything to find. Gloria is
vain and selfish, arrogant and narcissistic. But she isn't
stupid.

Besides, I don't think she had a chance to come back
here last night. She was at the restaurant with David and me
and then she was in jail. Judging by the looks of the place,
the hotel must have a concierge service on call to clean up
after a warrant search. The place is immaculate.

I pour myself a cup of coffee and doctor it with cream
(real, none of that flavored crap) and sugar, and have taken
a seat on a chaise on the terrace when Gloria rejoins me.
Her skin glows, her wet hair falls in waves around her face.
She has on pale yellow silk pajamas that look both tailored

and expensive. Wearily, she falls into a chair opposite me. She gestures toward my cup.

"Any more coffee?"

My evil twin wants to say, "Yeah, in the kitchen. Do I look like a gofer?" The fatigue in her eyes, however, unleashes a rare moment of compassion and I find myself getting up, going into the kitchen and pouring her a cup. I'm not compassionate enough to ask if she wants cream or sugar, though.

She accepts the black coffee with a grateful smile. After drinking a moment or two in silence, she says, "What do we do now?"

I place my cup down on the glass-topped table between us. "Now you tell me about Rory. Anything that will point me to someone other than you with a motive to want him dead."

She tilts her head, eyeing me over the cup. "I really don't know anything. We didn't tell each other personal things. There was no need."

I start to say something nasty about her lack of moral fiber when Lance and last night's escapade flashes into my head. Okay. So if you asked me to tell you anything personal about Lance, like where he lives or who his enemies are, I wouldn't be able to answer, either.

On the other hand, I didn't go into business with the guy or cheat on my boyfriend with him.

"I know you spent your time screwing, but you must have come up for air once in a while. Did you ever overhear a telephone conversation that seemed off? Ever see anything that particularly disturbed O'Sullivan or made him mad?"

Gloria ignores my tone and lets her gaze drift out across the sea. After a moment, she replies, "Not really."

"Not really? Come on, Gloria. Think. This is going to be the shortest investigation in history if you don't give me something to work with. The suit he threatened you with. He suspected you of embezzling?"

She waves a hand. "It was harassment. He kept the books, for god's sake. He knew there were no missing funds. It was another ploy to get me to back down. To resume our relationship."

"I'll need to see that note. Is it still at the restaurant?"

She nods. "I'll call the manager and tell him to give you access to the office. Is there anything else?"

"Is there anything else?" I'm having a hard time reconciling this lethargic Gloria with the sharp-tongued harpy I'm used to. "Yeah, Gloria, there's something else. Why did you go to Rory's house yesterday? He was blackmailing you for sex. He was alone. You weren't afraid he'd force himself on you?"

Gloria isn't listening. She's focusing on the coffee cup in her hand. A hand that begins to tremble. She places the cup carefully on the table.

That's when it hits me. "Did you take something, Gloria? A sedative or a tranquilizer?"

This time when she looks at me, I see it. The dilated pupils, the glassy stare. "You did, didn't you?"

"I didn't get a moment's sleep last night. I'm so tired."

Great. "Stay with me. Tell me about O'Sullivan's home life. How did his wife act toward you in public? Did she ever let on that she knew the two of you were fuck buddies?"

A spark of life. Gloria leans forward. "If Laura knew we were having an affair, she never let on. Never. We had dinner, the three of us, many times. Sometimes, in the beginning, David joined us, too."

"You had dinner with David and Rory and his wife while you were screwing Rory. Balls of steel, Gloria. No wonder his wife has it in for you."

"I know what she told the reporters," she says. "She lied. I don't think she knew a thing about Rory and me."

"At least until last night."

"Until last night."

I shake my head. "You're sure O'Sullivan didn't say anything to his wife sooner? She says he confessed the affair weeks ago and she forgave him."

Gloria narrows her eyes. "Let me ask you something. If your husband confessed he was having an affair, would you invite the woman to his birthday party? Or a few days ago, invite her to your home for lunch?"

"Only if strychnine was on the menu."

She bobs her head. "Exactly. I'm the actress. There's absolutely no way Laura could have treated me the way she did if she'd known Rory and I were having an affair. She's his second wife, by the way. The trophy wife. She knew him. She'd have her sensors out for any indication that he was being unfaithful. She'd recognize the signs. After all, it's how she hooked him. She worked as his personal assistant. Emphasis on the *personal*."

Gloria watches me as she spins her tale. It sounds like motive enough. The second wife protecting her turf against the perceived usurper. It's neat and tidy. It could well be true. All the same, Gloria seems to be overlooking one important fact. While the current Mrs. O'Sullivan may not be an actress, the story she spun for the police was convincing enough to land Gloria in jail.

"I'll look into the wife's background. See if she has a gun registered in her name."

"Your friend, Chief Williams, should be able to help you, right? He'll give you access to the police reports?"

I shake my head. "He's on administrative leave. I don't have a contact in the department right now. Your lawyer will have access to those things. Call Sutherland and have the reports faxed to my office. You have the number."

I drain the last of the coffee and stand.

Gloria does, too. She extends her hand. "I'll call right

now. Thank you, Anna. For doing this. I know you don't want to."

I return the handshake. Oh, but I do want to. The smile on my face must look to Gloria like a gesture of goodwill. The truth is, it's a gesture of good riddance. One way or the other, Gloria is soon to be history.

I can hardly wait for her to be gone.

CHAPTER 19

WHEN I LEAVE GLORIA, I HEAD TO MY OFFICE. I realize as soon as I'm in the car that she never answered the question of why she went to Rory's yesterday in the first place. She pulled a neat little trick, distracting me with the coffee cup and the trembling hands. She recovered herself quickly enough, though, when the questions shifted to Mrs. O'Sullivan.

She's hiding something. I'm tempted to turn around and go right back to the hotel, force her to tell me what O'Sullivan said that sent her scampering to his home. Truthfully, though, there's another matter I'm more interested in. I want to find out why Frey objected so strongly to my meeting with Sandra. Frey and I have fought some pretty dangerous characters—human and otherwise. He knows I can take care of myself. The fact that he reacted so negatively means something.

Should I take his advice? Call Williams? And yet, when I saw Williams last night, did he offer any advice? Issue any warnings about meeting with Sandra? No. In fact, all he did was push the same buttons. Warn me that I was living a lie and that I'd crawl back into the fold soon enough.

I think Frey *is* overreacting.

I glance at my watch. I'm not due at Mom's until later. I may as well resume my reading on the deck of our office. Then when Gloria's lawyer faxes me the reports, I can look them over right away and decide what to do next.

David and I share an office on Pacific Coast Highway. Close to Seaport Village. Our business, fugitive apprehension, bounty hunting, has boomed in the last year or so. It's the perfect career choice for two adrenaline junkies. David is an ex–pro football player who couldn't face the prospect of opening a car dealership or becoming a sportscaster when he retired. I was a schoolteacher who couldn't face another year of teenage angst.

My parents still don't understand how I could have made such a radical career change. They never recognized the wild child who only went into education to please her mother. From the beginning, teaching was an ill fit. When I found myself hating the classroom even more than some of my students, I knew it was time to quit. Meeting David in a kickboxing class and listening to his stories about bounty hunting was like a door opening into another world. I only had to throw his six-foot-six frame on his butt a couple of times to convince him to take me on as a partner.

That was almost four years ago.

Before I became vampire.

I unlock the door and step into the empty office. I miss David. Though our relationship isn't what it was before a rogue vamp attacked and turned me, we still share—what? Love of the chase. Freedom. An appreciation of what making good money does for your lifestyle. Now, with Gloria soon to be but a bitter memory and that point of contention gone, maybe we can start having fun together again.

Yeah. Fun that does not involve eating or showing how

strong and fast I've become or avoiding mirrored bars and backlit windows.

Not bloody likely.

The most I can hope for is that his next girlfriend doesn't make it her mission to get me out of his life. God knows, Gloria tried hard enough.

I trudge over to the slider and pull it open. The deck stretches the length of our office and is suspended over the bay. The sky above is deep blue and the water below white tipped and frothy.

We're in the corner office. The neighbor to our left, a real estate broker, has strung Christmas lights and installed a tree in the middle of his deck. His slider is open, too, and the not-so-soft strains of Christmas carols drift out. For once, it doesn't bother me. For once, I'm not dreading Christmas. For once I think maybe I won't fight with David about putting up our own tree.

That is assuming he comes back before Christmas.

I lean against the deck rail, relaxing for a minute. Since my body temperature is much, much cooler than the 98.6 degrees of a human, and the air feels slightly warm to my skin, I figure it must be in the sixties. A clear, perfect December day.

Frey's book calls to me. Not literally, although it wouldn't surprise me if it was capable of such a thing. I retrieve it from the desk, roll my chair out onto the deck and settle in.

Let's see—chapter two. I thumb to the page.

I skim the text, letting the salient points sink in and skipping the irrelevant.

When bitten by a werewolf, a person does not undergo a drastic change. Not at first. He or she is taken to the woods and left there by his "sire" with no weapon and no food. He is told he must obtain a belt of wolf fur. He must obtain that belt within fourteen days or before the full moon, whichever occurs first. If he does not kill a wolf in that time, he dies.

If he is successful, the pelt becomes his talisman. He is accepted into the werewolf community and is initiated into a pack. The pack is his family. He is free to choose a mate, but only from within the family. If there are not enough females in the pack, he must earn the right to bring another over. The subjugation of females is complete within a pack. Mating is for life. Werewolves only propagate by an exchange of blood. Once bitten and initiated, the werewolf must, within its lifetime, turn two others to complete the circle of life. The rule is strict—he may turn only two. Rogues who disobey this edict are dealt with severely. (No details are given, but since I've dealt with rogue vamps before I can imagine what it means—death.)

The chapter ends and I'm left fuzzy headed and confused, partly from the strain of interpreting the difficult text and partly because what I read contradicts everything I ever knew about werewolves.

As soon as that thought passes through my head, the absurdity of it makes me laugh. The same could be said about vampires. Until I became one, I had quite a different perspective on the subject. Hadn't almost everything I believed about vampires proven to be false? Why should the popular mythos about werewolves be any less false?

And yet, there is one glaring inconsistency. Sandra is the leader of a werewolf pack. She's female. Definitely, unquestionably female. From what I saw the other night, her pack is 90 percent female. There were maybe two or three males in Culebra's bar that night. Unremarkable males obviously because I can't remember what they looked like. I wonder their purpose? Sexual toys? Heavy lifters? Bike mechanics?

Hmmm.

Chapter three beckons so I prepare to continue reading

when the chime of the fax machine distracts me from the book.

Gloria's lawyer?

I go inside to watch the machine spit out page after page of grainy, handwritten forms. The first page is a note on the lawyer's letterhead. It requests I call with anything I learn—either to Gloria's advantage or not. It also adds that I am to invoice the law office and not Gloria for my services.

No problem. I don't care who writes the checks as long as they're written and don't bounce.

I gather up the pages and take them back out to the desk. Frey's book gets put aside.

It doesn't take me long to go through the stack. There's the original police report made on the scene. Harris caught the case. It came in on a 911 call from Mrs. O'Sullivan at 9:10 p.m.

Harris' notes are precise, detailed and objective. No weapon was found at the scene. The ME put time of death somewhere between 2:00 and 6:00 p.m. O'Sullivan was killed by a small-caliber weapon, one shot to the back of the head. No sign of forced entry. No obvious sign of a struggle. The only thing disturbed was a stack of papers on the desk.

The interview with Mrs. O'Sullivan is more interesting. She named Gloria as a suspect right off. Talked about the affair and hinted that there were improprieties in their business dealings as well. She said she didn't know the details, but her husband indicated he had hired a forensic accountant to go over the restaurant's books. She assumed he'd found something because the last few days Rory had been furious with Gloria and tried several times to get in touch with her.

The next interview was with the son, Jason. Fourteen years old. Home from Loyola Prep School for the holiday break. He and his stepmom had spent the afternoon shopping and then went to dinner. He said he didn't know anyone who would want to hurt his father. He was with his stepmother when she found the body.

There was no one else in the home. The staff had the day off. The house is secluded behind a gated brick wall and is not visible from the street. To gain access, a key card is needed. As far as she knew, Mrs. O'Sullivan said, all the cards were accounted for, but she couldn't be sure if Gloria had one. She thought she probably did . . .

I have to smile at that. Mrs. O'Sullivan was doing a masterful job of steering the investigation toward Gloria.

The rest of the pages include pictures of the crime scene, O'Sullivan slumped across his desk, close-ups and wide range shots. The room. The outside of the house showing the windows and the ground beneath. The ground was not disturbed, and the notes indicated the area was muddy because the sprinklers had run that morning. If someone had broken in through the windows, there would have been footprints.

There are booking files. There's a mug shot, but damn if Gloria doesn't look beautiful. In a mug shot. She stares right into the camera, eyes wide, head up. An expression of shock and bewilderment casts a shadow on those perfect features, but not a hair is out of place.

The last page is the result of the warrant search of Gloria's suite at the Four Seasons and her vehicle. Nothing of interest found. No weapon. No key card for O'Sullivan's home. A request is to be filed to search her L.A. residence. The restaurant.

And David's condo.

That brings me straight up in the chair. Naturally they'd include David's condo. Not only because David and Gloria are a well-known local celebrity couple, but because of the way David acted with Harris. Now with the revelation that

Gloria and O'Sullivan were lovers, this search may be a fishing expedition for an accomplice. Or worse. David may actually be a suspect.

Why didn't I think of that this morning?

I grab the phone and put a call into SDPD. When I ask to speak to Detective Harris, I get an officer in his unit that tells me he's not available.

I don't leave a message. I'm out of the office and into my car so fast, the detective on the other end of the line may not yet realize it's gone dead.

CHAPTER 20

D AVID'S CONDO IS DOWNTOWN, A QUICK TEN minutes from our office. On the way, I call his cell. It's still turned off but I leave a message, though I suspect he won't pick it up when he sees who it's from. He's being such an ass. I'd certainly want to know if the police were searching *my* home. I hope I get there before they do.

I don't. Harris is coming down the front steps with three uniforms. I slide into a loading zone parking space and propel myself out of the car.

"Detective Harris."

He stops when he hears his name and meets me at the bottom of the stairs. The uniforms at his side step between us, frowning, until he waves them off. He says something to them and they move away toward the waiting police cars. Then he turns his attention to me.

"Ms. Strong."

I gesture toward the building. "What were you doing in my partner's condo?"

He smiles. "You aren't that naive." He reaches into a

pocket and pulls out the search warrant. "I would give this to Mr. Ryan but he doesn't seem to be around. It's a copy of a search warrant. Duly executed. I left another in the apartment. Care to tell me where he's gone?"

I glance over the warrant. No surprises. It lists the same items as Gloria's. When I look back up, two more uniforms and another suit have come downstairs. Empty-handed.

Harris takes the warrant out of my hand. "Where is he, Ms. Strong?"

I put on an innocent face and shrug. "Don't know, Detective. He left town after you arrested his girlfriend. He was a bit upset."

Harris laughs. "I can imagine. You find out your girlfriend is unfaithful and a murderer all in the same evening. It would ruin my night."

The next instant the amusement is gone from his face. "That's assuming he hadn't learned about the affair earlier. If I find out he had, Mr. Ryan may have more to deal with than a broken heart."

He turns away then and rejoins the cop waiting by the patrol car. I watch them pull away. At least he didn't press me for information about David's whereabouts. Nor did he threaten me with obstruction. I guess Gloria is still number one on his hit parade.

I let myself into David's condo with my key. There are two ways to toss a place—the neat way if you don't want to make it obvious what you were looking for or the trash it way if you don't care.

Harris didn't care. Not that he broke anything or deliberately went out of his way to mess things up, but drawers and cabinets were left open, the clothes in the closet pushed to one side, items on David's desk rearranged. David, the neat freak, will not be happy.

I'm not going to straighten up. David should have been

here to supervise instead of slinking away like a whipped puppy. Serves him right to come home to a mess.

On my way out, I do stop, though, to scoop up the newspapers accumulating on the doorstep. He hadn't bothered to stop delivery. David takes both San Diego and L.A. papers, and when I toss them onto the living room coffee table, a picture on the front page of the *Los Angles Times* catches my eye.

More than catches my eye. Trips that memory switch I'd been waiting for.

Rory O'Sullivan and his wife and son.

Jason. The kid I saw on the court steps with Gloria.

CHAPTER 21

J ASON O'SULLIVAN. NOW I REALIZE WHERE I'D SEEN
him before. Not in person, but in media accounts of the
restaurant opening. He'd accompanied his parents that night.
Video of the three of them exiting a limo and being greeted
at the door by Gloria had run on every newscast.

So what was he doing this morning hugging the woman
accused of killing his father?

I pick up the phone and call the hotel. When I ask to be
connected to Gloria's room, I'm told she's left a "do not dis-
turb" message. Crap. I leave a message for her of my own—
"Call me. And do not ever have the operator refuse my calls
again."

I slam the receiver down. She's probably in a sedative-
induced coma. She made it clear on the courthouse steps that
she wasn't going to talk about Jason, which leaves only one
other person to ask.

Jason.

David doesn't have a desktop computer at home, only a

laptop, and it's nowhere in sight, so I figure he must have it with him. That means back to the office.

David and I are Mac people. We each have a monitor on opposite sides of our big, oak partner's desk. I power mine up.

I figure odds are against a listed telephone number, but check online anyway. I'm right. No listing in his name. I could ask Gloria's lawyer to get it for me, but then I'll have to explain why I want it. Since Jason is a minor, I'd rather not involve Gloria's lawyer, Jason's mother and the army of O'Sullivan lawyers no doubt on the family pay-roll when I talk to him. Time enough later to share information.

If it turns out there's anything to share.

I do know another way to track down a teenager.

I log on to MySpace. David and I got an account not long ago for this purpose—it's a great tracking tool. I do a search for "Jason O'Sullivan." I get ninety-four hits, including every variation of the name you can imagine. Sixteen actually are "Jason O'Sullivan's." It takes the better part of an hour to sort through some pretty whacked-out profiles to find one that seems promising. Says he's eighteen, naturally, looking for friends. Lives in L.A. The kid in the picture, though it's not a sharp image, looks like the kid I saw with Gloria today.

It's worth a shot.

I send an instant message: FRND OF GLORIA. RE-SPOND F U R 2.

I have no way of knowing if this is the right Jason or if he's online. Nothing to do now but wait.

So, it's back to Frey's book. I settle into my desk chair, prop my feet up on the desk and start to read.

A few paragraphs into chapter three, and I have dubbed this one "the care and feeding of werewolves." Werewolves are human in most aspects twenty-seven days out of the month. Except for not being able to make babies (something weres and vampires have in common), they work (or "toil" in the book's archaic turn of phrase) in jobs, can have a social life outside of the pack, attend church and perform "works of goodwill" in their communities.

It's the other three days that create problems.

Werewolves must make a change at least once a month, usually during the full moon. The moon, however, does not *cause* the change. It's the life cycle of the were that requires it. Since a transformation must take place at least once a month in order for the were to survive, the full moon is merely a way of calculating time. A lunar wake-up call.

If the were does not make the change, his body goes into "crisis" (a condition not described), from which he will not recover. He needs the belt of wolf fur to make the change. Without it, the animal cannot emerge. (What does this "belt" look like? Is it literally a belt of fur that can be taken off? Does it meld into his skin to precipitate the change? Damn. Not enough details here.) If he doesn't "metamorphose" at least one time a month, he dies.

However, if he is transformed during the full moon, the odds are increased that the were will do humans harm. Since early recorded history, it has been observed that many animals are more prone to bite during a full moon than any other time. In his animal form, the were is particularly vulnerable to this behavior. Ordinarily, the were will only do what wolves do—hunt, feed, mate in a pack. Food sources are what would be found in the woods: small rodents, birds, such game as they can bring down. Should a pack happen upon a human, however, while an ordinary animal might be frightened away by aggressive behavior or shouting, a were pack is more likely to attack. The majority of werewolf killings occur this way.

How does one recognize werewolves? Most obvious is to see a pack in an area or location where wolves should not be, specifically, in a town or village. If the animals are observed acting in ways that suggest a higher intelligence or unusual physical abilities, or if you strike one with a nonmetallic object and do no harm, or (I love this one) if you are in an area with a large concentration of immigrants from Eastern Europe, most likely you will have made contact with werewolves.

Silver offers protection against werewolves. (Finally, something in the lore that I recognize.) A silver-topped cane or silver saber or knife will dispatch a werewolf, as will silver bullets.

The most effective method of protecting oneself?

Avoidance. Simply put, all ye, stay away from werewolves.

I close the book and lay it on the desk.

Stay away from werewolves.

Good advice under most conditions, I'm sure. My meeting with Sandra has nothing to do with her being a werewolf and everything to do with finally freeing myself of Avery. When we fought and I killed him, I did it defending my life. I didn't do it to become heir to his fortune. I wasn't aware of the ancient vampiric law that bestowed his property on me as survivor of an unjust battle. I didn't ask for it. I didn't want it. I've spent the last six months trying to forget it.

As far as I'm concerned, Sandra's claiming title as Avery's wife is a relief.

There isn't a reason in the world why Sandra and I shouldn't part tonight as friends.

An urgent stirring sends heat flooding through me.

Maybe more than friends.

I stand up, stretch, move to the deck.

I need to move. I need air to clear my head. I need to

understand why once again, thoughts of Sandra spark such a powerful sexual response.

That I'm attracted to Sandra sexually is startling. I made fun of it with Culebra, blamed the feeling on a spell. I've almost finished Frey's reading assignment, however, and there has been no mention of werewolves being capable of casting love spells.

I think about seeing her in the bar. How I hadn't noticed her at first. Hadn't noticed her at all, really, until she wanted me to. Then she hit me with a psychic sexual punch so strong, it left me dizzy.

So strong, the sound of her voice made me agree to go to Avery's tonight, something I'd sworn never to do.

So strong, I get shivers of delight imagining how it would be to please her.

Like a junkie jonesing for a fix.

Doesn't make sense.

Until suddenly, it does.

· It's crystal clear.

I don't know how she's doing it, but I do know why. This compulsion to be with her, this need to please her, is a weapon. She either doesn't understand or doesn't believe that I'm not going to fight her claim for Avery's property. That I'm relieved to be free of it. So she's set this velvet-lined trap.

A damned effective one.

Tonight, all I need do is make her understand that she has nothing to fear from me. She can revoke the spell. I'll give her anything she wants. Willingly.

Anything.

CHAPTER 22

A CHIRP FROM INSIDE BRINGS ME BACK—BACK TO consciousness, back to the computer.

An instant message: HU R U?

I reply: FRIEND OF GLORIA.

Jason's answer comes scrolling back: WOT FRND?

My fingers tap out: SOME1 TRYING 2 HLP HER.

Jason: PRUV IT.

Me: GLORIA HIRED ME.

Jason: 2 DO?

Me: FIND OUT WHO REALLY KILLED YOUR DAD.

There is a pause here, so long I break it by typing: JASON, R U STILL THERE?

Finally, I get a response: CAN WE MEET?

Me: THE SOONER THE BETTER.

Jason: NOT 2DAY. 2MORO MORN?

Me: WHR & WEN?

Jason: 9 A.M. LESTAT'S? KNO IT?

The character name I know, any Anne Rice fan would. A place with that name? I type: NO.

Jason replies: COFFEE SHOP. ADAM'S AVE.

A coffee shop named Lestat's? And I'm being invited there? Oh, the irony. I type back: C U @ 9.

I'm ready to log off when one more message comes back: DON'T TELL ANY1.

I have to smile at Jason's dramatic parting shot. I suppose he doesn't want his stepmother to know he's consorting with the enemy. Which begs the question: why is he?

I'll get the answer tomorrow morning.

My thoughts shift back suddenly to Sandra. Now that I understand she's the source of this—whatever it is—I have to know how she's doing it. If it's not a spell, what? Power of suggestion? Can she tap into my sexual psyche and feel the hunger? At this moment, the image of her in my head is powerful enough to make me tremble. Is there a way to block those message receptors?

Words from the book spring unbidden: How best to protect yourself from werewolves? Stay away from them.

The office phone rings and I glance at the caller ID. Then at my watch. Yikes. I snatch up the receiver, "Sorry, Mom. Time got away from me. I'm on my way."

She laughs. "Good. We're giddy with excitement over here. Our lives are about to change. *Your* life is about to change. Hurry, Anna. We're waiting for you."

Giddy with excitement? Change my life? My mother is not one for hyperbole but here she is, sounding for all the world like a spokesperson for Publishers Clearing House. Is there a goofy-looking guy with bad hair and a toothy grin holding balloons and a big cardboard check lurking on our front porch?

"You didn't enter a sweepstakes, did you?"

Again, the silver lilt of her laughter. "Better. I'm not

going to tell you anything else. You need to come home. Now."

"Okay. On my—"

But she's already rung off.

Weird. Very weird.

CHAPTER 23

MOM, DAD AND TRISH RUSH OUT OF THE FRONT door and spill down the porch steps like lemmings over a cliff. I've barely gotten out of the car before I'm surrounded. They crackle with excitement. I feel it on my skin. Little electric shocks like static from a light switch.

"Whoa." I hold up both hands. "What's going on?"

Mom recovers first. She puts an arm around Trish's shoulders. "Anna, you won't believe what happened today."

"A lawyer came," Trish interjects, hopping around like an eager puppy.

"With news," my dad adds.

"From France," Mom says.

"We're going to live there," Trish says. "All of us."

"In a château," Dad says.

"Oh, Anna," my mom gushes. "It's so wonderful. We've inherited a winery."

A winery?

It takes some doing, but I finally get my family corralled and back up the porch steps and into the house. They never stop babbling. All three. All at once. I've never seen my parents so animated. Trish? She's jumping up and down.

I scoot them over to the couch and hold up a hand. "Sit."

They do, still chattering like agitated squirrels.

"Quiet."

The prattle dies away, leaving me staring at three glowing faces, bright with expectation and anticipation. They're waiting for me to ask questions. I hardly know where to begin.

"You said a lawyer came here? Today?"

They look at each other, and then Dad and Trish both look to Mom, making her the official spokesperson. She takes a deep breath and plunges in.

"Yes. He came to see me first yesterday at school. Asked me some questions. Mostly about my grandmother and her side of the family. I told him she died when I was young and my memories are vague. I gave him her maiden name and her place of birth. He wondered about my mother. I told him she died many years ago and as far as I know, we have no relatives left on that side of the family except us. He asked to make an appointment with your father and me this morning. Said he had some details to check, but he was fairly certain he'd have some good news for us when he saw us again."

She can sit still no longer. She jumps up and starts pacing. "Well, he showed up this morning and presented us with a thick portfolio of documents. He went through the papers one by one. There were birth records and death certificates. A family tree. Photos of my grandmother and *her* mother taken almost a century ago. In France. There's a will. The will of a great uncle I didn't know existed. An uncle who owned a great deal of property in France, including a working winery. An uncle who evidently has no living relatives left to inherit his estate."

She stops pacing, turns to face me, and her face is

once again wreathed in as joyful a smile as I've ever seen. "Wait until you see the pictures. It's unbelievably beautiful. There's a château on the property and a staff that's worked for the family for decades. They're waiting to meet us. We can go anytime. It's ours, Anna. All of it."

I was born a cynic, and becoming a vampire didn't temper my natural inclination to distrust anything that looks too good to be true. If anything, it's worse. So it's hard not to say, "Are you all crazy? People don't inherit property in France out of the blue. It's got to be some kind of scam."

But I can't say it out loud. I don't want to be the one responsible for eradicating the pure joy I see on the faces of the people I love most. It would be like stomping on a kitten.

My dad, who knows me too well, stands up and puts an arm around my shoulders.

"I know what you're thinking," he says. "It's too good to be true. I did my homework. I have business contacts in France, you know. I had them check out the lawyer. He's legitimate. Got a prospectus for the winery. It's well-known. Exports product to the United States. The château has been renovated and well maintained. It's fully furnished and staffed. I'm telling you, Anna, there's nothing bogus about this. Sometimes people really do get lucky."

He opens his other arm to Trish and Mom. They join us in a kind of awkward group hug. "I think this calls for a celebration," he says. "Let's get dressed up and go to Mister A's. Champagne on me." He plants a kiss on Trish's forehead. "Ginger ale for you, *ma petite chère.*"

That does it. Now my *father* is speaking French? I'm sick. With shock. With apprehension. My father may be right. This might be legitimate. I sincerely hope it is. The realist in me screams there's a better chance it's not.

CHAPTER 24

I LEAVE MY FAMILY, PROMISING TO JOIN THEM downtown in an hour. I know as I speak the words that I'll not be staying for the celebratory dinner. Once again, too many ways to give away the fact that I'm no longer human. I can fake it when I eat with them at home by taking small helpings and spreading the food around my plate. I've been known to sneak into the kitchen and dump a napkin full down the garbage disposal.

Can't do that in a restaurant. Especially one famous for large quantities of food, to say nothing of platter-size steaks. It'll be impossible to pretend. I've used the late lunch excuse too many times already to have it sound credible, especially since my mother specifically asked me for dinner tonight. No, better to come up with another reason for leaving before dinner.

Damn it, David. If you were home the way you should be, I could ask you to call me and say there's a fugitive who needs apprehending. Give me an excuse.

Makes me realize how completely I've cut myself off

from the few friends I had before the change. I can think of no one else to call and ask the favor. No one to rescue me.

Shit.

When I get back to the cottage, I shower and fluff dry my hair, then stand naked in front of my closet to decide what to wear. My wardrobe is limited. Jeans. Black, navy, tan. A few pairs of linen slacks with matching blazers (court attire). A few skirts, assorted blouses. One simple silk sheath, black, V-neck, narrow waist accented by a wide belt.

I choose the dress and slip it over my head. It's body hugging and soft against my skin. I have no way of knowing how I look in the dress, I bought it after becoming, but I know how it makes me feel. Slinky. Sexy. The skirt is midthigh length. I pair it with a pair of three-inch strappy Jimmy Choos. I bought them because the lady at the shoe store said I had pretty feet and trim ankles and they show them off. The skirt is short and the heels high.

All this for an evening with my folks?

Of course not.

I can't fool myself any more than I can change what I'm feeling. My blood is on fire. This prolonged anticipation is almost unbearable. The incongruity of what I'm thinking does nothing to mollify the mounting passion.

I make no attempt to understand or explain it. In fact, I can let myself enjoy it. It's been a long time since I've felt this kind of anticipation.

My hands skim the contours of my body, the silk cool and liquid and sensuous beneath my fingers.

This dress is for what happens *after* the evening with my folks.

This is for my evening with Sandra.

And since after tonight it will be over, why not enjoy it?

CHAPTER 25

M ISTER A'S OCCUPIES THE TOP FLOOR OF A building on Fifth Avenue. From Thanksgiving to New Year's, the entire building is decorated from top to bottom with Christmas lights. It's a gaudy over-the-top holiday display that's become a San Diego tradition. For the first time in years, it makes me smile. When my brother and I were growing up, we had a family tradition of our own: drive through Balboa Park to see Santa and his reindeer, then come to dinner here to see the lights.

I haven't had dinner at Mister A's in years. As far as I know, neither have my parents. That Dad should choose this restaurant to celebrate shows what Trish's existence has given back to the family.

There are three businessmen waiting with me for the elevator to the restaurant. If I wondered how I looked in the dress, any doubts are dispelled by the lingering, hungry looks I get from them. They'd like to see me on the menu, I think, served on a bed of—it wouldn't matter as long as it was a bed.

My father does a comic double take when I walk in. He stands when I approach the table and holds out a chair. "I almost didn't recognize you," he says.

"I've never seen you in a dress, Aunt Anna," Trish says. "I didn't know you owned one. Especially one like—"

"Okay," I hold up a hand. "Enough. So you don't often see me in a dress. Isn't this supposed to be a special night?"

"Anna is right," Mom says. "And I, for one, think you look beautiful. You should dress up more often. When we get to France, we'll go on a shopping spree. For you and for Trish."

"I'd love a dress like that," Trish says eagerly, eyeing my cleavage.

"Oh, no," Mom says, laughing. "You're much too young. I'm sure Anna and I can find something more appropriate for a teenager. Imagine, Anna, what shopping in Paris will be like."

It hits me then that they expect me to go to France with them. I stare at my mother. Maybe I'm misinterpreting her intention.

No.

It was in her voice, and it's right there in the way she's looking at me—with an expression that says no one in her right mind would pass up an opportunity to live in a château in France. I can't believe I didn't see this coming.

Worse, my dad and Trish are both looking at me the same way.

My shoulders tense.

I can't let them think for one moment that my going with them to France is a possibility. And yet—

Do I want to fight this fight tonight?

No. I won't ruin this evening any more than I have to. I put on a bright smile. "You all look pretty spiffy yourselves."

My mother is wearing a cream-colored silk pantsuit with a blouse of warm rose. Dad is wearing Hugo Boss, charcoal coat and slacks, white shirt, burgundy tie. Trish is lovely in dark slacks and a hand-knitted rainbow-hued angora sweater.

I'm not the only one who went all out for the evening.

Mom and Dad grin at the compliment; Trish touches the collar of her sweater as if self-conscious. "You don't think this sweater makes me look, you know, weird?"

I laugh. Typical teenager. "Why would you think it makes you look weird?"

"Well, it's *bright*."

"Bright is good. Bright is happiness and excitement. You three could light the city of San Diego tonight with your luminescence."

Trish giggles.

"You should be happy, too." Mom reaches over and touches my hand. Then she takes it in both of her own and rubs gently. "You are so cold, Anna. Do you feel all right?"

Crap. I didn't move fast enough. I forget at times to avoid skin contact. I pat her hands with my left and gently pull my right from her grasp. I fold my hands on my lap and nod. "I'm fine."

She doesn't look as if she believes me, but she picks up the thread of her conversation and adds, "This is a new beginning for all of us."

There. No possible way I could misinterpret that. I have to say something. I open my mouth, but the maître d' chooses that moment to announce that our table is ready. I've been granted another reprieve, however brief, to keep from breaking their hearts. That's the big break. The small one will come when I tell them that I'm leaving before the first course.

We take our seats at the table, the server places our napkins in our laps (Trish giggles unpretentiously and charmingly at that, too), and the sommelier approaches with a wine list. Dad waves it away and asks about champagne choices. He's given several that sound foreign and expensive. Not surprisingly, Dad orders real champagne, not a domestic clone. The sommelier bows away with a smile of approval and snaps his fingers for the servers to begin their preorder hovering with the rituals of water pouring, silverware straightening and candle lighting.

Trish watches it all with the curiosity and delight of one who has spent the better part of her life dining at McDonald's. It's a joy to see. I can only imagine her reactions to the marvels awaiting her in France. I'm struck by sudden and intense sadness that I will not be there to share in her journey of discovery.

If there is a journey of discovery. I'm still concerned that this is some elaborate hoax and when it comes to light, the disappointment will be as bitter as the excitement now is sweet.

"Anna?"

Mom's voice pulls me back.

"What's wrong? You have the strangest look on your face, and you're wringing that napkin like it's someone's neck."

Not a bad analogy. If this does turn out to be a hoax.

I refold the napkin, place it beside my plate and try to smile. "Just thinking of work."

"Work?" Mom echoes. "Why would you be thinking of work tonight?"

God. I steel myself to say it. "I'm really sorry, but I'm not going to be able to stay for dinner."

Three voices say, "Why not?"

"It's a job. David and I are heading up the coast to Del Mar. There's a guy we've been trying to grab and this is our chance. He's been seen hanging around a local watering hole." I make a sweeping gesture with my hand. "That's why this getup."

Trish leans forward eagerly. "Could I go with you? I'd love to watch you in action."

Mom and Dad both make gasping noises. Dad says, "I'm afraid that's not a good idea, is it, Anna?"

Before I can answer, Mom says, "Absolutely not, young lady." She half turns in her seat so that we're eye to eye. She's angry. Her voice quakes with it. "I can't believe you're leaving us tonight of all nights. This is a family celebration. You aren't going to need that job much longer. The sooner you tell your partner you're quitting, the sooner he can find a replacement. Call him. Tell him something came up and you can't make it."

Her vehemence catches me off guard. Suddenly I'm plunged right back to the time before Trish when we were never able to get together as a family without the inappropriateness of my work becoming a hot topic of conversation. Saving Trish masked it for a while, but I didn't realize until this moment how close to the surface the acrimony still boils.

Trish is stirring in her chair. She's gone pale, her expression anxious, as if afraid that Mom's displeasure will be turned on her. That the negative turn the evening has taken is somehow her fault.

Mom sees it, too, and reaches over to take Trish's hand. "I'm sorry, honey. Anna and her Dad and I should discuss this in private. I have no right to ruin our evening."

She doesn't look at me as she adds, "Well, if you must go, Anna. We're sorry you're not going to share in what promises to be a wonderful meal. There'll be plenty of family time when we're in France, though."

Dad stands up and comes to hold my chair for me as I prepare to leave the table. He squeezes my shoulder and kisses my cheek.

"Come by the house tomorrow. We'll talk. We have plans to make."

The lump in my throat prevents me from answering. I smile at Trish and she looks back with eyes wide and wet. I manage to croak, "I'll see you tomorrow, Trish. Promise."

Mom doesn't acknowledge my leaving. Dad resumes his place at the table. Trish follows me with her eyes.

There's a fissure, cold and brittle as ice, forming in my chest. It expands until my heart aches from the pressure.

I shouldn't have worried so much about breaking their hearts. I should have worried more about breaking my own.

CHAPTER 26

I SPOT WILLIAMS' TAIL FOR THE FIRST TIME WHEN I leave Mister A's.

The guy is seated at a table not far from ours. He has a forkful of salad halfway to his mouth when I sweep past him. I doubt I'd have noticed him at all except that in one second, he's arisen, pulled some money out of a pocket and slammed it down on the table before whirling after me.

His action pushes the sadness out of my head, at least for the moment, and jump-starts my internal warning system. Every probe I send out, though, returns nothing. The guy's human.

The concerned server follows after him, inquiring if anything was wrong and asking if he'd like his dinner boxed to take home.

He answers an abrupt "no" to each question.

To make it more embarrassing for him, when the elevator appears, the outside glass elevator to the parking lot, he has no choice but to step in with me.

Once the doors close, I can't help it. I laugh out loud.

This isn't the first time that Williams has had a mortal tailing me. It's not that surprising. If the guy was good (and up until now, he has been), there'd be no telltale vibe for me to pick up on. A vampire can shut down the conduit that prevents thought transference, but there's always the chance that distraction can cause the wall to slip. I'd be able to detect another vampire the second it did. Other supernaturals, like shape-shifters, project telepathic signatures that are stronger still.

So, here I am, in the elevator with the mortal who is supposed to be shadowing me, laughing like a crazy woman.

To his credit, he laughs, too.

"I figured you'd be spending the evening with your family," he says. "Guess I blew it."

"I guess you did." I turn and hold out my hand. "I'm Anna. You know that, though, don't you?"

He takes my hand. His grip is firm and dry and warm as only a mortal's can be. He doesn't pull his hand back or comment on the fact that mine is as firm, but cold as death.

He knows that I'm a vampire.

"Tom," he says in reply. "Well, Anna, it's been a pleasure. I imagine I'll be replaced as soon as I tell Williams how I botched it tonight."

I watch his reflection in the glass of the elevator. He's tall, stands at ease, his broad shoulders filling out the well-tailored coat he's wearing. His face is strong featured without being arrogant. Lined, as if he's spent a good deal of time in the sun. The expression reflected in his dark eyes and gently smiling mouth is one of quiet strength touched with amusement. He senses that I'm checking him out though he can't see me in the glass.

"Are you a private detective?"

He nods.

"How do you know Williams?"

"I used to be a cop."

I let a moment go by while I weigh my options. What's that old saying about the devil you know being better than the one you don't?

"Why don't we make a deal."

He raises an eyebrow. "What kind of deal?"

"I think we should let things stand. I won't tell Williams if you don't."

"Yeah? How is that going to work?"

I shrug. "The same way it's been working. I'll go about my business and you go about yours. I'll pretend this never happened."

He chuckles. "You're not going to try to lose me the first chance you get?"

"Why should I? You're supposed to watch me, right? Not interfere?"

He lifts one shoulder. "My instructions are to keep you in sight. Report who you meet with. I figured it was some kind of family thing. Williams' family since it came from him."

The way he says it makes me wonder what family he's referring to. Williams is a vampire married to a mortal. That this man knows about vampires means that Williams must trust him. Maybe Tom is a relative of his mortal wife.

The elevator stops. We step into the cool night air and are greeted by the valet. He takes both our tickets.

"May as well wait together for our cars," Tom says.

"Does that mean we have a deal?"

He smiles. "Care to tell me where you're headed from here?"

I look up at him, turning up my own smile a notch. "Now what fun would that be? Let's see how good you really are."

CHAPTER 27

MY CAR ARRIVES BEFORE TOM'S AND I THROW him a two-finger salute as I pull away. He looks chagrined that I'm getting the jump on him. Too bad. He can always call Williams, make up a story about losing me. I have no doubt Williams knows where I'm headed tonight. He and Culebra and Frey seem to make my business their own.

It's eight forty-five, already too late to make it to Avery's by nine. Impatience nips at me, but there's one more thing to do. I circle the block, come back and park a block away from the restaurant. When Tom pulls out in his big, black Escalade, I take note.

I know what kind of car to keep a watch for now.

He turns in the same direction I did moments before. The direction that takes him away from me.

Finally, I'm free.

Angst over what happened with my family, surprise at identifying Williams' tail, irritation at allowing myself to be drawn into Gloria's drama—everything is swept from my thoughts. Only anxiety, excitement and anticipation remain, making me feel like a teenager on a first date.

No, not exactly a first date.

Like the first time a girl knows she's going to sleep with someone and she's breathless with wanting.

Wanting it to be perfect.

Wanting not to be found lacking.

Jesus.

Sandra is female.

Doesn't matter.

It doesn't matter.

Concentrate on something else. Concentrate on driving.

There's not much traffic on the highway to take my mind off Sandra. I take 5 North from downtown and head toward La Jolla, doing my best to ignore the tight coil of uneasiness unraveling along with my self-confidence.

Anxiety over Sandra is giving way to the realization that I'm soon going to be setting foot in a house that holds dreadful memories. David almost died there, at the hands of a man who spun an intricate web of desire and intrigue. For a time, I was Avery's willing pupil, believing that he loved me and was honestly trying to help me understand my new nature. He was a doctor of medicine, devoted to the care of mortals. I thought he understood how important it was that I stay close to my human family.

Truth was, he did everything to sever those ties. He burnt down my home and kidnapped my partner, torturing him under the same roof where he made love to me. He played an elaborate charade, offering his help to find David when in reality he threw up one roadblock after another. He manipulated and controlled me.

And I let him.

More than let him. I was his eager protégée. I believed everything he told me. Questioned nothing. Blinded by a powerful sexual attraction and fueled by a new blood drive, I fed from him body and soul. It was powerful. It was an addiction.

It was wonderful beyond words.

Until I learned the truth.

Avery's house is on Mount Soledad. It sits behind a gated wall, perched high over the Pacific. The gate yawns open at my approach, but I see no one in the gatehouse. I steer the Jag up the long, palm-tree-lined driveway fighting a sudden impulse to turn the car around and race away.

As strong as that urge is, though, a burning desire to see Sandra is stronger. It propels me forward, sends fingers flying upward to smooth my hair, to touch my lips, to trace the curve of my breasts through the silk of my dress.

I can't control it.

My hands start to shake. I felt this way with Avery. Out of control. Bewitched.

I bang a fist on the steering wheel, hard enough to send a shiver of pain racing up my arm.

I won't let it happen again.

The house looms ahead. Light spills out of every window, warm, inviting shafts of light that signal welcome like a beacon. I pull up at the front door. There are no other cars or motorcycles in sight but there is a garage in back. Sandra must be parked there.

I climb out of the car, closing the door gently. She knows I'm here. Just as I know she's inside. I feel it like the breeze on my face. There's a tickle of scent on the air. Jasmine. Rose. Something more exotic. Frangipani. I breathe it in. Closing my eyes, tilting my face. Stalling.

When I open my eyes again, I see it. Rising over the roof of Avery's house. Sending clouds scurrying from its brilliance like rats from a golden scythe.

The full moon.

CHAPTER 28

THE FULL MOON.

I've never been a follower of astrological charts. Don't read my horoscope or follow lunar timetables to determine when to change the color of my hair or seek out new friends.

I didn't know the moon would be full.

Did Sandra? Is that why she wanted to see me tonight?

The book said the full moon, though a werewolf's reminder that he must change at least once a month, is not an edict. When I walk in, will I be met by an entirely different Sandra than the one I remember from Beso de la Muerte?

Do I care?

Not really.

I'm more concerned about how I'm going to handle being in Avery's house.

Unlike the gate at the front, the front door does not swing open at my approach. I press the bell with a hand that shakes in spite of my commanding it not to. I hear the chimes and, again, am transported back to the first time I found myself on Avery's doorstep.

Dread mixes with anticipation in a strange concoction of emotion that makes my stomach lurch at the same time my libido jumps into overdrive.

This is ridiculous.

Maybe I should turn around and go home. Let Sandra come to me. Meet on my turf. I haven't read that last chapter. Wait until I've read it. Wait until the goddamned full moon is past.

"Hello, Anna."

The melodious voice floats on the air, and for a moment, I look around stupidly thinking she must have snuck up behind me. Then reason returns and I remember the security camera over the door. I frown into the blinking lens.

"Are you going to let me in?"

She laughs. "Of course. I wanted to warn you first. I have a pet inside, and she tends to be protective. Be a good girl and you'll be perfectly safe."

What the fuck? A pet?

The door doesn't open. She's obviously waiting for me to agree not to attack her on sight. Why would I? She still doesn't get that I'm not going to fight her about Avery's estate. It's not lost on me, though, that in effect, *she's* threatening *me*. I've never suffered bullying well.

"Either you're going to let me in or I'm going home. Makes no difference to me. If I do come in, you might want to put a leash on that pet. You may have forgotten what I'm capable of. Avery made the same mistake."

There's a moment's silence, then the door opens.

Sandra stands in the doorway, backlit by the soft glow of a fireplace in the living room behind her. I get a flash of Avery in that same spot, inviting me in, a party in full swing behind him. I'm dizzy with conflicting emotions. I vowed never to come here again. The pain of finding David, of betrayal, of lost love sweeps over me with such force, it sends panic rioting through me.

As if reading what's in my head, Sandra lays a reassuring hand on my arm. "I understand it is difficult for you to be here. I promise to make it better. Please come in, Anna. We have much to discuss."

The touch of her hand, the touch of her voice reaching into my psyche brings me back with a jolt. Avery fades. The party fades. I'm back in the present staring into the eyes of a woman who seems able to read my soul.

But that's only the first shock.

When my senses return, and I look, really look, at Sandra, disbelief chases any other emotion right out of my head. She's wearing a red dress. A Badgley Mischka gown of silk cut low at the neck and slit high at the sides. The gown Avery gave me before our last meeting. The gown I threw in a wastebasket after I killed him.

CHAPTER 29

SANDRA TAKES A STEP BACK AND TWIRLS AROUND. "Isn't this the most beautiful gown? I found it in a closet upstairs. I couldn't resist trying it on. Fits me well, don't you think?"

The eyes are too wide, the voice too breathless, the innocence stamped on that smiling face too pronounced to be real. She knows exactly whose dress it is. Or was. Where did she get it? The last time I saw it, it was crumpled in a wastebasket in David's condo.

"How did you get that dress?" It erupts like a growl.

No pretense in the emotion that shows on her face this time. Cunning. Self-congratulatory pleasure in having shocked me. Arrogance in the belief that she now has the upper hand.

Mistaken arrogance.

I purposely keep my voice low. "How did you get the dress, Sandra?"

She blinks back to innocence. "I told you, Anna. In a closet upstairs."

She lets a heartbeat go by, then before I can reply, adds, "Why do you ask?" She lifts a hand, trailing a finger between her breasts. "Don't tell me. Was this your dress? Did Avery buy this for you? He has been a naughty boy, hasn't he?"

Her eyes have turned cold, glittering in the dim light of the foyer like blue diamonds on snow. She's watching me, head tilted, eyes narrowed, body still except for the fingers that continue to move in a provocative path down to the depths of her décolleté and up again.

When I move, it's so fast, she has no time to prepare. I grab that hand and bend it backward at the wrist. She flinches, gasping, trying to relieve the pressure. I step back with her, holding tight, and bring my face close to hers.

"Where did you get that dress?"

Then, before I can stop it, she's yanked her hand free and is pushing me, forcing me back until I'm rammed with ferocious force into the wall. Now it's her face that looms above me, her hands that hold mine in a grip I can't break, and her voice growling in my ear.

"I told you to play nice, Anna."

Her eyes are animal eyes. Her body has lost its softness, as if the feminine has been swallowed up by a hard and masculine anger. Her scent has changed. Gone is the sub-tlety of roses and pheromones, the promise of sex. In its place are musk and testosterone and an odor I don't recognize until I see the burning in her eyes. It's the smell of rage, sharp, pungent, threatening. Violence a flicker, a kiss, away.

I stand still and wait for it to pass. Wait for the instant she no longer perceives me as a threat and the animal retreats.

She burrows her face close to my neck. She inhales my scent, licks the skin, her tongue rests on my jugular. She's interpreting my intentions the same way I did hers.

At last, the fury drains from her body. I feel it, in my

head and in the physical release as her muscles lose their rigidity, and the softness, the feminine, returns.

She straightens up and stands back. She turns, head down as if embarrassed, and walks away, into the living room. She doesn't say a word or look around to see if I'm following.

I slump against the wall for a moment, waiting for my body to stop shaking and for my head to clear.

She's strong and fast. Faster than I am. Stronger? I'm not sure. She caught me off guard and tossed me into that wall like a rag doll. I've fought centuries-old vampires and won.

Not this time, though. The first round goes to Sandra. I realize now I cannot let my guard down for a moment with this one. Not if I want to survive.

I watch her, in front of the fireplace, her back to me, her posture relaxed. She raises her hands and runs her fingers through her hair. She stands with one hip slightly thrust forward, a model's stance that draws one's eyes to the curves of her body. It's a cultivated pose. She knows I'm watching.

The siren is back.

CHAPTER 30

I PASS A HAND OVER MY FACE TO GATHER MY WITS, clear my head before moving to stand beside her at the fireplace. She does not acknowledge my presence. She's grown still. She's staring into the fire, eyes dreamy and unfocused, head tilted, her thoughts obviously turned inward. She seems to be *listening*. To what or to whom, I have no idea.

"Sandra?"

The sound of my voice brings her back. It's subtle. Her shoulders straighten a bit, her eyes brighten. She half turns toward me, an eyebrow arched, as if trying to remember who I am or why I'm here.

The ambiguity passes quickly.

"Anna." She gestures toward one of the chairs placed on either side of a large coffee table. "Please, sit down. We have business to discuss."

No indication, no mention of what transpired between us. She gathers the long folds of the gown and eases herself into a chair, waiting for me to do the same.

"I want to know about the dress," I say, still standing.

She looks up at me with a hint of impatience drawing the corners of her mouth into a small frown. "I told you. I found it upstairs."

"Not possible. It was my gown, and I know where I left it. It was not in this house."

She waves a hand. "God. What difference does it make where you left it? It may not be the same dress."

"It's the same. It was an original." I hesitate a moment, wondering if I should say anything else. When the expression on her face darkens into irritation, it trips my own. "I know it because Avery told me it was. The night he gave it to me."

"And you believed everything he told you. How did that work out for you?"

Her fingers begin to move restlessly, picking at the dress, pinching the silk, plucking at the neckline. It's as if they are acting to relieve the agitation I see building again in her eyes. She's fighting to control—what? Herself? Me? I'm having a hard time recognizing the woman who bewitched me in Culebra's bar with the sound of her voice, the warmth of her smile. Suddenly, I feel foolish. Why am I standing here dressed to seduce or be seduced by a woman who doesn't seem capable of either?

I feel her watching me. When I meet her eyes, the frantic movements have stopped. Her expression is once again calm, detached. Then, as if having conjured up my last thought, she rises from the chair.

"We can do whatever you want, Anna," she says, her voice rough as new wine. She slips the straps of the gown off her shoulders, and it falls in a silken puddle to her feet. "All you have to do is ask."

CHAPTER 31

I DRAW A QUICK, SHARP BREATH. HER BODY IS MORE beautiful than I imagined. Reflected light from the fireplace bathes her in a golden, flickering aura. It catches highlights in her hair and throws them back like quick, bright sparks. She's slim where she should be, trim waist, sculpted hips and thighs, and lush where she should be, perfect breasts, firm, round ass. She has no pubic hair, no body hair at all. In spite of the woman's body, it gives her an air of innocence, of vulnerability. I want to cover her nakedness. Ask her to slip the gown back on. To protect her.

Sandra lets me look at her, drink her in. She knows I have no choice, that I can't look away. She fills my mind, whirlwinds my senses.

In the next instant, everything changes.

Now I'm panting with desire. My blood races, my skin heats up with such intense passion, I'm on fire, from within and without. The vampire is dangerously close to taking what it wants. The human Anna, the Anna whose common sense is screaming to get out of here, is slipping away. I no longer want to protect Sandra. I want nothing more than to cover her nakedness with my own. To explore her depths with fingers and tongue. Taste her. Find her pleasure points and make her cry out with the same aching need possessing me.

"What are you waiting for, Anna?" She opens her arms, inviting me closer. "You want me. I feel it."

I do. More than I've wanted anyone since—

Her eyes burn into mine. *Her* eyes but different. Familiar. Threatening.

"It would have been so good, Anna. I waited so long for a worthy companion. I reveled in finding you, in showing you what could be. I loved you. I loved you."

Her voice. Her voice but different. The words spoken with anger, disappointment, unbearable sadness.

My god.

I take a step back, mind reeling. Sandra's face, *Sandra's* face, is devoid of expression. Only her eyes are different. They're his eyes, sparked with life. They're his words. His last words.

Avery.

CHAPTER 32

I MAKE NO CONSCIOUS DECISION TO FLEE. ONE moment, I'm staring into Sandra's face, into Avery's wide, unforgiving eyes and the next, I'm racing out the front door, into the night, away from the apparition.

I know in my head what I saw wasn't real. My heart, though, is sending adrenaline pumping and thundering the message to get away. The animal fights for self-preservation. I'm in my car and spinning out of the driveway, tires screaming in protest, and miles down the road before rational thought returns.

With it comes the shaking. It starts with my hands, jerking on the wheel, then my body spasms with such a visceral physical reaction that I have to pull over. I stumble to the side of the road and retch until my ribs throb with the effort. I vomit blood, black, thick, burning my throat like acid.

I fed from Lance last night, but blood is absorbed directly into my system. There's no detour through a digestive tract like food in a human. Where this blood is coming from, I don't know.

I don't care. I'm too sick too care. Too weak from the exertion. I fall to my knees, clutching my stomach, head falling forward to the pavement, and pray that this sickness will pass.

From far away, like sound muffled by water, I hear the approach of a motorcycle, the deep, guttural roar of a Harley. Fear that it might be Sandra brings me staggering to my feet. I get back behind the wheel of the Jag and slide down until I'm hidden, waiting for the bike to pass.

It does.

I sit up and stare at the figure riding away from me.

Long, black hair flows from underneath a helmet. A broad, masculine back hunches over the handlebars.

A stranger.

Not Sandra.

Relief, then a deep feeling of futility washes over me. What did I do? Did I think Sandra would not have recognized my car at the side of the road? Was slinking down in the seat supposed to protect me?

I lean my head against the steering wheel. I have to get control of myself. I don't know what happened back at that house—at Avery's house—but I do know I'll never let it happen again. I'll never go back.

I also know that Sandra's hold over me is broken. Whatever magic she possesses, I won't give the bitch a second chance at me.

My heart has stopped its wild pounding. My body no longer jerks and quakes. It's time to go home.

CHAPTER 33

I'VE NEVER BEEN SO HAPPY TO BE HOME. IT'S EARLY, only ten o'clock but I head right upstairs. I brush my teeth until my gums bleed, and then I rinse until I can no longer taste the blood. I strip off my clothes and climb into bed. I lie there, covers pulled up to my chin, trying to make sense out of the day. How could things have gotten so crazy? What happened to me at Avery's? How did Sandra make it happen?

I think about Frey's book. Maybe the answers I need are in that damned chapter seventeen—the one I haven't yet read. I start to get up, to get it, when I realize I've left it at the office. Damn. I don't have the energy to get out of bed and drive back to the office.

A car alarm shrieks. I jump at the noise, sitting straight up in bed. Has Sandra followed me here?

Then I collapse back into the pillows. Damn it. It's out on Mission, not the alley in back of my house, and it's certainly not my car, locked in the garage.

Locked.

Did I lock the doors downstairs? The windows?

Frantic drumming starts again in my chest.

What the hell is wrong with me?

I throw off the covers, no longer wanting to sleep. I grab my purse and dump the contents on the floor. Start shuffling through the contents.

There it is.

I snatch up my phone and dial the number printed on the card in my hand.

Please let him be home.

"Hello?"

"Lance. It's Anna. What are you doing right now?"

There's a lilting laugh. "Coming to see you?"

I release a pent-up sigh of relief. "How soon can you get here?"

CHAPTER 34

I GREET LANCE AT THE FRONT DOOR WET FROM A shower, towel twisted like a sarong around my body.

He's in jeans and a black T-shirt, flip-flops on his feet. He doesn't say a word, lets me draw him inside. When the door is closed, he kicks off the flip-flops, pulls the tee over his head. He reaches for the towel.

I stop him. The memory of being sick beside the road is still fresh in my memory. "I don't want to feed. I want the sex."

He smiles. "I think I can accommodate you," he says. He unzips his jeans, peels them off. He's already hard. This time when he reaches for the towel, I let him snatch it away.

His hands start their exploration while his mouth covers mine, his kiss urgent and savage. One hand holds me at the hollow of my back, pressing his body against mine, letting me feel his hardness against my thigh. The other goes to work, massaging my breasts, pinching my nipples, tracing a path down my stomach. I try to hold back, to control the tidal wave building too soon, but when his fingers find their way inside me, desire, hunger and turbulent need take over. I pull Lance down to the floor, lock my legs around his waist and force him between my thighs. Only when he's inside, matching his movements to mine, do I relinquish the lead. His movements become deliciously slow and deliberate. Teasing, languid. He's watching me through the veil of his hair, his eyes glowing.

The pressure builds. For him, too, I feel his sex swell, filling me.

Still, he holds back. He wants me to cry out for release and when I can no longer bite back long, shuddering moans, he brings me to the brink and over. With a single thrust, he comes so deep inside, I feel it to my very core.

After, he waits for me to grow still, for the heat to subside. My muscles refuse to relax. I'm reluctant to let go of him. He's in no hurry. He moves gently, lowering himself on his hands until our faces are within inches of each other. He kisses my forehead, my cheeks, the tip of my nose.

"You are beautiful, Anna Strong," he whispers. "Why are you so alone?"

The question raises the hackles at the back of my neck. I put both hands on his shoulders and push him up and away. "I'm not alone."

An eyebrow arches. "Oh?" He makes a parody of looking around. "There's a husband I don't know about? A boyfriend? A steady fuck buddy?"

I start to protest, but he's hard again and he moves just enough so that the hot, wet friction sends ripples radiating through me. He smiles and rocks a little faster.

"I'm not alone," I whisper again.

He isn't listening. He doesn't care.

In another second, neither do I.

CHAPTER 35

WHEN I AWAKEN THE NEXT MORNING, LANCE IS gone. I didn't hear him leave. The emotional exchange with my parents at dinner, the terror I felt at Sandra's, the mind-numbing relief of sex with Lance left me exhausted. When I finally succumbed, it was like falling into a great dreamless pit.

The sleep of the dead.

I only wish I felt rested. Instead, I feel restless. Restless and full of dread for a day that holds no promise of resolution for any of my problems. When my eyes drift to a bedside clock, however, those feelings are swallowed up by a moment of panic.

Shit.

It's eight thirty. I'm supposed to meet Jason at the coffeehouse at nine.

I throw back the covers and head for the shower. Lance's smell is strong on me—the musk of sex and sweat and healthy male vampire. I'm not about to go out smelling like I spent the night doing what I did. Especially when meeting a teenage boy.

I turn the shower on full force and hot. Since I don't have the body temperature of a human, I can stand under a steamy hot shower and not feel the burn. I lather up head to toe, paying particular attention to the nether regions, rinse off, and jump out.

Slather on perfumed body lotion. Comb out my hair. Pull on jeans, a T-shirt and black leather boots. Grab a leather jacket, and I'm out the door by eight fifty.

Lestat's. The onboard GPS tells me the address is 3343 Adams Avenue. The Normal Heights area. It's Sunday, so though I know I won't make it by nine, I also know I shouldn't be too late.

At nine ten, I'm pulling up in front. The storefront has big picture windows, and through them, I can see an array of well-worn couches and chairs clustered around well-worn tables. Not many people inside. Two hippie types in a corner. No Jason.

Did he think I wasn't coming and leave? Would he do that after only ten minutes?

Cursing myself for being late and Jason for being on time, I climb out of the car and dart across the street.

The first surprise comes when I walk in. The shop is a long, narrow space with the counter area along one wall. There's a guy with his back to me pouring beans into a grinder. He gives a start, puts the bag down, doesn't turn around.

Vampire?

It's my turn to be startled. The guy looks at me over his shoulder. He's a nerdy-looking, chunky fellow with dark hair combed across a wide forehead, black horn-rim glasses perched on a narrow nose and thick lips.

I nod. *This your shop?*

He turns toward me. His name tag reads "Gordon." He shrugs. *I wish. I work here. Pretty cool decor, huh?*

The walls are hung with original art along with a few scattered crucifixes, an assortment of miniature cast-iron "death skulls," a half dozen ornate mirrors (I send Gordon a raised eyebrow at those although I notice they're set high enough that you'd have to be ten feet tall to see your reflection—or not) and a crystal chandelier over the wood-and-glass alcove where the two guys I spotted before are playing chess.

There are also festoons of garlic. I don't smell or feel anything. Another raised eyebrow gets this response: *They're artificial. Made of raffia. Look real, though, don't they?*

Too real. Are you trying to keep vamps out?

He shakes his head. *I don't like it, either. It's my cousin's idea. He owns the shop.*

He's not a vamp, I take it?

A nod. *He imagines himself a rogue vampire slayer. He'll be in soon. Dressed in black with a stake in a holster and pretending to be all broody and shit. He gets his ideas about what a vampire is from Anne Rice. I think it's pretty funny, really.*

You're not worried he'll find out about you?

He blows air through pursed lips. It comes out a disdainful *pffft.*

Look at me? Do I look like a vampire to you? When I decided to change, I thought I'd get all buff and cool looking. I was hoping for Spike and got Xander. The only thing that got buffed was my brain. I'm smarter and faster but no less nerdy looking. Go figure.

I give him a sympathetic shrug. *At least you had a choice in becoming.*

You didn't?

I don't want to talk about that, so I look around. The windows are covered with something that looks like amber Saran Wrap. The two humans playing chess in the corner don't cast a reflection.

How'd you do that with the windows?

He smiles. *Nonreflective film. Told my cousin it would decrease the heat and glare in here. It does, but it also allows me to be in here during the day or night.*

Before he can say anything else, a couple steps up to the counter. They have short, unisex haircuts and are dressed in silk sweat suits that scream uptown chic. I move aside so they can place their order. The case under the counter is full of baked goods and they take their time making a decision. I don't blame them. The stuff looks so good I wish I could eat again. Once they have their goodies in hand (lattes and chocolate muffins), they move off to a table.

I want to ask Gordon how he came to be a vampire. I don't get many opportunities to talk, really talk, with other vamps. There are more people outside, though, getting ready to come in. Time to get down to business. I jab a thumb toward the door.

I'm supposed to meet a kid here. He's about fourteen, blond, stands about five feet tall. Have you seen him?

He points behind me. *You mean him?*

Jason has come in and is looking around the shop, a hesitant expression on his face. He doesn't see me at first, his eyes flit from the couple who just sat down in front to the long hairs playing chess. Then he spies me at the counter and walks straight back.

"I'm Jason. Sorry I'm late. The bus—"

He's held out a hand. I take it without thinking. "I'm Anna, Gloria's friend."

He pulls his hand back out of mine. "Your hands are really cold."

"Sorry." Shit. Gotta learn to curb that reflex. I rub the offending hand on my jeans. "Poor circulation."

He shrugs. "Do you want some coffee?"

I'm surprised and impressed that he made the offer first. Shows maturity. "Yes." I look over to Gordon. "Coffee, double cream, one sugar."

"You want something to eat?" Jason says.

Gordon, meanwhile, is smiling at me. *You dog. Isn't he a teeny bit young for you?*

This is business, Gordon. "No thanks, Jason. Coffee is fine. You get something if you're hungry."

Jason orders a double espresso and a whole-wheat blueberry scone. When I make a move to pay, he holds out money to Gordon and says, "No. This is on me." Then he looks around again, and points to a table in the back of the café. "Let's sit over there."

I let him take the lead. The last time I saw him, he was in a panic, running up the court steps to Gloria and collapsing in her arms. Today, he's calm and composed. He's dressed exactly like a rich teenager on holiday break from prep school would be: Abercrombie & Fitch baggy jeans, red polo with the collar up, Vans with the laces untied. His young face is drawn, however, and he's projecting the manner of someone much older—fourteen going on forty.

Maybe that's what finding your father's dead body does to you.

Once we're seated, he starts right in. "How do you know Gloria?"

"She's my business partner's girlfriend."

"What's his name?"

"David Ryan."

"What did he used to be?"

"A football player. For the Denver Broncos."

"What's he do now?"

"He's a bounty hunter."

He pauses. I guess I passed the audition because then he blurts, "Gloria didn't kill my father."

I stir my coffee, watching his face. "Your mother seems to think she did."

"*Step*mother. My real mother died two years ago. Right after my dad left us."

The words are heated, but his face remains impassive, aloof.

"I'm sorry, Jason. I didn't know about your mom."

He shrugs. "She was sick. Had been for a long time. Timing sucked, though. You'd think my dad could have waited before leaving us. He knew how sick she was, but he had a new girlfriend and I guess he wasn't thinking too clearly."

Again, no rebuke, no real emotion in his response. Is it an act for my benefit? I pause a heartbeat before saying, "Must have made you pretty mad when he left."

He meets my gaze. "My mom and dad had problems for a long time. Laura wasn't his first girlfriend. Mom should have left his sorry ass years before he walked out. He was my dad and I guess I loved him, but he wasn't nice."

The answer is well thought out and delivered so calmly that I'm unsure how to proceed. Something about this kid's demeanor is setting off warning bells in my head. No fourteen-year-old is this poised two days after his father's murder. Maybe I should switch gears. "And Gloria? How do you know her?"

"She's my dad's business partner—" He pauses, re-phrases. "*Was* my dad's business partner."

"That's it?"

"What do you mean?"

"I saw you with her at the courthouse. You looked pretty upset."

He picks at his scone. He hadn't yet touched it or taken a sip of his coffee. Now he breaks off a tiny piece and raises it to his mouth. He doesn't take a bite, though, and his hand falls back to the table. "I like Gloria. She's nice. She always treats me like an adult. I know she was spending time with my dad. I know they had a relationship. She couldn't have killed him."

"And you know this . . . how?"

He folds his hands and places them in his lap. His shoulders hunch. "Because I know who the killer is."

I raise an eyebrow. "You do?"

He sets his jaw. "It's my stepmom. It's Laura."

"I thought you were with your stepmother all day. At least that's what you told the police."

For the first time, his composure slips. His eyes widen, fill with tears. "I don't care. She did it. I know she did it. I even know why."

I nod for him to go on.

"It's because of the trouble my dad was in. I think he was going to be arrested. He was going to jail."

Jason looks close to breaking down. I don't want him to become so flustered that he runs out on me so I sit still and give him a moment to collect himself. He does. More quickly than I would have expected. The eyes lose their panic, his face relaxes.

Tentatively, I begin. "Why do you think your dad was going to be arrested? I don't remember seeing that mentioned in any of the newspaper articles. It's something I'm pretty sure the police would have known."

He blows out a breath. "Maybe not. I heard Dad and Laura the morning he was killed. They were talking in the study and didn't know I'd come in. I could hear it all from the hall. Dad said something was about to come out. Something bad. Dad said we had to leave the country now. Laura didn't want to."

"Did he say what the trouble was?"

"No. Only that we couldn't stay here. If we did, we'd

lose everything. Laura was furious. Said he was exaggerating. She said her life was here and she'd leave over his dead body." He puts subtle emphasis on the last words. "That's why I know she did it. I just don't know how."

I lean in toward him. "Why didn't you tell the police what you just told me?"

His expression shifts, back to anger. "Would the cops believe a kid? And I told you, we were together all day. I'm her alibi. I don't have any proof. But you can investigate. You can find something to prove Laura is the one who killed my dad."

I sit back in my chair, studying Jason. He's doing the same—studying me. Gauging my reaction to his charge that his stepmother killed his father. Hefty charge. He's got his jaws clamped so tight, I see the muscles twitch.

After a moment, he says, "You believe me, don't you?"

I'd like to. It would make more sense than Gloria killing O'Sullivan over—well, over anything. The realist in me knows that thinking something and proving it are two different things.

CHAPTER 36

I'VE WAITED TOO LONG TO ANSWER. EITHER THAT, or my expression isn't reassuring enough because Jason bangs a fist on the table. Our coffee cups, dishes and everyone in the place jump. Me included.

Gordon says, *Everything all right over there?*

Yeah. Sorry.

He turns back to his customers, but I feel his mind probing into my head. Great. Now I have to make sure I don't project anything I don't want him to pick up on. *This is private, Gordon.*

He doesn't shut down right away, but finally, after a moment of dead air, his attention is back on coffee and scones and I feel the conduit close.

"Jason," I say sharply. "Getting pissed is not going to help."

"Then what is? You don't believe me. I can see it on your face. You're going to let Gloria be blamed for this and I'm telling you, she didn't do it. Laura did."

I hold up a hand. "I didn't say I don't believe you. Gloria

doesn't have a motive for killing your dad. At least not a credible one."

Relief softens his face and shoulders. "The love affair thing? It's bullshit. Laura didn't know anything about Dad and Gloria. She couldn't have. She wouldn't have been so nice to her when Gloria came over to discuss business with Dad."

"Well, she sure knew two days ago. Any idea how she found out?"

He shakes his head. "The only thing I can figure is that she must have started having Dad followed."

"By a private detective? Why would she if she didn't suspect an affair?"

He fiddles with his still untouched coffee cup. "Maybe she did suspect something. Not with Gloria . . . necessarily."

I peer at him. "Your dad was seeing someone else besides Gloria?"

Jason's eyes fill again. He looks down at the table. "I think he was seeing one of his lawyers, too."

"What makes you think that?"

Again, he doesn't look at me. "I walked in on him once. At the office. We were supposed to meet for lunch and I was early. He and this woman were kissing. They made some lame excuse that he was helping her get something out of her eye." He grunts. "Yeah. Her eye. His hand was on her boob. How stupid do they think I am?"

"Did you tell your stepmom?"

He shakes his head. "No."

His expression is suddenly cautious, hesitant and shadowed by guilt.

"You think you should have?"

"Maybe." Again, he's avoiding my eyes. "Truth is, I was happy to see it. I don't like Laura. Never did. I thought if Dad was seeing someone else, it meant he and Laura were having problems."

I dig in my purse and pull out a small notepad and pen. "What was the lawyer's name?"

"Connie Crandall."

"She works at your dad's office?"

He nods.

I give Jason a sympathetic smile. "Were there any other women?"

He shakes his head. "I'm not sure but I can find out."

Uh-oh. "What do you mean?"

Eagerness replaces the uncertainty of before. "If Laura did hire a private detective, there's got to be a paper trail, right?"

Paper trail? He's been watching too much television. Before I can comment, though, he's already forging ahead.

"I'll go through her desk. Look for a bill or a canceled check."

I hold up a hand to stem his enthusiasm. "Uh-uh," I say firmly. "No. I don't want you to do anything. If your step-mom was involved in your dad's death, she's dangerous. Let me take care of it."

"But how—?" A craftiness creeps into his expression. "I know. Laura and I have to go to the funeral home today. To make arrangements. I'll leave Dad's study door open and you can come inside. Laura's office is off their bedroom upstairs. We'll be gone at least two hours."

"What about the staff?"

"Laura gave them the day off. Some of them have been with Dad and me for a long time. They were all pretty shook up by what happened."

I can't believe I'm actually considering his suggestion, but it does make sense. More sense than my trying to break into their house on my own or calling every private eye in the San Diego area to see if Laura is a customer. Something they may or may not tell me. Unless the price is right.

"Okay. What time are you leaving?"

"Two."

"Here." I dip a hand back into my purse and pull out a business card. I circle my cell number. "Take this. If your plans change or you come back sooner than four, call me. I'll make sure I'm in and out by then."

Jason takes the card, then gestures for my pen. I hand it over. He scribbles a set of numbers on a napkin. "The security code for the front gate."

I slip the napkin into my pocket.

Jason is looking at my business card. "Bail enforcement. You're a bounty hunter, too?" he says. "Very cool."

Yeah. Bounty hunter turned private detective. Very cool.

CHAPTER 37

I LEAVE JASON AT THE COFFEEHOUSE. HE'S FINALLY started in on the scone, his demeanor calm, almost detached. Not normal for a kid who spent the last hour discussing who could have killed his father.

And yet, how should he be acting? He's doing what I'd do in the same situation. Especially if I suspected my stepmother had engineered my dad's death.

I'm hardly normal, though, am I? Probably not a good idea to compare what I'd do in any situation.

Maybe his detachment can be credited to shock. Jason has had a rough couple of days. It could also be something more sinister. I don't want to believe it, but I know it's possible that Jason had a hand in whatever happened to his dad. He stood to lose as much as his stepmother if his father was indeed in trouble with the law. If that's true, going to the house this afternoon could be risky. Could even be a setup, a trap to make Gloria look guiltier. I can see the headline now: Gloria Estrella's friend caught breaking into O'Sullivan home.

Well, nothing to do but take the chance. I have no other leads. Now the quest becomes to discover what kind of trouble his dad was in.

I know who might be able to help me.

The question is, after last night, am I ready?

Gordon throws me a parting invitation to come again when we can talk and then I'm back in my car, wondering if I have the courage to face my family and knowing I have no choice. Reluctantly, I crank over the engine and head for La Mesa.

SUNDAY MORNING USED TO BE SPECIAL IN THE Strong household. When I was a kid, we'd go to early Mass at St. John's in Lemon Grove, pick up donuts at the parish hall after and head for home. Steve and I always managed to wolf down a donut or two on the way, even though we knew we were supposed to wait until after we had a "good" breakfast of pancakes or eggs or French toast. We'd sit in the backseat trying to be sneaky, giggling at how we were fooling our parents even though we knew the three feet separating us in the backseat was hardly distance enough to muffle the sound of the paper bag rustling or our greedy chomping on hot, jelly-filled donuts. Mom and Dad always let us get away with it. Never mentioned the jelly stains or powdered-sugar mustaches.

Steve went away to college. Mom, Dad and I still went to church, but it wasn't nearly as much fun sitting in the backseat alone with that greasy bag. I waited until we got home and proper breakfast was consumed before nibbling on a plain cake donut.

Then Steve got killed.

We stopped going to church. We no longer ate donuts over the Sunday paper. It became another morning to get through, prelude to another day without Steve. Another day without warmth, without joy.

Over time, things returned to a kind of normalcy. Dad went back to his job, Mom went back to work, and I went back to school. There was a gaping hole in our lives, but to their credit, my parents rallied. For my benefit, I know. I'll always be grateful to them for that.

Some things, however, were not as before. After the funeral, we never went back to St. John's. The parish priest tried many times to coax my folks back, but the answer was always the same. Like Steve, God vanished from our lives. Utterly and completely.

I missed Steve much more than I ever missed God.

Now, approaching the house, I'm haunted by the past and nervous at what awaits me. My mother was so angry with me. Will she still be? Will Trish? Will they forgive me for ruining their evening?

I never should have left them last night. The meeting with Sandra was a disaster, accomplishing nothing except making me feel like a fool this morning. I don't know what happened. I don't care. I only know the spell is broken, not in the way I'd planned, but broken all the same. I'll never step foot in Avery's house again.

By the time I pull up in my parents' driveway, I've worked myself into such a state of anxiety, I debate the wisdom of coming here at all. In fact, when I go up to the front door and let myself in and find that they're not at home, I wilt in relief. I scribble a note to let them know that I was here, then beat it back out to my car.

I did what I promised last night. I came over. As far as I'm concerned, the ball is now in their court.

I'll call Dad tomorrow at his office and ask him if he'd heard about Rory O'Sullivan being in trouble. He's an investment banker. He knows the dirt.

Relief that I don't have to face my mother is tempered by unhappiness that I won't see Trish. I scared her last night. Made her afraid the bubble of happiness she'd been so carefully constructing was about to burst.

And for what? Sexual delusions about a woman who is obviously psychotic.

Good job, Anna.

I almost make a clean getaway. I've got the Jag turned around in the driveway and am halfway to the road when my folks come back. If they'd been thirty seconds later, I would have made it.

Shit.

I put a smile on my face and the Jag in reverse, and back up the driveway. Mom and Dad pull up front and park beside me. Trish opens the rear passenger door and jumps out, a relieved smile brightening her face.

"I'm so glad you're here," she says. She lofts something for me to see. "We bought donuts after Mass. They're still hot. You're just in time."

She lifts a brown paper bag.

CHAPTER 38

TRISH LINKS HER ARM WITH MINE AND PULLS ME along and up the front stairs. Mom still hasn't said anything, but at the door, Dad plants a kiss on my cheek and gives my arm a squeeze.

"We're glad to see you, honey."

I know he means it but I'm feeling so disoriented by the realization that they've started going back to church that I find myself blurting, "How long have you and Mom—?" I point to the bag.

He looks puzzled for a moment, then smiles. "How long have we been going to church? I don't know, Anna, a long time."

Mom finds her tongue. "Since about the time you moved out," she says.

It's ridiculous, I know, but I feel betrayed. "You never mentioned it."

"Should we have?" Mom asks.

I find myself sputtering. "Well . . . yes."

She looks at me with a small, puzzled frown. "What

difference does it make if we started back to church? You were off to college, living in your grandmother's cottage at the beach. We hardly saw you. In fact, we've seen you more in the last few months than we had in the five years before that."

It's true, I know. Becoming a vampire changes your priorities pretty quickly. Especially priorities involving a family you know you're going to lose.

We've moved inside and into the living room. Mom goes to the kitchen without another word and Trish goes to her bedroom to change. Dad and I are left by ourselves. I'm still smarting from my mother's rebuke but this seems the perfect opportunity to ask him about O'Sullivan.

"Dad, can I speak to you a minute?"

He gives me a sympathetic smile and says, "Don't let your mother get to you, honey. You know how she is. If she had her way, you'd have never left the nest."

I return the smile. "I know, but it's not about that. It's a business thing."

He nods. "Then let's go to my den."

Dad leads the way to the back of the house and one of my favorite rooms. It's small and intimate and such a reflection of his personality that when Steve and I were children, and Dad was off on one of his business trips, we'd sneak in here to play. Breathing "his" air made him seem closer.

The room hasn't changed much since I was small. The smell of leather and aftershave, the nautical pictures on the wall, the desk piled with books and magazines. The furniture has been updated, and there's a computer now, but it's still my father's room.

He shuts the door and takes a seat behind his desk, motioning me into one of the seats in front of it. "What's going on?"

I fill him in on what I'm doing for Gloria and my interview with Jason this morning. I finish with Jason's charge that his father was in trouble, maybe with the law, and ask if he'd heard any rumors to that effect.

Before he answers, he narrows his eyes. "Kind of out of your range of expertise, isn't it? Are you and David—"

"Not David," I interject quickly. "I'm on my own in this."

He frowns. "I don't understand. Isn't David Gloria's boyfriend?"

I sigh. "It's complicated, Dad. No one is more surprised than I am to have gotten involved in Gloria's drama. The truth is, I don't believe she killed O'Sullivan. After what Jason told me this morning, I think there may be someone else that has far better motive to want him dead."

His frown deepens. "That may be true, but why didn't he go to the police? Why did he come to you?"

"He's fourteen, Dad. He's accusing his stepmother. Why do you think he didn't go to the police?"

Dad nods and shrugs. "I can see how he would be reluctant to make an accusation without proof. I take it that's where you come in?"

My turn to nod. "Can you tell me anything about O'Sullivan's business dealings? Anything that's happened lately that seems off?"

Dad takes a moment, his eyes on me. "You're not putting yourself in harm's way over this, are you?"

His solemn expression makes me smile. "No, Dad. This is purely a fact-finding expedition. If I find anything, I'll turn it over to the police. I won't take any unnecessary risks; I promise."

Not a lie. Jason, after all, is leaving the door open for me this afternoon. No risk there.

Dad nods, accepting what I say to be true. "Something

strange did happen a few months ago. Involved O'Sullivan and a company called Benton Pharmaceuticals."

"I don't know the name."

"Not many people do. I only know of it because a prospectus came across my desk when O'Sullivan was preparing to take the company public. He was the primary investor in a research lab working on one product. A cure for HIV. They claimed they found one."

A cure for HIV? That gets my attention. I sit up straighter. "Wow. That'd be big news. Why haven't I heard about it?"

Dad rises and comes around the desk. He perches himself on the corner and folds his arms. "The FDA was scheduled to begin running trials, a process that could take years and millions of dollars. The reason for taking the company public was to raise that capital. The prospectus sounded promising. It appeared as if Benton might have discovered a treatment that not only managed HIV, but cured it."

"They must have had investors lining up around the block."

"Indeed. It would have been the medical find of the decade."

"Would have been?"

"The company never went ahead with the clinical trials. The offering was pulled. The company, at least as far as I can determine, went belly-up."

"Why, do you think? Was the preliminary data skewed in some way? Was it a hoax?"

Dad shakes his head. "Can't answer that. I can only tell you when our pharmaceutical-industry analysts looked at it, they were excited by what they saw. We were ready to give the investment a stamp of approval. Hell, I was ready to buy the stock myself."

That's an impressive endorsement. In Dad's business, he sees hundreds of potential investments a year. He doesn't consider investing his own money in many. "How much money do you think O'Sullivan had invested before pulling the plug?"

Dad shrugs. "To fund research like that? Would have been millions."

"In the tens of millions?"

"Try hundreds of millions."

"God. So O'Sullivan lost a shitload of money on Benton. Who else might have gotten hurt when the company went under?"

Dad thinks about it a minute. "Well, O'Sullivan was the primary moneyman. But the research director and his staff would most likely have taken part of their compensation as equity in the company."

"Like the Microsoft people in the eighties?" I ask. "When the company went public, secretaries retired in their thirties as millionaires."

"Good analogy. Unfortunately, the opposite is also true. When Benton went under, the equity became worthless."

"But it doesn't sound like O'Sullivan did anything illegal, does it? Why would he get in trouble over something like that?"

He shakes his head. "That I can't answer. As far as I know, O'Sullivan, apart from losing a hell of a lot of his own money, did nothing wrong."

There's a timid knock on the door, and Trish peeks in. "Mom says breakfast is ready."

Dad smiles at her. "We'll be right there, honey."

He stands away from the desk and waits for me to lead the way out of the den. "You know," he says, "this Benton thing may not have anything at all to do with whatever trouble O'Sullivan had gotten himself into. I only mentioned it because it was odd. He was too good a businessman to take a company as far as he had only to dump the thing at the last minute. Something was off."

I acknowledge his last remark with a nod, filing the information away. My mind, however, has already moved on. To a more immediate problem. One that awaits me in the kitchen. How am I going to get out of here without insulting my mother yet again by refusing food?

CHAPTER 39

TURNS OUT TO BE FAR EASIER THAN I THOUGHT. Mom is gathering purse and keys when Dad and I enter the kitchen. She throws me an apologetic smile.

"I'm sorry, Anna. I promised one of the women from church I'd help organize a fund-raiser for the new parish hall. I'm meeting her in about ten minutes. You visit with Trish and Dad, and I'll try to get back as soon as I can."

Her attitude has softened, going from stiffly formal when she greeted me at the car, to being almost friendly. Is it for Trish's benefit? I don't care. I give her a quick hug and tell her if I'm not here when she gets back, I'll be in touch soon.

I spend a few minutes sipping coffee and visiting with Dad and Trish before excusing myself. Trish is smiling and relaxed when I leave, making plans with Dad to go to a bookstore to find books on France. It's the only mention of the upcoming move. I'm much happier with this image of my family than the one I left with last night.

I head downtown to see Gloria. I'll tell her about my

meetings with Jason and my dad, and ask if she's heard anything about O'Sullivan and Benton Pharmaceuticals. I'm about to pull under the portico at the Four Seasons and let the valet park my car when a cop waves me off. The hotel entrance is clogged with police cars and rescue vehicles. Most likely some overweight tourist suffered a sun-and-booze-induced heart attack. Happens all the time. I make a U-turn and park on the street.

I dodge through the crowd that's gathered in the lobby and make my way to a house phone. I have to dial the operator to be connected with the penthouse. There's the briefest of hesitations before the smooth voice on the other end of the line tells me she'll put the call through.

Looks like Gloria did add me to the list of people she'd deign to talk to. Good thing.

The phone rings three times before it is picked up.

"Gloria. It's Anna. I need to speak to you."

"Ms. Strong," a male voice answers. "Come up."

I don't recognize the voice. One of Gloria's lawyers maybe? "Who is this?"

"Detective Harris," he replies. "I'll tell the patrolman downstairs to show you right up."

Detective Harris? Shit. What did Gloria do now? "Why are you with Gloria?" I ask. "She didn't try to leave town, did she?"

"Depends on what you mean," he says, his voice gruff. "Ms. Estrella tried to kill herself."

I don't wait to hear anything else but hang up and head directly for the penthouse elevators. Harris didn't say she committed suicide, he said she *tried* to. Explains all the commotion in the lobby.

Now Gloria killing herself is about as plausible as Gloria killing O'Sullivan because he dumped her. She's much too self-absorbed to do either, but I wouldn't put it past her to stage a fake suicide in an attempt to get sympathy. Especially from David. That does sound like her. Ignore the deal we made. Attempt to influence the jury pool. I can think of a dozen reasons she might think a suicide attempt was a good idea.

I'm gearing myself up to lash out at her for being such a fucking idiot when Detective Harris meets me at the door.

"Where is she?"

He jabs a thumb toward the bedroom. "In there. She's in pretty bad shape."

"Will she live?"

He looks surprised at my tone. "Looks like it. I thought you were her friend."

I push past him, insides curdling with anger. I start yelling even before I get to the door. "If you think I'm going to run to David and tell him how you—"

The words die in my throat, choked off by what I see when I stomp into the room. Gloria is on the floor, propped up against the footboard of the bed. Her hair is matted and her makeup is in streaks. She has on a nightgown that's torn at the shoulder. Scattered around her are pill bottles and a single, empty bottle of scotch. She's been vomiting; it pools around her and drips down her mouth and chin. She holds a wet rag in a limp hand. The paramedics have stopped doing whatever it was they'd been doing before I arrived. They're standing back, keeping an eye on her, but gathering together their equipment. She doesn't seem to know that I've come into the room.

I turn to the one closest to me. "What happened?"

He's sliding a stethoscope into a bag. "Looks like she overdosed. On everything and anything she could find in the medicine cabinet. All over-the-counter stuff. Weird, really."

"Why?"

"Because she had much stronger prescription medicine in her handbag." He holds out a bottle of Valium. "If she'd taken the contents of this, we'd be wheeling out a corpse."

I watch as they make final preparations to leave. The paramedic's words seem to confirm my suspicion that Gloria staged this. A stunt to gain attention and sympathy.

Except for one thing.

If Gloria was going to put on this kind of show, she'd have damn well staged it better. She'd be dressed to the nines, hair and makeup perfect. No way would a narcissistic woman like Gloria allow anyone to find her with vomit on her face and a torn, stained nightgown on that Barbie-doll body.

Detective Harris moves into the room to stand beside me.

"What happens now?" I ask.

"She'll be taken to the hospital, kept under guard."

"Will you revoke her bail?"

"Depends on what the court-appointed shrink says after he talks with her. If he feels she's not a danger to herself, he'll let her come home. Assuming she has someone to come home to."

He says the last in a way that suggests I'm supposed to be the one she comes home to. I don't intend to commit to that now, but at the same time, I don't want to see Gloria in jail. I have too many questions to ask her. I answer Harris by saying nothing at all.

He lets a minute go by before reaching into his jacket and pulling out a notebook. He flips over pages until he finds what he's looking for. "I'm going to have to notify the DA about this," he says.

I turn to look at him, understanding full well the implications of a murder suspect attempting suicide. "I know what you're thinking, Detective Harris. You don't know Gloria the way I do. This isn't her style."

Then he surprises me by saying, "I don't think so, either."

One of the paramedics hands Harris a plastic bag with the discarded pill bottles. Aspirin, cold remedies and some kind of decongestant. The guy was right. If Gloria was attempting suicide for real, those were weird choices considering she had Valium.

The ambulance attendants lift Gloria onto a stretcher. Harris moves out of the way, giving me no opportunity to ask about his last remark. Obviously, I'm not the only one who feels there's something off about this scenario. Of course, we may both be wrong and Gloria took stuff she thought would only make her sick, not dead. She may not have gauged just how "sick" that would be.

But right now, the attendants are securing Gloria to the stretcher, pulling a blanket up around her shoulders. They act as if they're ready to take her downstairs. I stop them with a hand on the cot.

"Aren't you going to clean her up?" I ask, hardly recognizing that it's my own voice making the suggestion.

They cast questioning glances at each other, then at me.

"You know who she is, don't you? She wouldn't want to be seen like this."

I can't believe I'm actually feeling sympathy for her. It's good that she doesn't realize it. Still, the two attendants aren't making any move to do anything. I take the wet cloth from her hand and wipe the mess off her mouth and chin, dab the makeup smears off her cheeks and do my best to smooth her hair. Her eyes follow my hands, but there's no spark of life, no animation.

"What's wrong with her?" I ask, alarmed at her lack of responsiveness. She should be grabbing at my hand or yelling.

One of the attendants shrugs. "Combination of the effects of the drugs and shock," he says. "She'll come around soon." He takes a card from a pocket. "We'll be taking her to County General. She'll be examined and held overnight for observation. You can check on her tomorrow morning."

I slip the card into a pocket of my jeans and watch as they wheel Gloria out. Harris follows, then one by one, the room empties until I'm the last person left.

I look around at the mess, pick up the phone and call housekeeping. Whatever they pay maids in this place, it isn't enough.

CHAPTER 40

WHILE I WAIT FOR THE MAIDS, I GATHER UP GLOria's jewelry case and handbag and put them in a small Louis Vuitton canvas bag I find in the closet. I'll take it to her at the hospital when I see her tomorrow.

Tomorrow. If she's allowed to come home, who's going to babysit her? I'm not going to do it. I hate like hell to be considering it, but I think it's time to enlist the help of the one who got me into this predicament to begin with. David. He brought Gloria into our lives. Much as I hate to throw them together, I don't know anyone else to ask.

The thought makes me twitchy with aggravation, but David is the one who came running when Gloria crooked her finger. He's the one who kept secret the fact that he'd been pursuing her all the time I was being sweet and sympathetic because I could see her absence was killing him. Gloria will live up to her bargain. I fully intend to tell David exactly what I'm doing and why I'm doing it. In the meantime, though, David can damn well accept some of the responsibility to see that she's okay.

I glance at my watch. It's eleven thirty. Enough time to make the trip up to his cabin before keeping my house-breaking appointment at Chez O'Sullivan. If David was answering his damned phone, I wouldn't have to go at all. Still, seeing him in person is better. If he gives me any trouble, I'll drag him back by the hair.

I take a last look around the bedroom, wondering if there's anything else I should take. I open the drawers next to the bed, checking for stray jewelry or cell phones or stacks of cash. I find none of those. I do find three hotel tele-phone message sheets. The ones she palmed yesterday?

The first is from her agent. I wonder how getting arrested for murder affects your marketability?

The second and third are from Jason. Marked urgent. Dated yesterday.

Did she return his calls?

The maids arrive, interrupting my train of thought, and I take my leave. The lobby is still crowded with reporters and hotel guests drawn to the commotion. Until this moment, I don't think anyone knew where Gloria was staying. Now the whole world knows.

I leave the hotel by a back entrance and start for my car. I'm fifty feet away when I spot her.

Tamara. Sandra's muscle-bound werewolf pal.

Sitting on the hood of my car.

Sitting on the hood of *my* car.

She's dressed in leathers, and even from this distance, I can see the long, thin scratches made from the studs on those pants when she scooted herself up on the hood.

A surge of white-hot fury races along my spine.

She's Sandra's friend. She scratched my car.

I'm not sure what makes me angrier.

I move so fast, she never sees me coming. I hook my hands under her arms and lift her off the car, turn and dump her on the sidewalk. She makes one, short, startled yelp as her ass hits the concrete. She bounces once, like a big, dumb Nerf ball.

Two kids are skateboarding on the other side of the street. One lifts his fist in a salute. "That was awesome, dude," he yells.

Yeah. Awesome.

My eyes never leave Tamara's face. If she's here, where is Sandra? My blood races, senses leap to high alert. In one blinding moment of rage, the vampire takes control.

I look around.

Tamara is stumbling to her feet, scrambling backward, out of my reach. The fall knocked the wind out of her. Her mouth is open, her eyes wide. No sign of the bully who challenged me in Culebra's bar.

"Where is she? Where is Sandra?"

Tamara is having a hard time catching her breath. She's got a hand to her throat and one to her chest. She's gulping air, her face contorts with the effort.

I wait. I'm trembling as much as Tamara. The uncontrollable panic I felt last night is battling with the anger. Fear is winning. I want nothing more than to run away, to hide, because I know if Tamara is here, Sandra must be, too.

I grab Tamara, shake her until her teeth rattle. "Where is she?"

Tamara flinches. She raises both hands and tries to push me away. She can't. Finally, she gives up, drops her hands. "She's not here," she says.

I don't let go. I squeeze and slide my fingers up her collarbone until they're around her throat. "Where is she?"

Tamara's eyes flash. She's recovering. I sense it—the shift from being caught off guard by my attack to getting pissed because I coldcocked her. I tighten my grip until color floods her face and she's gasping again for air. No way am I going to let her regain enough strength to fight me. I remember her from the bar—she outweighs and outmuscles me—and I remember Sandra's strength last night.

She's pulling at my hands. Her eyes are wide again, pleading.

I relax my grip. Not much, enough for her to be able to draw an uneven breath. I lean my face close to hers.

"I'm going to ask you one more time. Is Sandra here?"

She shakes her head.

"Then why are you?"

She gestures to my hands, a plea to let her go.

My turn to shake my head. "Not likely."

A movement behind me and to my left draws my attention. I take a quick look. The skateboarder and his buddy have circled around and are coming back. They're whooping and pointing at us like we're an opening act for pro wrestling. It's drawing the attention of people coming out of the hotel.

Great.

I keep one hand on Tamara's arm while I open my car's passenger door with the other. I shove her inside. Then I snatch up Gloria's suitcase, run around to the driver's side and throw myself into the seat. In a second, we're hauling ass away from the curb.

CHAPTER 41

TAMARA HAS ONE HAND ON THE DASH, ONE AT her throat, massaging bruises already starting to form. "You're insane, you know that? You almost killed me back there."

Her voice sounds like it hurts to talk, like she's scraping the words across sandpaper. Good.

"Almost being the operative word. What were you doing at the hotel?"

"What do you think I was doing? I was there to see you."

"Did Sandra send you?"

She shakes her head.

"So, what? You tracked me down to finish what you started in the bar?"

For a moment she looks puzzled at the question. Then she smiles. "Crap. If I wanted to fight you, you'd already be bleeding in the dirt."

I jab the side of her head with a finger. She flinches, recovers and then smiles again, ruefully this time.

"Okay. You got the best of me back there, but only because I didn't see it coming. Would've never happened otherwise."

"Right. You do know what I am, don't you?"

"A hot-shit vampire? Is that supposed to scare me?"

"Unless you really are dumber than you look."

Tamara stops massaging her throat. I feel her tense. She's tired of my insults, tired of the verbal sparring. "So. You want to throw down? Pull the fucking car over and we'll do it."

For one second, I actually consider it. Beating the shit out of Sandra's minion would really feel good. Except that I have no quarrel with Tamara. My quarrel is with Sandra.

"I don't want to fight you. I want you to tell me what you were doing sitting on the hood of my car. Think you can handle answering that simple question?"

Tamara is glaring at me. "I was ready to tell you that back at the hotel. Before you dumped my ass on the sidewalk. You didn't ask then, though, did you?"

"No," I say through gritted teeth. "You scratched my car with those fucking chaps. What were you thinking?"

"It's only a car," she shoots back.

"Yeah, well, remember that sentiment when I drop-kick that Harley of yours from here to tomorrow."

For once, she doesn't have a comeback. In fact, when I sneak a look at her, she has a pensive look on her face. I don't know what surprises me more, that she might be considering the possibility that I feel about my car the way she does her Harley or that she's capable of thinking at all.

I'll give her the benefit of the doubt. "Let's start over. Why did you want to see me?"

But before she answers, she sits up in the seat. "Where are we going?"

She's finally noticed that we're heading out of the city. I'd hopped on 5 North and now swerve toward the Interstate 8 East exchange. "We're taking a drive to the mountains."

"The mountains? Why?"

"I've got someone to see."

"I don't want to go to the mountains."

"I don't remember asking you. I had only two hours to get up there and back. You made me late."

She snorts. "You'll never make it in two hours. Not in this."

"You insulting my car again?"

"Calling it like I see it. You want to make it to the mountains and back in two hours? I'll take you. On my bike."

I look over at her. I know she's right. The Jag's fast. On the highway. Half the trip to the cabin is on back roads. Dirt roads. I barely had enough time to get to David's cabin and back before my run-in with Tamara. If I want to get into Jason's house, I have to be back here as close to two as possible.

I don't remember seeing Tamara's bike parked anywhere near my car. As that thought percolates, I realize I'm going to accept her suggestion. Why not? Now I know I can take her. She's not Sandra.

And I'm curious. She still hasn't told me why she's here.

"Where's your bike?"

She smiles. "Pull off at the next exit and go back. I'm a block from the hotel."

I do it, putting as much menace as I can into my tone when I say, "You'd better not be fucking with me or . . ."

"Yadda, yadda, yadda," she says. "I know. You'll beat the crap out of me and kick my bike. Christ, you vampires are all alike."

It takes us exactly fifteen minutes to get back to the hotel, find Tamara's bike and prepare to head out again. In the car I told her where we were going so I swing behind her on the Harley, watch while she slips on her helmet and ask if she has one for me. Now safety is not a concern for me. If we crashed, it'd take my landing on a wooden fence post to hurt me, but there are helmet laws in California and getting stopped by a cop would be one more delay.

When I mention that to Tamara, she reaches into a saddlebag and hands me an orange knit cap, hand knit it appears, with head flaps. Along with a headset. "So we can talk on the way," she says.

No kidding. I slip on the headset and adjust the microphone, eyeing the cap. "Jayne's mom know you have this?"

She doesn't say anything. Probably never saw *Serenity*. I jam the cap on my head, asking, "This really passes for a helmet?"

"If you're going fast enough."

Then she proves what she means by gunning away from the curb at fifty miles an hour.

Obviously, cops aren't the concern to Tamara they are to me. She weaves in and out of city traffic, hits the freeway going about eighty and launches that Harley like a rocket once we hit open road. With all that, she doesn't draw as much as a raised eyebrow from the motorists we fly past. It's like we've become invisible.

Once I've gotten used to the breakneck speed, I relax my grip on her waist and sit up straighter.

"It's about time," she grumbles. "You were about to cut off my circulation."

I can hear her loud and clear through the headset but the knit cap offers no protection from the wind. My eyes are soon streaming. "I feel like an idiot in this cap."

She doesn't laugh out loud, but I feel her shoulders shake. "You should see how you look."

I resist the urge to smack her. "Not a good idea to piss off a vampire," I growl. "I could break your neck and take that helmet before your brain knows you're dead."

She's quiet for a moment, then she blows out a breath. "Listen, as much as I enjoy trading insults with you, there was a reason I came to see you today. I'm worried about Sandra."

Not exactly what I wanted to hear. My shoulders tighten, my stomach lurches. "And you're coming to me because Sandra and I are such good buddies?"

She shakes her head. "No, I'm coming to you because you're the only one who can save her."

That does provoke a laugh. "You can't be serious. Do you know what happened last night? She worked some kind of spell on me. She had me seeing and hearing things. Things I didn't ever want to see or hear again. I've told everyone I know that I don't want Avery's estate. She can have it. All I want is for that bitch to leave me alone."

I can't see Tamara's face, but I feel her back stiffen, see her hands tighten on the handgrips. "It wasn't Sandra," she says.

"Oh, right. It wasn't Sandra. Listen, I don't know exactly how she did it, but somehow she knew things Avery said to me. She even wore a copy of the damned dress he gave me. She scared the shit out of me, and I don't like being scared. So, if Sandra really is in some kind of trouble . . . Gee, how can I put this? I don't give a fuck."

"You should." Tamara's voice has become hard. "Didn't you wonder how she did it? How she knew so much about you and Avery?"

"I know how she did it. Listen, since I've become vampire I've seen all kinds of weird shit. I've seen witches raise demons. I've seen shape-shifters shift. I know empaths and psychics. I know how she did it. It was a spell. I have no intention of ever letting her get close enough to do it to me again."

"It wasn't Sandra," Tamara says, more forcefully this time.

"Then who was it?" I'm so angry, blood pounds at my temples. I'm shaking at the memory of the wrenching terror that had me vomiting at the side of the road. "If it wasn't Sandra, who the fuck was it?"

"And you called me stupid," Tamara snaps. "It was Avery."

"Avery?" I repeat, loading the word with as much scorn as I possibly can. "You mean the Avery I staked during the fight that almost killed me? The Avery that dissolved into dust and blew away on a puff of air? That Avery?"

That's what I say to Tamara. Inside my head, though, a sudden, startling kernel of doubt turns my thoughts in a disturbing direction. When Sandra looked at me, when she spoke Avery's words, she looked and sounded different. That had to be part of the spell, though, right? If possession was even remotely possible, Williams or Frey would have said something.

"Do you get it now?" Tamara says after a moment. "Avery has taken over Sandra's body. He's doing it to get back at you. He hates you so much he'll do anything, even kill Sandra to do it."

No. I shake off the doubt. It's not possible. "Avery is dead." It's unequivocal. "I killed him. I thought Sandra was psychotic. She's delusional as well. So are you if you believe what she's telling you. We're almost at my partner's cabin. I'll drive back with him. You want to take a message to Sandra? How about this? I don't want to see either of you ever again. If I do, I'll kill you both."

CHAPTER 42

TAMARA STARTS TO SAY SOMETHING, BUT I CUT her off. "I know what Sandra is doing. She's getting revenge because her cheating husband was getting ready to dump her ass. It's the only thing that makes sense. How she found out about Avery and me in such detail, I don't know. Maybe she's a voyeur and she was there that night watching us. Maybe that's how she gets her rocks off. What I do know is that possession isn't possible. I staked Avery and he didn't disappear or fly away or turn into a rat. He dissolved into dust. Into dust."

"You don't understand," Tamara says.

The vibe she's sending off is hostile, anxious and powerful as a bad smell.

It triggers defense mechanisms of my own. If she tries anything, the vampire Anna is ready. I lean forward, tighten my grip around her waist again until she whimpers, and whisper, "I don't want to understand."

Tamara grows quiet. We're approaching the turnoff that takes us off the highway, into the woods. For the next fifteen minutes we bounce along on a dirt road. Then, dead ahead is the last turnoff to David's cabin. It's not marked, so I drop my hands, touch Tamara's shoulder and point to the left. She maneuvers the Harley smoothly into the turn. I had braced myself because I wasn't sure she would. I figured she might take it at breakneck speed, bank sharply and dump me off the bike.

The dirt road drops off after about half a mile and becomes hard-packed gravel. Tamara downshifts and reduces speed. She can't see the cabin. It's set back about a mile and completely hidden in the pines. I remember how I felt when I saw it for the first time. Tamara is in for a surprise.

I point to the left again, to a paved driveway. She takes it, and I wait for her reaction when we round the last bend and the cabin comes into view.

Predictably, her shoulders jump. If I could see her face, I'm sure the eyes would be big and the mouth agape.

The "cabin" is a two-story affair, about twelve rooms and three thousand square feet. It's made of pine, stained a color close to that of a setting sun—or blood. David's father built it in the early seventies, right after the birth of his son, from logs harvested from their own land. Then David invested a lot of money during his football years to upgrade and renovate the place. There are two big stone chimneys, one at each end, and a wraparound porch in front. The windows are all open, and sheer curtains move with the breeze.

Tamara stops the bike in front and dismounts. "Who owns this place?" she asks.

I swing off the back and pull the cap off my head. "A friend."

I start away from the bike, but Tamara puts a hand on my arm. "This isn't over." It's spoken quietly, but the harshness of the threat comes through.

I shake off her hand. She's probably right. The next time I face Sandra, though, it will be on my terms.

I head toward the front door but sounds from the back stop me: the rhythmic swish of an ax through the air and the crack as it hits wood. I switch directions.

David is splitting logs in a clearing behind the cabin. He's bare chested, sweaty and oblivious to our approach. Earbuds attached to an iPod at his waist explain why. I can hear the music. I could hear the music even without vampire hearing. He's got the volume turned way up. He's listening to Incubus, one of his favorite alternative/rock/trash/whatever groups.

He's really gotta be depressed.

"That's your friend?"

I turn to look at her. Tamara is staring, her mouth open. "Why are you still here?"

She doesn't answer, which makes me take another look at David. I guess I've known him for so long, I've become oblivious to how he must appear to other women. He's a big guy, hard muscled, broad shouldered, lean. He's wearing a pair of jeans, tennis shoes, no socks. His face is darkly handsome, strong mouth and jaw, full lips, blue eyes, cross-cropped dark hair. He swings the ax with easy grace, the muscles on his bare arms barely rippling with the effort. He's not aware that he has an audience, so there's no self-consciousness, no coyness in the way he's attacking that woodpile.

And attacking is what he's doing. I bet I know who he's thinking about.

Tamara is still staring. She's making no move to leave, so I tell her to stay here while I get his attention. No sense scaring the shit out of him and maybe getting bashed in the head in the process.

I cross around in front. He's so engrossed in the work and lost in the music I realize calling out to him isn't going to do it. I wave my hands and jump up and down until he catches the movement and looks my way.

His face turns red. He holds the ax in front of him like a weapon. "What the fuck are you doing here?"

"Good to see you, too. Want to put the ax down so we can talk?"

He's still glaring when Tamara moves to join me. She's grinning like an idiot. "You're David Ryan, right? Heisman Trophy winner? Played tight end for the Broncos?"

Now it's my turn to stare—at Tamara. "You know who he is?"

David switches his gaze from me to Tamara. Curiosity softens the anger. The ax falls to his side and he pulls the earphones from his head. "And you are?"

She thrusts out her hand and takes a step toward him. "Name's Tamara. People call me Tammy. I brought Anna up here. Didn't have any idea who we were coming to visit though. I can't tell you how thrilled I am to meet you."

I'm listening to this openmouthed. People call me Tammy? That's like calling a tiger "pussy."

David is smiling. He takes Tamara's hand and shakes it. "Football was another lifetime ago. I hardly think about it anymore."

"No way," Tamara says. "You were a great player. If you hadn't gotten hit in that Giants game and hurt your knee, you'd still be playing. It was a cheap shot, and Rutherford should have been thrown out of the league."

I can't believe what I'm hearing and seeing. Talking to David, Tamara's demeanor softens and damn, if she doesn't even look different. Prettier, somehow, more feminine. Christ, is this another spell? Here I am listening to a muscle-bound Amazon, a werewolf, no less (and one I would have sworn had a lesbian thing for Sandra), gushing over a muscle-bound, strictly heterosexual ex-jock whose chest is starting to swell like an overinflated inner tube.

Her sense of purpose in bringing me here seems to have vanished.

"You know how I got hurt?" David asks, clearly flattered that she does.

That's it. I step between them. "Hey. I came up here for a reason, and I don't have all day. You two can continue this trip down memory lane another time. David, we have to talk."

The pleasant face he's showing Tamara morphs into the angry face he wore the first moment he saw me. "I told you to leave me alone."

"Believe me, I'd love to. Unfortunately, I can't. Gloria needs you. Another thing I can't believe I'm saying. You have to come back to San Diego now."

It's David's turn to look incredulous. "What are you talking about? Why would you think I'd be interested in anything to do with Gloria? Are you nuts?"

"You get that question a lot, don't you?" Tamara says to me with a smirk.

I ignore her and focus on David. "Gloria is in trouble."

"No shit. She's in jail for murder."

I shake my head. "She's out on bail, but she may not be for long. She's at County General Hospital. The official story is she tried to commit suicide."

Emotions play across David's face like a fast-forward slide show—fury, hesitation, concern, distrust. "I don't believe it. Gloria would never try to kill herself. Is this a trick?"

"Good question. Detective Harris is working on that now. The important thing is, if she doesn't have anyone to stay with her, they may revoke her bail. I can't do it. I'm working on something else. You could. Will you?"

David slams the ax into the log he was splitting when we arrived. "Let's go."

No questions, no indecision, no wavering.

David goes inside to grab a shirt.

Tamara watches as he walks away. I think she's forgotten I'm here. She's focused on the door David disappeared through like a puppy eagerly awaiting her master's return.

David is back in two minutes. He secures the cabin and comes down the steps, pointing to the Harley. "That your bike, Tammy?"

She nods. He fishes keys out of the pocket of his jeans and tosses them to me. "I'll ride back with her. You take the Hummer."

Tamara beams, David takes her arm and steers her toward the bike, and I'm left standing alone on the porch.

Nice to see he's over Gloria.

CHAPTER 43

I WATCH DAVID AND TAMARA PEEL AWAY DOWN THE driveway with a rooster tail of flying gravel. Have I fallen down the rabbit hole? It occurs to me that I didn't tell her not to mention the fact that I'm a vampire to David. Or to warn her what will happen if she's entertaining thoughts of delivering David to Sandra to use as leverage against me. But I remember the stupid way she looked; her brain was vapor locked by giddiness. What are the odds my name will even come up?

Any skepticism I had that Tamara and Sandra cooked up this visit today to trap me into another meeting vanished with the look of pure delight on Tamara's face when David wrapped his arms around her waist. I wonder how she's going to explain her distraction to Sandra? Or is Sandra a football fan, too?

Christ.

I walk around back to the carport and climb into David's Hummer. After my Jag, driving it is like wrestling alligators.

It does better on the open road, though, and I head right for the O'Sullivan house.

The O'Sullivans live in Fairbanks Ranch, a wealthy enclave in northern San Diego County. It's two fifteen when I pull up a block away from the O'Sullivan compound. Fairbanks Ranch is not a gated community. It doesn't have to be. Each residence has a gate and fence all its own.

I'm debating whether to walk from here or drive up to the house. I have a better chance of getting in and out without notice if I walk. On the other hand, the streets of Fairbanks Ranch are wide and tree lined and patrolled regularly by a security company. If I leave the Hummer here, will it attract notice?

The answer comes immediately. A sedan marked "Fisher Home Security" has passed by twice in the five minutes since I arrived. The second time, the car pulls to a stop behind the Hummer and the driver's door opens.

I watch in the rearview mirror as the uniformed guard approaches. He's middle-aged, gray, balding, with a slight paunch. His bearing suggests a military background, erect, stern. He has one hand on his belt, resting on the handle of a long flashlight, the mannerism of one who was used to carrying a gun. The military was most likely followed by a stint as a cop.

I roll down my window and wait.

The guy touches two fingers to his forehead in a greeting. "Afternoon, ma'am. Are you here to visit a resident?"

Behind his dark sunglasses, the eyes are cautious. I guess they have to be when you're responsible for the security in a neighborhood where the median price of a house is three million dollars.

I put on a bright smile. "Yes, sir. I'm visiting my aunt. I've had a bit of car trouble. I called my boyfriend, and he's sending a tow truck. It shouldn't be too long."

He casts an eye toward the hood of the Hummer. "Want me to take a look for you?"

"No, thanks. It's not necessary. This has happened before. I'm going to walk on over to my aunt's and wait there for the truck."

"I'd be happy to drive you," he says. "Want to give me the address?"

"Actually, it's right around the corner and I don't mind walking. It's so beautiful here."

He is studying me, no doubt wondering if I look like an ax murderer or a burglar or, even worse, a vagrant. Evidently, I pass inspection because I get the two-finger salute again and he leaves me with a curt "Have a nice day, miss."

He returns to the car, and I notice he takes the time to write down the Hummer's license plate. I notice because he wants me to. In fact, he makes an obvious show of it before getting into the car, a not-so-subtle message that I shouldn't try anything because he has my number. The fact that I'm driving a seventy-thousand-dollar automobile does not make me above suspicion here at Fairbanks Ranch.

I half expect him to shadow me when I get out of the car, which would pose a problem. He watches me lock the Hummer, and I feel those eyes follow as I walk up the sidewalk. In a second, though, he starts the car and pulls around me, sending me another of those quasi-salutes.

I trot up to the O'Sullivan gate. There's a camera, but it's focused on the gate, not the keypad, and it doesn't swing toward me when I punch in the code. Jason's doing? If he thought to disable the camera, too, he's one smart kid.

The gate swings open and I sprint inside, keeping to the bushes that line the drive. I don't know how many security cameras they have on the property and I doubt Jason does, either. The one on the gate is obvious.

From the road, you can't see the house, but I know what

to expect and I'm not disappointed. The O'Sullivans live in a big, square Tudor set in the middle of an acre of manicured lawn. From the outside, the house appears to have a hundred rooms. The paving stone driveway circles the house. Jason said his dad's study was in the back. I head in that direction.

The ground level of the house has about two dozen sets of French doors. I have to peek into each room before I find the one that matches the pictures of the crime scene. I wish I had gloves. Unfortunately, I didn't expect to be driving the Hummer. I expected to be driving my Jag, which is where the gloves are. So I do the next best thing. I pull the hem of my T-shirt free and cover my fingers with the cloth to try the door.

It opens.

I step inside, close the door and wait to see if I'm greeted by the shriek of alarms.

Nothing. So far, so good.

The den looks exactly like it did in the pictures—except O'Sullivan's body is no longer sprawled on the desk. The forensic team evidently released it as a crime scene because there is no yellow tape and the room has been cleaned. It appears the desk blotter has been removed, and there is a piece of carpet cut out from the area where O'Sullivan's chair rested. The chair is gone as well. There's a box of Kleenex on a sideboard. I pull one out. Since I doubt I'll find anything of interest here, I move out of the room, using the tissue on the doorknob, and try to locate Mrs. O'Sullivan's office.

Jason said it was upstairs. The first challenge is to find the stairs. The den opens into a gallery almost as wide as my living room. It's paneled in dark mahogany, lined with portraits. The combination of dark paneling and a collection of intricately framed gloomy portraits of stuffy-looking gentlemen in early eighteenth-century garb sucks the air right out of the room.

I hurry through and try the door at the other end. Success. This door leads to the entry hall. There are rooms on each side and in the middle, a double curved staircase right out of *Gone With the Wind*. I ignore the flanking rooms and run up the stairs.

I should have asked Jason to draw me a map or at least tell me which of the twenty closed doors I'm looking at is his stepmother's office. Since I didn't, and I've never met her, I can't rely on my sense of smell to ferret her out. At the head of the stairs, though, I pick up a flowery citrus scent. Feminine and subtle. Expensive. I follow it to the third room on the left.

This is definitely a woman's room. Rose-colored wallpaper, blond French Provincial furniture. Bedroom furniture. Mr. and Mrs. O'Sullivan must have had separate bedrooms. My hunch is confirmed when I open the connecting door to my left. This is a man's bedroom, heavy, dark furniture, hunting scenes on the walls, the scent of musk.

I close the door. There's a deadbolt on Mrs. O'Sullivan's side.

Interesting.

On the opposite side of the room is another door. This leads through a massive walk-in closet. Must be a thousand pairs of shoes. At the far end, is one more door. I try the handle.

It's locked.

Shit. I wasn't expecting that. I could easily break down the door, but that wouldn't be very subtle, now would it?

I kneel down to examine the lock. It's a simple key and tumbler. No deadbolt. In my day job, David and I have jimmied this type of lock a million times. The only problem is I left my purse in the Jag back in town and in it, my set of picklocks. Maybe I can do it the way they do in movies—use a knife from the kitchen or a nail file from Mrs. O'Sullivan's bathroom.

I go in search. First, the bathroom since I'm here. Either she never does her own nails, or she carries her only nail file with her because a cursory search of her bathroom vanity finds nothing. I'm not about to turn her drawers inside out. I run back down the steps to the kitchen.

It takes me a while to find it. I've never understood why anyone would want to live in a house so big that it takes a map to navigate the maze of rooms. It's getting close to three o'clock, and I want to get out of here as soon as I can. After several false starts through living rooms and dining rooms and media rooms and rooms whose purpose I can't fathom, I finally find the kitchen.

A kitchen about fifty yards long with a hundred places to hide the knives.

Shit again. I start pulling open drawers. The tissue is about in shreds and the idea of kicking down the door is looking better and better when I find a silverware drawer with something that looks like it could work. It's a thin-bladed butter knife. I grab it and run.

Picking the lock is not as easy with a knife as it looks on television. It takes several attempts at wedging the blade between the doorjamb and the lock before I get the feel of what I need to do. Even then, the knife blade slips, leaving thin scratches on the woodwork. Finally, I feel the lock give and the handle turns at my touch. Unfortunately, the blade of the knife breaks at the same time and I'm left with pieces that I stuff in my jacket to discard later. Hope Mrs. O'Sullivan doesn't count the silverware.

It's three fifteen.

Mrs. O'Sullivan's office is not what I expect. Compared to the carefully appointed and immaculately clean rooms in the rest of the house, this room is furnished in early American yard sale and cluttered with dusty piles of old magazines, newspapers, scrapbooks, photo albums—the detritus of her thirty some years of life *before* she became Mrs.

Rory O'Sullivan. There are framed pictures of beauty pageants, glittery rhinestone tiaras, ribbons marking her progression from Miss El Cajon to Miss San Diego to Miss California, and culminating in the title of runner-up to Miss America. They stop there. Photos show her with Mr. O'Sullivan, one of the celebrity judges for that pageant. Her life as a beauty queen ended with a runner-up sash and the biggest prize of all.

I maneuver my way through the stuff to a desk thrust against the wall. It's as piled with junk as the rest of the room. There's nothing of obvious interest on top and everything is so dust laden, I wonder if she ever comes in here.

I try the drawers. The middle holds nothing but pencils, pens, paper clips, broken rubber bands.

The right-hand drawer is a file drawer. From the dates on file tabs, nothing has been added to categories such as "Bills Paid," "Recipes" and "Misc" since 2003, the year she met O'Sullivan. No tab marked "PI Investigating My Cheating Husband." Too bad. It would have made my life so much easier.

The left side of the desk holds two drawers. The first is empty.

The second is empty, too.

Except for one item.

A gun.

CHAPTER 44

I STARE INTO THE DRAWER. I'M LOOKING AT A SMALL-caliber handgun. O'Sullivan was killed with a small-caliber handgun. If this is the weapon, am I the best investigator in the world or the luckiest?

I take a pencil from the middle drawer and pick up the gun by lacing the pencil through the trigger guard. It's a .22-caliber minirevolver. A lady's gun.

What to do now? Call the cops?

How do I explain being here?

Leave it and risk Mrs. O'Sullivan getting rid of it at the first opportunity?

Leaving it isn't the best choice, but self-preservation is a strong motivator. I don't want to go to jail. On the other hand, if it's the murder weapon, I'm holding the only tangible link to the killer.

I look around the small, cramped room. There's no obvious place to hide the gun. Except—

There's a stack of manila envelopes on the floor. I take one and slide the gun inside. Then I shove the envelope under the pile of bulging scrapbooks and photo albums against the far wall. Not bad. I doubt even Mrs. O'Sullivan would notice the new addition to that mess.

Now what?

My watch says it's 3:40 p.m. Time to go. I back out through the door. I can't relock it. The fact that someone has come into this room will be evident the first time Mrs. O'Sullivan tries the door.

It's so quiet in the house, my nerves start to tingle. Now that I've done what I set out to do, with remarkable results, getting out should be the focus of my attention. The nagging thought that this was too easy, that I'm missing something even more important makes me pause at the top of the stairs to consider what I should do next.

Two possibilities present themselves. Check out O'Sullivan's office downstairs.

Or check out Jason's bedroom.

I turn back to the hallway. I close my eyes and let my senses "taste" the air. This morning, Jason smelled of Safeguard soap, Redken shampoo and CK One deodorant. I follow the same scent trail to the third door on the left at the end of the hall.

The door is not locked. When I step inside, I step into every teen's dream room. An LCD wide-screen TV hangs on the wall opposite the bed. A Bang & Olufsen system connects computer and TV and every conceivable music source imaginable. There's a desk and a small love seat. The desktop is clear except for the computer monitor. No bookcase. Nothing personal on the walls, only what looks like LeRoy Neiman sports prints. I recognize the collection because David has them, too. It's the Football Suite and when I look closer, I realize these are probably the original lithographs.

I move to the desk, open drawers, carefully shuffle contents although I have no idea what I'm looking for or why I think I should be looking here at all.

In the bottom right-hand drawer, under a stack of *Playboy* magazines, I find an engraved envelope addressed to Jason's dad. I know as soon as I touch it that it's important—it's the old spidey sense again. The same kind of intuition that tells you to slow down because there's a cop up ahead or not answer the phone because there's someone you don't want to talk to on the other end.

I lift it from the drawer and open it.

An invitation.

From a pharmaceutical group in France.

Inviting Jason's dad to a press party introducing the world's first cure for HIV.

Is this why O'Sullivan dropped the Benton Pharmaceuticals deal? Did another company find a formula to rival the one they had been developing and beat them to production?

I'm staring at the invitation, trying to figure if this could fit into O'Sullivan's murder when the sound of a car door shatters my concentration and brings me back to the moment with a jolt.

Shit.

I peek out Jason's window. I'm two stories up, facing the back of the house. The front door is already opening, and I can hear Jason and his stepmother in heated conversation. I don't wait to try and determine what they're fighting about. I quietly shut Jason's door, take another quick look at the invitation, memorizing the company name, and slip it back where I found it. Then I open his window, climb out onto a narrow ledge under it and slide the window closed again moments before Jason trudges into his room.

He goes into his bathroom and slams the door.

With an eye on the ground, I leap off the ledge.

CHAPTER 45

THERE ARE SOME THINGS ABOUT BEING A VAMPIRE
that I've begun to take for granted. For instance, I can
leap off a two-story building with perfect confidence that I
won't break anything major. It's hard to describe what being airborne feels like—something between hovering like
a helicopter and gliding like a bird. Since I have neither ro-
tors nor wings, I don't know how I'm able to defy the laws
of gravity. I simply know that I can.

I land on my feet with barely a jolt. I glance up to see if
Jason caught my aerodynamic display, but luckily, he's not
at the window. I take to the bushes and work my way back
to the gate. This time, I don't want to risk opening it so I
follow the brick wall until I come to a place that I estimate
is close to where I left the Hummer. There's a tree on this
side that I shimmy up to survey the road. The Hummer is a
half block away. No security car in sight. It's a quick hop to
the ground and I'm on my way.

I drive out of Fairbanks Ranch before I pull over to
consider what I should do next. My first impulse, to call

Detective Harris and tell him about the gun, is stifled by the questions he's bound to ask. Like where I found it, how I knew where to look for it and how I got into the O'Sullivan house in the first place. Questions I'm not willing to answer. I could tell Gloria's lawyer. He could go to the DA's office and ask them to issue a search warrant. Would they, though, with no other evidence except the word of a person who conducted an illegal search?

What if Gloria's fingerprints are on the gun?

What if this is a setup?

I have no answers so I head for town. I'll let Gloria's attorney figure it out.

I remember from his letterhead that his address is in the Darth Vader building. I debate stopping at the hospital to see how Gloria is doing, but logically, getting the gun to the police should be first priority. I have no idea how often Mrs. O'Sullivan goes into her office. She'll notice the broken lock as soon as she does.

It isn't until I'm downtown and stalled in holiday-shopping traffic that I remember. It's Sunday afternoon.

Great.

As soon as the opportunity presents itself, I disentangle myself and get off Harbor Drive, heading for Pacific Coast Highway. I'll stop at the office and leave a message for Gloria's lawyer to contact me as soon as possible.

My own telephone message light is blinking when I get to the office. There are two messages: One from David asking me to meet him at the hospital. The second is from my dad.

"Anna," he says. "Take a look at the business section of today's paper. I think you'll find something of interest. Call me if you have any questions."

The paper is still outside; I hadn't bothered to pick it up. Now I retrieve it and spread it open on the desk. I have to sort through all the junk ads and flyers before finding the business section.

Something of interest?

You betcha.

The lead story is about the late Rory O'Sullivan and his aborted foray into the pharmaceutical business.

And the suit being brought against his estate by the officers of Benton Pharmaceuticals, charging that O'Sullivan stole the formula for their HIV cure and sold it to a foreign country.

Stole the formula? I remember what my dad said about O'Sullivan being the financier behind Benton. If that was true, knowing how shrewd a businessman he was, wouldn't the contract have stipulated that the formula belonged to him? I can see how the officers of the company would be enraged by getting cut out of a deal, but would they have legal basis for a lawsuit? And what benefit would O'Sullivan gain by selling such a valuable formula to a foreign entity instead of marketing it here in this country?

It also puts a new slant on what I found hidden in Jason's drawer. The name of the company on the invitation was Pharmaceutique Bouvier Compagnie de la France. Is this the foreign company O'Sullivan is suspected of selling the formula to? It's not named in the newspaper article. Maybe those bringing the suit don't yet know it.

Why would Jason hide that invitation? I'm beginning to suspect Jason's mom isn't the only one trying to steer the investigation in a certain direction. It makes me wonder if he was truthful about what he heard outside his father's den that morning.

I need to talk to my own dad. A glance at my watch shows it's getting close to dinnertime. No way am I going to risk having to decline another of my mom's meal invitations. We parted on friendly terms this morning. I won't push my luck. What I will do is call Dad at his office tomorrow—or maybe drop by in person after seeing Gloria's lawyer.

Which leaves me nothing more to do except head for

the hospital. Before I leave, I put that call through to Gloria's lawyer. An answering service picks up, and I leave my name and number.

DAVID IS STANDING OUTSIDE GLORIA'S HOSPITAL room door. He doesn't see me at first. He's leaning against the wall, head down, shoulders slumped. He looks sad and my heart jumps.

I rush up to him. "What's the matter? Is it Gloria?"

He straightens with a sudden jerk. "Where did you come from?"

"You told me to meet you here, remember? Why are you standing outside? Did something happen to Gloria?" I move to look through the window in the door. There are two people standing in my line of sight, their backs to me. A man I recognize dressed in an off-the-rack suit, Harris, and a woman I don't with smooth, shoulder-length black hair who's decked out in a red Versace power suit and Ferragamo pumps. "I can't see Gloria; Harris is in the way. Is she all right?"

David waves a hand. "Slow down. She's fine. She's with her lawyer. Harris arrived a minute ago."

The Versace suit is her lawyer? "That's Jamie Sutherland? Gloria never mentioned that her lawyer was a woman. I assumed—"

"That Jamie was a man. Happens all the time."

I turn away from the window and focus my attention on David. "I'm sorry for dragging you back here. You know I wouldn't have if I'd been able to come up with anyone else. I don't suppose Gloria told you what I've been doing?"

He nods. "She said you're working for her. Trying to prove her innocence. You helping Gloria. A surprising turn of events, wouldn't you say?"

But he's smiling, which makes me smile, too. With relief. "No kidding. When I started the investigation, I didn't really care how it turned out because Gloria and I made a pact. Did she tell you about that, as well?"

He nods, eyes serious once again. "She did. When this is over, she's gone. For good."

I'm not sure how to interpret his expression. Is it relief or sadness? I'm glad Gloria was honest with him for once. "You know, all that aside, I don't think Gloria killed O'Sullivan. I think she's being framed."

David looks past me into the room. "She didn't try to kill herself, either," he says quietly.

Shit. All the good feelings I had for the woman are swallowed up in a rush of anger. My first instincts had been right. "Damn it. You mean she really did fake it? Is that woman stupid or delusional?"

David stops me with an upturned hand. "No. I don't mean she faked it. I mean it wasn't suicide. Somebody tried to kill her."

CHAPTER 46

"SOMEONE TRIED TO KILL GLORIA?" MY FEELINGS are boomeranging. I realize I'm more comfortable thinking it was a botched fake suicide than a murder attempt. I always thought I was the only one with motive enough to want her dead.

David either isn't paying any attention to the lack of concern in my voice for Gloria's plight, or he's too distracted to comment. "She said someone came into her suite while she was asleep," he says. "A man in a hotel bellman's uniform wearing a mask. He chloroformed her and dragged her out of bed. He fed her pills and whiskey before he left. The next thing she knew, the paramedics were forcing a tube down her throat, and she was puking her guts out."

"Does she know who called the paramedics?"

David shakes his head. "No. Harris says it was an anonymous nine-one-one call from a pay phone in the hotel lobby."

"What about the bellman's uniform? Anyone report one missing?"

"The manager said the uniforms are picked up each Friday afternoon by a dry-cleaning company and returned on Saturday. They're left in an employee's lounge. Anyone could walk in and pick one up. It's a big hotel with a large staff. The people working day shift aren't familiar with people working the night shift and vice versa. No one claims to have seen anyone acting suspiciously."

"But how did he get into Gloria's suite? He must have had a passkey. Surely somebody keeps track of those."

David nods. "The manager is looking into that." He looks past me into Gloria's room. "It doesn't make sense. Why would someone hurt Gloria, then call for help."

I remember Harris' comment that he would have to tell the DA that Gloria attempted suicide. "Maybe because if people think Gloria tried to kill herself, it would make her look guilty." I'm thinking of Laura now, the jealous stepmother. Wanting Gloria to suffer the humiliation of a trial might be just her style.

"If they wanted her out of the way, why not kill her when they had the chance."

I shrug. David doesn't know about Jason or his suspicions about his stepmother. I want to speak with Gloria's lawyer before I voice my own opinions, so I add, "Maybe whoever is responsible didn't want Gloria dead. They wanted her in jail. Whatever the motive, it was a clumsy attempt."

Or juvenile. Jason? How hard would it have been for him to buy over-the-counter drugs, take a bottle of liquor from home, steal a bellman's uniform? No, any smart kid could have done that. Now, getting his hands on a passkey is another story. That would have taken some ingenuity.

I give myself a mental thump on the head. It couldn't have been Jason. He was genuinely concerned about Gloria. He might have faked it when we met at Lestat's, but that display on the courthouse steps? He had no idea I was watching. He wouldn't risk hurting her or worse if the plan went wrong.

"Anna?"

David's voice pulls me back.

"What are you thinking?"

Nothing I want to share. I turn my attention to the room. It looks as if Harris and the lawyer are getting ready to leave. I gesture vaguely at the window. "Let's see what Harris has to say."

Harris comes to the door, then stands back to allow Jamie Sutherland through first. She looks at me with calm brown eyes and holds out her hand.

"Are you Anna Strong?"

I nod and return a brief handshake. Jamie Sutherland is thirtysomething, tall, lithe, possessed of great cheekbones and arresting but irregular features. Wide eyes, small, straight nose, a generous but rather thin-lipped mouth. Along with that sweep of black hair, I'm guessing Eurasian ancestry.

Harris greets me with a nod, too, as he closes his notebook and slips it into his jacket. "I've taken Ms. Estrella's statement. As soon as the doctor gives his okay, she's free to go. Bail conditions remain the same. She's not to leave the jurisdiction."

"What about the attempt on her life?"

David's tone is belligerent and confrontational. Obviously, he and Harris didn't mend any fences while I was gone.

Harris doesn't rise to the bait. Worse, he ignores David completely. He looks instead at Jamie Sutherland. "Counselor, we'll be in touch?"

When she nods, he steps around us all and makes his way to the exit.

David looks as if he's about to charge after him. I stop him with a hand on his arm. "Go see Gloria," I say. "I want to talk to Ms. Sutherland."

He shakes off my restraining hand but doesn't argue. With a grunt, he pushes open the hospital room door and steps inside.

Sutherland throws a wry smile my way. "Well. Looks like someone has finally tamed the Ryan beast."

It's an odd thing to say and suggests a familiarity with David that catches me off guard. "You and David . . . ?"

She laughs. "No. Not an ex. David and I met at Notre Dame. He was a senior and I was a first-year law student. We had friends in common, that's all. Ah, but that temper. Got him in trouble more than once."

Well. I definitely want to hear more about that. Later. Right now, I want to tell her about the gun and get Gloria on her way out of our lives.

"Want to get some coffee?" I suggest. When she gestures to lead the way, I do, telling her as we make our way to the basement cafeteria about my conversation with Jason and what I found in his house.

I don't tell her everything. I'm purposefully vague about how I found the gun and might have given her the impression that Jason was at the house at the time I did my non–breaking and entering.

She's watching me the way an eagle watches a mouse. I get the feeling I'm not fooling her.

"So," she says when I pause for air. "You were in the O'Sullivan house at the minor son's invitation because he suspects his stepmother killed his father, and found yourself in Mrs. O'Sullivan's private office where you stumbled upon a small-caliber gun in a desk drawer. That about sum it up?"

Except for what I found in Jason's room. Don't think I'll mention that right now, either. "That's it." I feel like I should be batting my eyelashes and winking.

She's quiet for a moment, drawing slow circles in her coffee with a spoon. Finally, she taps the spoon on the edge of the cup, sets it down on the table and raises the cup to her lips. Instead of drinking, though, she eyes me over the rim. "As an officer of the court, I'm compelled to tell you that you should have called the police the minute you found the gun. The evidence, exculpatory or not, may now be considered tainted because of the way it was handled."

I stop her with an upturned hand. "I didn't touch the gun. I was careful not to. I put it into an envelope and hid it. That's all. I didn't remove it from the premises."

She shakes her head and the cup descends back to the table, coffee untouched. "It doesn't matter. The courts have strict rules regarding chain of custody. Even if it turns out that Gloria's fingerprints are not on the gun, that the only prints belong to Mrs. O'Sullivan, if it becomes known that you moved the gun from its original hiding place, it may never be admitted as evidence in any trial."

"What about ballistics? The police have the bullet that killed O'Sullivan. I couldn't tamper with the insides of the damned barrel, could I?"

"No." She draws the word out as if sifting possibilities through her head before framing her next response. "Okay, Anna," she says. "Here's what we're going to do. I'll tell Harris about the gun. He'll ask how I know about it. I'll say confidential informant. We'll do a dance over that, but I think he'll get that search warrant. Once he has the gun, he'll have ballistics and fingerprints run. If we're lucky, and it's the murder weapon and it's registered to Mrs. O'Sullivan, he'll drop the charges against Gloria."

She gathers up her briefcase and takes one sip of coffee. "First, though, we go talk to Gloria. Let's hope O'Sullivan didn't take her target shooting or try to impress her by picking squirrels out of a tree. If she says she handled a gun in his house, even once, it may not matter what the evidence shows, the gun won't do us a damned bit of good."

CHAPTER 47

WHEN WE GET BACK TO THE ROOM, THERE'S SO much tension between David and Gloria it's like walking into a Deepfreeze. David is seated at the end of the bed, chair flat against the wall, as if trying to put as much distance as possible between the two of them and still be in the same room. Gloria is looking out the window, mouth pursed in a tight frown, avoiding David's eyes like a rat in a cobra's cage.

At least she looks better physically than the last time I saw her at the hotel. She's clean, her hair slicked back in a ponytail, but she's still pale. The lines of her face are drawn with anxiety and fatigue.

They both brighten when Jamie and I walk in.

Gloria scoots herself up in the bed so she's sitting up straighter. She looks at me. "Did you speak with Jason?"

I never had a chance to tell her that I was meeting with the kid. Only one way she could have known. "Yes. Obviously, so have you. What did he tell you?"

The corners of her eyes tighten a fraction as if she's suddenly aware she may have said something she shouldn't have. She recovers quickly, though, and moves her shoulders in an offhanded shrug. "Jason said that he was meeting with you this morning. He and I are friends. He knows I couldn't have killed his father."

Her voice drops off, waiting for me to pick up the thread, to share with David and her lawyer Jason's belief that it was his stepmother, not Gloria, who killed his father.

After all, it would sound so much more convincing coming from me.

"Anna told me what Jason believes," Jamie interjects. "He believes his stepmother is involved because he overheard them discussing a legal problem that could bankrupt the family. He thinks her motive was greed."

That's all she says. Nothing about my searching the O'Sullivan house or finding a gun.

Gloria's expression wavers. She's expecting more. It's clear she's talked to Jason. When? Before I met with him or after?

In either case, finding that gun feels more and more like a setup.

It must feel the same way to Gloria's lawyer. She asks Gloria a few questions about how many times she was in the O'Sullivan house and if she ever saw or handled a gun there. The questions are couched in general terms and when Gloria responds that no, she never saw or handled a gun, Jamie lets the matter drop.

To Gloria's obvious surprise and consternation. "That's it?" Color floods her face. "You're not going to tell Detective Harris about Laura O'Sullivan? About what Jason said to Anna? Shouldn't the police search the house for a gun? She obviously set me up. She even tried to have me killed. Someone has to make the police see that I'm being set up."

Jamie pulls a chair up to Gloria's bedside and leans her

face close. "Isn't that what you and Jason are doing as well?" she asks quietly. "Gloria, I don't believe you killed Rory O'Sullivan, but what you and that boy are doing to *prove* your innocence is only going to get you both in trouble."

CHAPTER 48

GLORIA DOESN'T REACT TO JAMIE'S WORDS. HER face reflects neither anger at, nor denial of, the accusation. It reflects nothing at all.

Gloria is an actress. Her life is played out in drama. This lack of animation is scary—the deadly calm at the center of a hurricane.

It also gives her away.

David, as always, is oblivious. He's looking at Jamie, indignation tightening the corners of his mouth. "You don't really believe Gloria staged a suicide attempt, do you? With the help of a teenager, yet?"

Good old David. Even now he comes to her defense. For me, though, each puzzle piece is falling into place. "Let's look at it objectively, David. The amateurish choice of drugs, stealing the bellman's uniform, Gloria could easily have set that up. Jason didn't need a passkey to get into the suite. Gloria let him in."

Gloria stares down at her hands, twisting the sheet into knots, lips compressed in a hard line.

"When David and I were talking about what happened," I continue. "We thought trying to kill Gloria and then calling for help made no sense. It wasn't a murder attempt; it was a diversionary tactic. Jason didn't do it because he wanted to hurt her; he did it because he thought he was helping." I shake my head. "Gloria, you took a chance, like flipping a coin. Heads, being the victim of a murder attempt makes you look innocent to a jury. Tails, if it's determined you did this to yourself, you come off looking guilty as hell."

Gloria stirs, opens her mouth, but Jamie shakes her head and puts a finger to her lips in a signal to stay quiet. She releases a long breath and gets to her feet.

"I'm going to leave now. Anything I heard here this evening is protected under the client/attorney privilege. I have to ask Anna and David to respect that. If the police determine Gloria played a part in a staged suicide attempt, they will bring charges. Gloria, I advise you to remain silent." She picks up her briefcase and turns to David. "Did the doctor tell you when she can go home?"

David hasn't taken his eyes off Gloria. He drags them away now to look at Jamie. "Tomorrow morning."

"Will you pick her up?"

He hesitates and for a minute, I'm afraid he's going to refuse. "Yes," he says finally. "I'll be here."

Jamie closes the door quietly behind her. When I look at David, he's staring again at Gloria, his face clouded with anger. He sees it now. All of it.

Gloria feels the shift, too. She looks up. "I didn't kill O'Sullivan," she says quietly. "You have to believe that."

David shakes his head slowly and pushes up from the chair. "I don't *have* to believe anything," he says.

He has a hand on the door. "Anna, I'll take you to your car. I'll wait for you outside."

Gloria watches him go. "He must know I couldn't have

killed anyone. You believe me, don't you, Anna?" She's crying, making no attempt to wipe away the tears.

"I do. I think, deep down, David does, too. But Gloria, I don't think it matters to him anymore."

I let a heartbeat go by.

"You and Jason. You two have been in contact since the beginning. You wanted us to meet. What would you have done if I hadn't been able to track him down?"

Gloria is still looking at the door. Her voice is soft, wistful. "I knew you'd find him. I've watched you and David in the office. Tracking people down. It's what you do, isn't it?"

"And if I hadn't?"

She shrugs. "He would have called you."

Of course he would have. I can't believe I fell into Gloria's trap.

I feel like a fool. I watch Gloria, still staring at the door, still waiting for David, her David, to rush back in and make everything all right.

I let myself out.

Not happening, Gloria.

DAVID IS WAITING FOR ME AT THE END OF THE HALL, slumped on a bench, his head in his hands.

I was an idiot to think he could get over his obsession with Gloria this fast.

He doesn't notice my approach and when I place a hand on his shoulder, he jumps.

I sit down beside him. "You can go back to your cabin. I shouldn't have brought you here. I'm sorry I did."

He swivels on the bench to look at me. "What? An apology? You must really feel guilty. Good. When this is over, you'll owe me. Big time."

He crosses his arms and leans back. "No. I'm glad you brought me back. I needed to see Gloria the way you evidently have since the beginning. She's so selfish she'll draw anyone into her web if she thinks it will benefit her— even a fourteen-year-old kid. God, what was she thinking?"

I shrug. "She was desperate and scared. Honestly, I don't believe she killed O'Sullivan."

"You sound as if you're going to keep digging. Are you?"

"I guess I am. She's paying me two hundred an hour plus expenses. May as well earn a few bucks I don't have to split with my partner."

He smiles and stands up. "Let's get you back to your car. I have a date, and I want to go home and shower first."

"A date? So soon? Is this a rebound thing?"

"Don't know yet. It's our first date."

We're walking toward the entrance. A tremor of uneasiness slithers along my spine. "Who is this mystery woman? Have I met her?"

"In fact, you introduced us. This afternoon."

I stop, grab his arm. "Tamara? You're going on a date with Tamara?"

He looks down at my hand on his arm, then up at my face. "What's the matter with you? You look sick. Is there a reason I shouldn't go out with her?"

A reason? Jesus. I could give him ten, the first and foremost being his new friend Tamara happens to be a fucking werewolf.

CHAPTER 49

THOUGHTS SPIN AROUND MY HEAD. WHAT CAN I say to convince David that a date with Tamara is not just a bad idea, it might be a fatal one?

I panic when I realize I'm not coming up with anything that makes sense. The panic grows when we step outside and the first thing I see is a huge moon rising over the city like a silver balloon.

The second night of the full moon.

What is Tamara planning for tonight? I remember how she looked at David. I remember how few men were with the pack at Culebra's. Frey's book said werewolves have the right to take and turn a mate. Does the rule apply to female weres as well? Is that how she sees David?

We're at the Hummer. I don't know how we got here and I don't realize David is standing in front of me holding out his hand for his keys until he clears his throat.

"What is it with you?" he says, taking the keys I hand him. "You're pale as a ghost."

He uses the remote to unlock the doors and opens the

passenger side for me before crossing to take his place in the driver's seat. He takes a minute to readjust the seat and steering wheel. While he's doing that, he says, "Is there something I should know about Tamara? She's not married, is she? Or divorced with ten kids? Not that I mind kids but I don't know what kind of father I'd be. I've had friends with stepkids and it doesn't always work out well. 'Course, that—"

"Jesus, David." My voice is high-pitched and screechy. "This is a fucking first date. You don't even know the woman. I haven't known her for long. What if she's a flake? Don't you think you should go to lunch maybe or coffee before taking her out at night?"

David looks over with an expression that makes me want to smack him. He's trying hard not to laugh. "Go to lunch or coffee before taking her out at night? What are we, twelve? You want to come along to chaperone?"

Not a bad idea. Well, not coming along to chaperone exactly, but I could follow them. Make sure Tamara keeps her skin on.

David is eyeballing me again. "Come on, Anna. Spill it. You have something against Tamara? I suppose if you do I should hear it. You certainly had Gloria pegged."

Now that I've decided on a course of action, I relax and smile over at him. "No. Get me to my car and you can go on your date. It's a block or so from the Four Seasons. I'll direct you."

David drives with one eye on the road and one on me. I don't reverse myself often. It's amusing to feel his confusion. What wouldn't be amusing is Tamara turning into a werewolf and attacking him. I'm not sure how I'll tail them since he knows my car, but I'll figure something out.

We're about a block from my car when David slows the Hummer. "Holy shit. Is that the Jag? What the hell happened to it?"

His tone snaps me from my reverie. I follow his gaze.

I can't believe what I'm seeing.

The Jag is parked where I left it. Under a streetlight, a block from the hotel.

It's been trashed. The paint is scored with thousands of scratches, every inch of the body scraped and cut. Not even the windows escaped. The ones not shattered outright bear deep nicks and abrasions.

David's voice is hushed. "It looks like it was attacked by a pack of wild dogs."

I'm too stunned to respond, words just won't come, but I know he's right. It was attacked by animals.

Not dogs, though.

Wolves.

CHAPTER 50

LIGHTNING FAST, SHOCK VEERS TO ANGER. "I'M GO-ing to kill her."

I didn't mean to speak the words out loud.

David is no longer looking at the car. He's staring at me. "Kill *her*? Kill who?"

I've stumbled out of the Hummer and am standing in stunned silence beside my car. I love this car. It was the first really nice car I ever bought—my dream car. Sandra trashed it. The musk of wolf hanging in the air confirms it.

David joins me at the front of the Hummer. "Anna? You know who did this? We'll call the police. Anybody this twisted should be locked up."

He's reaching for his cell phone. I grab his hand. "No police. I'll take care of this."

"Are you kidding? What do you mean, no police? I've never seen damage like this. I can't even imagine what was used. A trowel? A knife? A bat? Jesus. You'd think some-one would have noticed a car being vandalized like this."

David's outrage is escalating. So is my own; my insides are seething with it. Except that I know there's nothing the cops can do except take a report. It was Sandra and her pack. How they managed in daylight on a busy side street, I can't even imagine. I do know that if she's capable of the things I saw and felt last night, she's capable of creating the kind of glamour that would render her invisible.

David is waiting. What kind of explanation can I give him for not wanting to call the cops? I give voice to the first thing that pops to mind. "It's been a long day. What happened to my car is bad enough. Standing here for an hour doing paperwork is worse."

David doesn't look convinced, but he doesn't argue. I can tell by his expression that my outburst when I saw the car is replaying in his head. I can also tell that he's filing it away for a future conversation. He says, "What do you want to do?"

I'm suddenly conscious of tears running down my cheeks. Stupid. Crying over a car. I swipe at them with the back of my hand. "Call a tow truck, I guess."

David has his cell phone out again. "I can do better than that. I have a friend who owns a body shop. High end. I'll call him. He'll come get the car."

"It's Sunday night."

"Doesn't matter." David is scrolling through his address book. "He and I played for the Broncos. If he's not in the hospital or dead, he'll come."

I rest my butt against the side of the Jag, running a hand along the damaged door, listening to David's side of the conversation. In less than two minutes, he snaps shut his phone.

"He'll be here in twenty minutes."

Guess the football fraternity runs deep. I glance at my watch. I know in my gut that Tamara had a part in what happened to my car. At least the one good thing that could come out of this would be David canceling his date. I give him a forlorn smile. "What about your date? Aren't you going to be late?"

David is on the phone again. "Hey, Tamara. David. Listen, I have to cancel tonight. There's been an accident. No. Nothing serious. Can we postpone until tomorrow night?"

Evidently she agrees because he's smiling and nodding. "Great. Pick you up at seven."

He pockets the phone and joins me.

I've got a twenty-four-hour reprieve.

"Where does Tamara live?" I ask.

He looks surprised. "You don't know? She's staying with a friend at some doctor's house in La Jolla. Quite a place to hear her tell it."

Oh, yes. Quite a place. What David doesn't realize is that he's been there before. At Avery's house. That's where he was taken when Avery kidnapped and almost killed him.

It's where I'll go soon.

After I finish doing what I should have done this morning.

Read that damned chapter seventeen in Frey's book.

CHAPTER 51

I'VE NEVER BEEN ONE FOR SMALL TALK. LUCKILY, neither is David. We stand together beside the Hummer waiting in silence for his friend. I don't know what he's thinking about. I'm thinking about the various, creative ways I will kill Sandra should the opportunity present itself.

David's friend is punctual. He turns out to be another example of that rare and remarkable American breed: the giant pro football player. He's a good four inches taller than David, outweighs him by seventy-five pounds. He's dressed in jeans that fit too well to be anything but custom tailored and a tee under a denim jacket. His hands are encased in leather driving gloves and his feet in reptile-skin boots. He walks like the Hulk. Must have been a defensive end.

David introduces him as "Charmer Moss."

"Charmer?" I say, returning a firm handshake. His hand is the size of a dinner plate. "For real?"

He smiles. His skin is rich dark mahogany and the contrast of perfect, white teeth in the handsome face is dazzling. "My wife says that's more my mother's editorial comment on my father than any reflection on me."

"What do you think?"

He shrugs. "Don't know. My father died before I was born."

He looks past me to my car and the smile fades. "Shit. What the hell happened to your car?"

David and I watch as he surveys the damage. He makes a complete circle of the car. "Never seen anything like this. You get caught in a dust storm? Sometimes high wind and sand can scour the paint right off a car."

I wish it were something as simple as a dust storm. "No. No dust storms. Can you fix it?"

That brings back the smile. "Didn't David tell you? I can fix anything. If it's cosmetic, the way it looks, I can repaint and replace the windows. Only take about a week. Do you need a loaner? I've got a sweet '69 Mustang convertible you can have for the duration."

"Shit," David says. "I'll take the Mustang. Anna can drive my Hummer."

"In your dreams. I spent the afternoon driving that colossus of yours." I turn to Charmer. "I'll take the Mustang."

He returns to the cab of the tow truck and comes back with a clipboard. He asks and I answer insurance questions, give him my personal information, and arrange to be at his shop tomorrow morning to pick up the Mustang. David says he'll bring me to the shop himself before going to the hospital for Gloria.

"So you're still seeing her, huh?" Charmer says. He gives David a sideways squint. "Heard she got herself in some trouble."

David looks down and away. "Yeah. You might say that."

He doesn't elaborate, and, living up to his name, Charmer doesn't push. His mama would be proud.

I get my purse and Gloria's things out of the trunk. I slip the ignition key off the key chain, and David and I stand aside as Charmer maneuvers the tow truck into position and starts the Jag. I don't realize I've been holding my breath until he drives the Jag up onto the bed. The engine sounds fine. At least that's something. Charmer secures the car and in another ten minutes, he's on his way.

"Nice guy."

David nods. "The best. It's early yet. Want to get some dinner?"

My automatic response to human offers of food revs up to spout the usual litany of excuses why I can't. Except for one thing. David is right about it being early. I'm not about to give him a reason to call Tamara back tonight because he's free sooner than he expected. Especially with no way to keep an eye on them.

"Sure. I ate a late lunch, so I'm not particularly hungry but I could use a beer."

He smiles. "Good. It's been a while since I've been to Luigi's. It's in your neighborhood. How about it?"

Great. I nod and attempt a smile back at him. Now let's hope I can restrain from projectile vomiting at the smell in the one Mission Beach restaurant whose motto is "If you don't like garlic, go home."

My plan is to keep David occupied until it's too late for him to consider contacting Tamara. I figure until ten or so. Then I'll read that last chapter in Frey's book.

When I face Sandra the next time, I'll be prepared.

To do that, I have David swing by the office on our way to Luigi's. I tell him I want to pick up the papers Jamie's office faxed to me yesterday.

Yesterday? Has it only been one day?

He waits for me in the car while I run inside. I do grab the papers along with Frey's book and stuff them in a brief-case. Then we're off to a place that used to be my favorite eating joint.

Luigi's is a block from my cottage. It's small, dark, cramped and always busy. The owner is not Italian at all, but Greek. He's a short, middle-aged guy with a penchant for long-sleeved designer shirts and well-pressed jeans. He runs his place like a general commanding troops. But Ted can cook. His meatballs are world renowned—at least to hear him tell it—and I can personally attest that there are none better in San Diego. I've eaten my fair share.

Before the vampire thing turned garlic into a weapon, that is.

Ted is behind the bar when David and I walk in. He does a double take and slams a glass down on the counter so hard, it shatters. He snaps his finger to the barkeep to clean up the glass and stomps out to meet us, scowling.

"So. You aren't dead, after all. Figured you had to be, it's been so long since you dropped by. So what was it? Amne-sia? You forget your friends in the neighborhood now that you have a fancy office downtown? You find another place that feeds you better than Luigi's?"

He looks like he's winding up for a long tirade. I can't speak the smell is so offensive. At the moment I think I'm going to have to run out or puke all over his Gucci loafers. He takes David's arm in one hand and mine in the other and steers us to a booth by an open window. It's already occupied, mind you, but that doesn't stop Ted from shoo-ing the couple out, gathering up their dishes, and plunking them down on a table in the center of the place. They're too stunned to object. Even if they did, Ted wouldn't care. He's a force of nature. His place, his rules.

David and I slide in. Neither of us has spoken a word.

Ted's storm passes as quickly as a cloudburst, and by the time he's signaled for the busboy to wipe down our table and bring setups, he's beaming at us.

"How about a nice Chianti?" he says. "For the antipasti. Then I'm going to cook something special for you. You two leave everything to Ted."

He heads for the kitchen like a robin after a worm. At least here by the window, I can smell fresh air. I scoot as close as possible to it and gulp down the nausea. What I do to protect my friends. This is not going to be fun.

CHAPTER 52

T HE CHIANTI IS SMOOTH, FULL-BODIED, GOES
down easy. I had planned to drink beer, but Ted sends
a bottle over and before we know it, it's empty and David is
calling for a second. By the time the first course arrives,
huge plates of pasta with rich, red marinara sauce chunky
with tomatoes and meat, David is on the third bottle. He's
nice and relaxed. He's also famished. Chopping wood and
Gloria's angst have obviously built up a tremendous ap-
petite. Lucky for me, he's hungry enough to consume both
our dinners, hardly noticing that I keep ladling my portions
onto his plate. Having a big guy as a partner has its perks. I
can sit here sipping wine while he does the heavy lifting.

Keeping my nose pointed to the window, I start in on a
third glass of wine. Three glasses out of three bottles. It occurs to me that David is starting to look bleary-eyed. Even
with all the food, three bottles of wine take a toll. I don't
think David will be driving home tonight.

We finish up. I pay the bill minus the wine, which was

on Ted, and I end up helping David out of the restaurant. Ted tells us not to be strangers. David goes for his keys.

"No way. We're only a block from the cottage. You can crash at my place tonight."

David seems to be considering it, though I can't be sure if the vacant look is a thought being processed or the slide into a wine-and-food-induced stupor. It doesn't matter. He comes along at my urging, and we're halfway down the block when he stops. His eyes clear for a minute, and he looks at me with a frown of concentration, like he's remembering something important. He jabs a thumb back toward Luigi's.

"Wait. I can't leave my car out on the street."

At first, I don't understand. Then an image of my Jag flashes, and I realize he's concerned if there's some crazy out there vandalizing nice cars, his might be the next target.

Like, even if it hadn't been personal, a Hummer is in the same class as a Jaguar. We're talking elephant versus, well, jaguar.

"It's okay. I'll get you to the cottage and come back for the Hummer. I'll park it in the garage."

That appeases him. The frown smoothes back into blankness. We continue down the sidewalk, David under his own swaying steam. I unlock the door to the cottage, lead David to the couch, give him a push. He sits down abruptly.

"I'll go move the car," I say. "Then I'll come back and make up the bed in the guest room. You sit here until I get back, okay?"

His eyes are open and he appears to be listening, but I could swear he's already fast asleep.

I dig his keys out of the pocket of his jacket along with his wallet and cell phone. He doesn't stir. There's a "missed call" message flashing. It's pure nosiness that makes me hit the "hear now" button and press the phone to my ear.

"Hey, David, it's Tamara. If you get in before eleven, call me. I'm a night owl. Maybe we can still get together."

I erase the message and close the phone. My instincts were right. I'm glad David is here with me.

I put the phone on silent mode and place it along with his wallet on the coffee table. The keys I take with me on the run back to the parking lot behind Luigi's. In five minutes I'm cramming that tank into my garage. Lucky for me I had the garage built higher and longer than average. Otherwise, the Hummer would never fit. As it is, it's like squeezing paste into a toothpaste tube.

Another five minutes and I'm back in the house. David hasn't moved. He's still sitting up, his eyes are still half-open but he's snoring. I've never seen anyone sleep with his eyes open. I stare at him for a minute, trying to decide if I should carry him up the stairs to the guest room. What happens, though, if he awakens in my arms? No, better to lay him out here and cover him up with a blanket.

Which is what I do.

Finally, at eleven thirty, I'm in a pair of sweats and curled up in my bed with Frey's book open on my lap.

Here we go—chapter seventeen.

CHAPTER 53

THERE'S NO HEADING TO THE CHAPTER, NO HINT of what it contains. Once my brain has adjusted yet again to the difficulty that comes from deciphering calligraphy, I'm plunged into a history of demons in the world.

In the beginning (according to this text) was not the word. In the beginning were the demons, the first species in human form to populate the earth. They were the spawn of the fallen angels sent to a harsh and unforgiving new world to survive or perish on their own. Among the first demons were the vampires. They were the strongest and most vicious of the predators and soon held dominion over all the beasts. Their reign lasted for a thousand years.

Then the gods (and it's plural) decided the now warm and abundant earth had become a paradise, too good for the demons. They sent man, possessed him of brain and brawn, allowed him to multiply. They set him against the demons. Man triumphed. The demons were banished under-

ground, to the realm of darkness. Here the vampire stayed, coming forth only to hunt and feed, for a millennium.

The great flood came. Vampires survived in greater number than humans and once more, they walked in daylight. But humans were scarce, the vampire needed beasts to hunt. The werewolf was fashioned from man by the vampire with the help of powerful black magic. The half man, half beast was made to be the servant of the vampire. In human form, he could integrate into man's society. In wolf form, he could hunt and capture prey for the vampire master.

The vampire's curse is that he cannot propagate save through the transference of blood. The werewolf, created by a spell, could only exist at the will of the vampire.

Until the time of the change.

The gods were angry that the vampires once more held dominion over their earth. They saw the balance changing and knew the humans were soon to become fodder for a stronger demon race. They knew the balance could only be restored by introducing an enemy, one capable of defeating the vampire, one who did not live off the blood of their beloved humans.

They allowed the werewolf to evolve into a creature that could "reproduce" on its own, through its bite with the power of a talisman. Soon, the werewolf numbers increased until they were no longer a slave to the vampire but a formidable enemy. When the battle came, the werewolves proved too strong and their superior numbers drove the vampire underground once more.

A were's strength is in his animal form. It is also his vulnerability. Man soon learned to hunt the beast and the weres numbers were decimated. Because the vampire exists in human form, he could walk among man unnoticed. If he was careful and cunning, his identity as a demon would not be revealed. The vampire flourished, learning to live among his human hosts, learning to assimilate into man's culture, sacrificing the were to his adopted human family.

From that time forward, there existed a mutual enmity between vampire and werewolf. But there is also a psychic connection. A powerful vampire can control a were, take over its will. Make it do its bidding. It need only possess the were's talisman. Without the talisman, the were cannot make the change, giving the vampire the absolute power of life and death over it. The power transcends time and space, it is all encompassing and cannot be broken until the vampire is killed or until the were regains possession of the talisman. In either case, once the werewolf regains control, it is the vampire that perishes.

The chapter ends there. I close the book and let it rest on my lap. Is it possible? Could Avery have somehow transported his spirit or soul at the moment of his second death to Sandra? Is that what Tamara meant when she said it was Avery, not Sandra, speaking to me last night?

Why be so damned cryptic? Why not come out and say it? If it's true, when and how would Avery have taken possession of Sandra's talisman? She wasn't here when I was with him.

Was she? Was what I said to Tamara on the ride to David's cabin true? Was Sandra watching us the whole time I was with Avery? It makes my affair with him even creepier.

I need to talk to Tamara.

David's phone. I fling back the covers and run downstairs. I erased the message but he must have her number stored since he called her this evening. Sure enough, it's there. I memorize it to punch into my own phone when I return upstairs.

The phone rings five times before voice messaging picks up.

"Hi there. You've reached Tamara. If I don't answer, I

may be out baying at the moon. Leave me a message after the beep and I'll get back to you."

"Baying at the moon? Cute, Tamara. It's Anna. Call me."

I ring off and try to settle down to sleep. My mind, however, refuses to settle down. The idea that Avery could be alive in Sandra, able to control my emotions and project such fear, leaves me sick with dread.

IT'S A LONG NIGHT. WHEN I FINALLY NOD OFF, I'M awakened with a start by a sound from downstairs. It takes me a minute to realize it's not Avery come to get me, but the sound of running water. I glance at the clock. 7:00 a.m. David must have awakened, moved from the living room to the kitchen, and is making coffee.

Shit. I throw off the covers and jump out of bed. If he's going through cupboards or the refrigerator, he's going to notice I have no food. None. I know I should keep something around for this sort of human/vampire contact, but I never think of it. The only place I shop now is Starbucks.

When I appear beside him in the kitchen, the question is stamped all over his face.

"No wonder you're so skinny," he says, standing before the open refrigerator with the bag of coffee in his hand. "You have no food. Jesus, Anna, how can anyone have no food?"

I snatch the bag from his hand and take it over to the coffeemaker. "I've never liked to cook, you know that. I eat out. So what? I didn't expect to have a houseguest this morning. You should be thanking me for taking care of your drunken ass last night instead of criticizing me."

A flush like a shadow creeps over his cheeks. "I don't know what happened. I couldn't have had that much to drink."

"Try three bottles of Chianti. Ted's treat."

"Three? Bottles? By myself? Weren't you drinking?"

Should I tell him the truth? That I only had one glass from each bottle? Make me look like a wuss? Nah. "I had my share."

He rubs a hand over his forehead. "We split three bottles? How come my head feels like this and yours doesn't?"

"Isn't it obvious? I hold my liquor better than you."

He grunts and takes a seat at the table. While the coffee perks, I get two mugs down from a nearly empty cupboard. It's a good thing I caught him before he started going through the cupboards. Otherwise, he'd be making some comment about the lack of dishes right along with the lack of food. Everything I'd had was destroyed in the fire. I never got around to replacing them. I will now. I'll buy some dishes and a few canned goods.

Soon.

Today I have to track down Tamara. Kick her ass for what was done to my car. I should see Jason again, too, and call my dad about O'Sullivan and the "stolen" formula.

It's going to be a long day.

CHAPTER 54

DAVID LEAVES AT EIGHT, AFTER COFFEE, TO GO home and change. The body shop opens at nine, which gives him enough time to take me to Charmer's for the loaner and be at the hospital to speak to Gloria's doctors at ten.

His day will be far less complicated than mine, though I see how uneasy he is with the prospect of being alone again with Gloria. Magnanimously, I offer to stay with her tonight when he's on his date with Tamara. He immediately thanks me for the offer and accepts. Considering I don't intend to let that date happen, I should feel guilty about the deception.

I should feel guilty.

I don't.

When he's gone, I debate trying to reach Tamara again, but decide instead to call Frey. He gave me the book. Maybe there's more he can tell me about devamping a werewolf. I go upstairs to make the call.

Layla, his girlfriend, picks up. "Hello, Anna," she says with a decided lack of enthusiasm.

"Has Frey left for school yet? I need to speak with him."

She sighs into the phone. "Today is a teacher workday. He doesn't have to be on campus until ten."

"May I speak to him please?"

She slams the phone down on some hard surface with enough force to make me wince. Nice talking to you, too, Layla.

In a moment, Frey is on the line. "Anna?" He sounds relieved. "Are you all right?"

"Why wouldn't I be?"

"Why? You were meeting a werewolf. Did you read the book?"

"That's why I'm calling. I need more information about vampires and werewolves. The book says a powerful vampire can psychically control a were. What about physically?"

"Physically?"

"Is it possible for a vampire to—I don't know how to put this—*teleport* his spirit or soul to a were? So that the vampire is actually in control of the werewolf both mentally and physically?"

There's a long minute of silence. "What vampire? What werewolf?"

"Can you answer the damned question? Is such a thing possible?"

"Are you speaking of Avery?"

Frey is a member of the Watchers, a group of supernatural beings whose purpose is to protect mortals against creatures who would prey on them. I used to be a member, too. He knows my history. What I didn't tell him myself, Williams did, so it doesn't surprise me that he'd assume I might be talking about Avery. Because of that, I answer simply, "Yes."

I fidget impatiently through another protracted silence, finally breaking it myself to say, "I don't know why you're taking so long to answer the question. Either it's possible or it's not."

"Anna, you were the instrument of Avery's second death," Frey replies. "Why would you ask such a question?"

Another evasion. I swallow my impatience and tell him. All of it. Who Sandra is. How her eyes and voice became different when she repeated words Avery had spoken to me that last evening. How she was wearing the same dress I had on that night, a dress Avery had given me. How my body's sexual response to her is the same as it was with Avery. How the fear I felt before I ran away was exactly the mind-numbing fear I felt when fighting him for my life.

All of it.

When I'm finished, Frey's hushed tone frightens me as much as his words when he says, "You must be careful, Anna. If Avery is powerful enough to do as you suggest, you are in grave danger."

"If? You don't know if it's possible?"

"It's never been recorded. There have been rumors. I know of two that speak of vampires inhabiting a were-wolf's body at the moment of second death. Neither ended well. If Avery accomplished such a thing, he could live on in Sandra's body indefinitely as long as he allows her to make the change. If he does not, she will die and he may jump to another host."

I take a moment to process what he's telling me. "The book says the vampire can be exorcised. How?"

"That magic has been lost. Probably just as well. It would be powerful and black and not easily invoked. There would be violent repercussions to the one casting the spell, perhaps lethal repercussions. Exorcism is not an option."

Which leaves only one. Find the talisman. Free Sandra. "Finding the talisman is the only way to stop him."

Frey's silence confirms it.

"Then I know what I have to do, don't I?"

Frey lets a heartbeat go by before he says, "There is something else you should know. Something not in the book."

"I don't like the way you say that. What is it?"

"Through the centuries, vampire physiology hasn't changed. Adaptation allows you to walk in daylight, but most things are the same as they were in the beginning. Your system absorbs nutrients from ingested blood without benefit of a digestive tract, you have superhuman strength and agility and heightened senses, and you are invulnerable to *mortal* disease. But there is one thing, a toxin, that the vampire is vulnerable to and once infected, there is no cure."

"Why are you telling me this now?"

"Because it's something you need to know before you face the were again. There is one way the toxin is introduced and one way only. Through the bite of a werewolf."

I'd moved to the deck outside my bedroom, watching a cold December morning break over the water. Frey's words echo in my head, triggering two different emotions as the implication of what he's telling me becomes clear. The first is anger. Much of my adjustment to life as a vampire has been forged on the anvil of anger. Its burn is familiar, almost reassuring. I've grown used to it.

But the second emotion, disappointment, is far more devastating. That Frey would withhold something this important is incomprehensible. When I try to speak, the sense of betrayal rises in my throat and words won't come.

"Anna?" Frey's voice is gentle, prodding.

My impulse is to hang up. Instead, I swallow hard and manage to say, "Why didn't you tell me this before? When you gave me the book, for instance?"

A pause. "You told me you had *business* with a were. I thought if you read the book, you'd rethink doing any kind of business with a were. You didn't say it was personal. You didn't say it was a were with a vendetta. I should have told you. I'm sorry."

A comforting tide of rising anger swamps betrayal. "You should have told me? A werewolf bite is deadly to a vampire. Why the fuck isn't that in your books?"

"It's a rather new development," he says, retreating into a professorial tone from the guilt laden. "The pathology only showed up in the last hundred years or so. The book was written in the fifteen hundreds."

"Does Williams know about this toxin?"

A hesitation. "I don't know."

The hesitation gives it away. "A vampire as old as Williams? What are the odds he doesn't know?"

Frey doesn't let himself get drawn in. He must sense where I'm going with this because he adds, "I can't believe Williams would ever deliberately put you in danger. Anything he's done, he's done with your best interest at heart."

Best interest? As a human or a vampire? I can think of several things he's done that were definitely not in the human Anna's best interest. Because of it, and because of his arrogance, I'm not convinced Williams has a heart.

I'm not convinced Frey is telling the truth, either.

I hear Frye's quiet breathing on the other end of the line. I've made him uncomfortable, questioning Williams' motives in keeping me in the dark. Not that it matters. My path is clear.

"Are all weres infected?"

"I don't know for sure," Frey answers. He sounds relieved that I've changed the subject. "It's best to assume they are. The only accounts we have are of deaths that have occurred. There are none of vampires surviving a bite."

Great. "Is there anything else you've neglected to tell me?"

"Just be careful, Anna. I wish you could walk away from the were but if what you suspect is true, if Avery has taken over Sandra's body and mind, I know that's not possible. He would have killed David to sever the bond between you. He is as powerful and vengeful now as he was then. Who knows who he will target this time to get back at you."

CHAPTER 55

AFTER I HANG UP, IT TAKES A MINUTE TO GALVA-nize myself into action. The resentment I feel, toward Frey for not simply telling me everything when I was at his house instead of giving me that damned book and toward Williams for letting me blunder off to meet Sandra without a warning, takes some swallowing. I want to call Williams, confront him because I will never believe he didn't know about the toxin. The question is why he wouldn't tell me about it. He's always looking for ways to draw me into the fold. Or to scare me.

I trudge upstairs and into the shower, head still spinning with possibilities.

There could be other reasons he might not tell me.

One terrible reason. Frey asked a very important question: if it is Avery, who else might he target to get back at me? He already went after David. Would my family be next? Might Williams let that happen? Might he see that as a way to sever the last links I have with humanity? Or might it be that Williams is sick of our sparring and wants to be rid of *me* once and for all? Let me tangle with the were, get bitten, and watch me die. Either way, his problem is solved. We began as enemies; maybe we've come full circle.

By the time the front doorbell rings, promptly at nine, I've showered, changed, but am far from ready. I'm sick with the implications of Williams' treachery and know I have to confront him. But right now, I open the door to find David talking on his cell, a stupid grin on his face. He rings off and slips the phone into his jacket.

"Tamara," he says, though I didn't ask. "We've moved our date up to four. Going back to the cabin. I'm going to cook her dinner."

"Four? That's pretty early. I do have things to do today, you know."

He looks down at me. "You said you'd stay with Gloria. You owe me this, remember?"

Shit. I grab my jacket and purse from the back of the couch. I do owe him. My timetable got moved up: Call Jason, see my dad, find that damned talisman without being attacked and bitten by a werewolf. Go after Williams. All in time to make sure Sandra and her crew are out of town before 4:00 p.m.

Bloody piece of cake.

CHAPTER 56

CHARMER'S BODY SHOP IS IN A STRIP MALL RIGHT off the South Bay Freeway in Chula Vista. At first, the inconspicuous location and modest look of the place makes me wonder if I was wise in trusting my car to a local instead of taking it to the dealership. Once inside the big prefab building, however, my misgivings are put to rest. Workers in spotless white jumpsuits swarm over a Ferrari, a Mercedes, a vintage Corvette and my Jag. It's already up on risers, the prep work for the new paint job under way.

Charmer smiles a greeting and jabs a thumb toward the car. "Forgot to ask you last night. Same color? We can change it if you'd like."

I shake my head, unable to drag my eyes off the damage that was done to my car. It looks even worse under the harsh glare of overhead lights. "No. The original British Racing Green."

He nods his approval and leads us out of the building to the back. He hands me the keys to the loaner. The candy-apple red Mustang sparkles under the overcast sky like a jewel. Seeing it lifts my spirits.

"Sure you don't want to take the Hummer?" David asks in a wistful voice.

I snatch the keys from Charmer before David can. "No. Thanks." I look up at Charmer. "You sure it's all right for me to take this? It's such a beautiful car."

"You're not going to let it get trashed, too, are you?" His face is serious, but his tone is not. He grins. "Of course. Have fun with it."

The Mustang engine growls to life when I turn the ignition. David still has that little-boy look of yearning on his face when I pull out. I wave to them both, then double-clutch it when I hit the road. The Mustang responds like a race car. I feel like Steve McQueen.

At least one thing will be fun today.

I head back downtown to the office to call Jason.

When I pull into my office parking space, I notice a car parked in David's. It's one of those hybrid models, painted a dull pastel green. Looks anemic beside the Mustang. I don't recognize it. David won't be happy, especially since both our spaces are clearly marked "reserved." He can take care of it. I need to get in and out.

The keys are in my hand and I'm right at the door when someone steps out from the bay side of the building.

"Jason?"

He looks tired and scared, and I open the door and motion him inside.

"What's the matter?"

The kid stares down at his shoes and I realize he's wearing the same clothes he had on when I saw him at his house yesterday. I point to a chair. "Sit. I'll make coffee." I get it going and check out the small, under-the-counter refrigerator we keep in the office. "There's not much here, but there are some day-old bagels. Are you hungry?"

He still hasn't said a word. I go ahead and pull out the bag and a carton of cream cheese. Having a human partner who eats real food has come in handy twice now in the last twenty-four hours. Thank you, David.

I don't press Jason until he's eaten half a bagel and had a few swallows of coffee. Then I sit down opposite him. "What happened to you?"

Jason finally meets my eyes. "I didn't tell you everything," he says.

"About?"

"My stepmother. Gloria. What I overheard the day my dad was killed."

"Want to tell me the truth now?"

He nods, starts fiddling with the coffee cup.

"Tell me."

"I did overhear my dad and Laura the morning he was killed," he says. "It wasn't about any kind of criminal investigation. He was arguing with her about something he'd done to a colleague. I don't know the details. It didn't make sense then. Whatever he did cost somebody a lot of money, and Dad thought the guy was coming after him. He sounded scared. He wanted us to leave. Laura said she wouldn't go. She ran out, and Dad ran after her."

"What happened then?"

"I went into his study. I found something."

He dips a hand into his pocket and pulls out an envelope. I recognize it as the one I found in his room. He offers it to me, and I take it.

While I open it, he says, "I didn't know what it meant until I saw the newspaper yesterday."

My own paper is open on the desk where I left it after getting Dad's call. He taps the article about his father. "I think they were right. I think Dad took the formula and sold it. I think somebody at that Benton company killed him."

CHAPTER 57

"SO WHY THE LIES, JASON?"

He frowns bitterly. "I hate Laura. She doesn't even try to be nice. When she moved in, the first thing she did was go through the house and throw away anything that belonged to my mother. Do you know what she said to me last night? She said the best thing my dad could have done for us was to die. That it saved us a lot of trouble."

He wipes a hand across his eyes. "She didn't know about the lawsuit or what Dad had done. She didn't really care who killed him, she just wanted to make Gloria look guilty."

"So, you know for sure that she found out about Gloria and your father?"

"She must have. My dad told her someone was after him. She lied to the police anyway."

"And the gun, did you plant that so I'd find it?"

"Yeah. I figured you'd found it when I checked last night and it was gone. I kept waiting for the police to show up."

"Where did you get it?"

"It's Laura's. She keeps it in the glove compartment of her car."

"Which you saw when you were out shopping with her. You've known all along it wasn't the murder weapon." Only a kid's logic would make moving it and planting it in so obvious a place seem a reasonable thing to do.

Jason is quiet for a moment. "What's going to happen now?"

"Good question. Gloria's lawyer is attempting to get a search warrant as we speak. It will take the police about five minutes to prove it wasn't the murder weapon." I lean back in my chair, eyeing him. "Why didn't you go home last night?"

He looks at me as if I've performed a magic trick.

"I saw you yesterday. You came home before I could leave. You were wearing the same clothes you're wearing now."

"But I never saw you."

"You weren't supposed to. Now answer my question."

His features contort with an expression that's half panic, half anger. "Laura heard me talking to Gloria last night. She knows I planted the gun. She threw me out of the house."

"Where did you spend the night?"

"Here. I got the address from your card. I didn't know where else to go, and I thought I should talk to you this morning."

"How did you get here? It's a damn long walk from Fairbanks Ranch."

He reaches into his jeans and pulls out a set of car keys.

"You drove? Jason, you're fourteen. Where did you get the car?"

He mumbles something I don't quite catch. The key chain's logo matches the hybrid in David's parking space. "You didn't steal a car, did you?"

He shakes his head. "No. It was my dad's. I've been driving since I was twelve. Learned on our ranch in Wyoming. We have so many cars, I doubt anyone will even notice it's gone."

I stand up, grab both sets of keys, his and mine, and motion for him to join me. "Come on. We'll worry about returning the car later. Right now we're going to see Gloria's lawyer and you're going to tell her what you told me. After, we'll get you home. I'm pretty sure Laura can't keep you out. She's committed a crime by deliberately lying to the police. If anyone will be spending the night away from home tonight, it's likely to be her."

There is one other thing.

"How involved are you in Gloria's suicide attempt?"

A half shrug. "I only bought the pills and made the nine-one-one call. She made me leave before she started taking them."

"The police have the pills. Are they going to find your fingerprints?"

A smile. "No. I bought everything in boxes. Paid cash at different grocery stores. When I got them home, I took out the bottles wearing rubber gloves. I burned the boxes and the bellman uniform. I didn't touch anything in the room. There shouldn't be anything to connect Gloria and me in that hotel."

Thank you, *Law and Order*. At least some of the lessons sunk in. Jason missed the episodes about ballistics, but he learned how to cover his tracks. Unless he got caught on a hotel security camera. If he did, we'll hear about it soon enough.

God, what was Gloria thinking? Jason is a kid, but she certainly should have known better. There'll still be a phone record of calls between them, although that can be explained away because Jason and Gloria know each other through his father. Condolence calls, Detective Harris, that's all.

"Okay, let's go see Gloria's lawyer. Don't talk about anything except what you heard the day your father was killed. Don't volunteer anything about the gun. She knows I found one. Let's hope she hasn't already reported it to Detective Harris. No more lies. No more saying what you think will get Gloria off."

I take him by the shoulders and make him look me in the eye. "There isn't anything else, is there?"

He looks ready to cry. "I wanted to help Gloria. I wanted to make the police look somewhere besides at Gloria. Now all I've done is screw things up and make her look guiltier. Why are the police going to believe anything I have to say now? Unless Laura backs me up, it's my word against hers."

"Not necessarily." I tap the newspaper. "You may have corroboration. Right here."

CHAPTER 58

J AMIE SUTHERLAND'S OFFICE IS LOCATED ON ONE of the posh top floors of a high-rise that has come to be known as the Darth Vader building. It's tall, black and pierces the skyline like a sword. Her door says "Sutherland, Talmadge and Gates, Attorneys at Law." Her name is first. Senior partner. For one so young, it's quite impressive.

I called to let her know we were on the way and she's waiting for us in the reception area. I introduce her to Jason as she leads us into a book-lined corner office with a view as impressive as her title. Once we're settled into richly up-holstered visitors' chairs, she urges Jason to begin.

Jamie listens to Jason's story with sober concentration. She lets him talk without comment or interruption. For his part, Jason does exactly what I told him. He doesn't men-tion the gun or the hotel room. When he's done, she crosses her arms over her chest and leans back in her chair.

"When your father was telling your mother that he thought someone was after him, did he mention a name?"

Jason frowns. "I don't remember—" He lapses into silence, then after a moment, sits up straighter in his chair. "Wait. He didn't mention a name exactly, but he did say it was a doctor on the research team, one of the directors, I think."

I point to the newspaper I brought with us. "All the directors are listed in this article. They're also all plaintiffs in the suit being brought against O'Sullivan's estate."

She picks up the article. "Well, being cut out of a billion-dollar deal would definitely cause hard feelings. What I'm wondering, though, is why kill him if you're planning to sue?"

I think of the questions I was going to ask my dad when I read the article the first time. "What if the suit had no merit? Jason said his dad told Laura he'd cost a colleague a lot of money. It seems to me that O'Sullivan was a shrewd enough businessman to have made sure he owned the rights to any marketable formulas his team came up with. So maybe what he did wasn't illegal, but it certainly would have pissed off somebody who'd expected to share in the profits. With O'Sullivan dead, it'd be far easier to deal with Mrs. O'Sullivan, coerce her to settle simply to avoid a nasty court battle."

"Laura definitely wouldn't want a battle," Jason says bitterly. "Dad's only been gone a couple of days and she's already got lawyers checking into how much of my father's estate I'm entitled to and how much is hers. She's even contacted my grandparents to see if I can live with them. She wants to get me out of her life as quickly as she can. She'll want to get this suit settled, too."

Jamie taps a manicured fingernail against the arm of her chair. "I'm going to call Detective Harris. Jason, I want you to tell him what you told me. He's already suspicious of some of the things your stepmother said. For instance, the police have determined there were no irregularities with the books at the restaurant. There is no proof that your father and Gloria were having an affair. Now that he's gone, all she has is suspicion. Gloria certainly won't testify about it. We won't get Gloria off this minute, but we can point Harris in another direction. It's a start."

Jason doesn't look convinced, but he does agree to talk to Harris. While Jamie makes the arrangements, I ask him if he wants me to stay. I'm relieved when he says no. I still have business to settle with Sandra, and the sooner I attend to it, the sooner I'll feel safe in my own skin.

Before I leave the lawyer's office, I take Jamie aside. I give her my father's number in case she has questions about O'Sullivan's dealings with Benton Pharmaceuticals. I also give her the invitation. She recognizes the implications immediately. Then I tell her where Jason spent last night. She doesn't ask why or if Laura kicked him out, and I don't volunteer it. Jason is a minor, and she says she'll make sure he gets home when they're finished. From her tone, I have a feeling she's hoping Laura will give her a reason to exercise some legal muscle against her. I do, too.

After that, I'm on my own. Up to this point I've given no thought as to how I'm going to take care of my problem with Sandra. I know what I have to do, find that talisman. Maybe Tamara can help.

This time, when I call her, she picks up.

"Anna. I was about to call you."

"Yeah. I'm sure."

"Did David tell you he's cooking dinner for me tonight?"

Not if I can help it. "Yes, but I need to talk to you first. About Sandra's problem."

There's a moment of dead air. "You believe me now?"

"Yes."

"Why?"

"Is that important? Do you want my help or not?"
"Where are you?"
"On my way to Avery's."
"Good. We'll be waiting."

CHAPTER 59

$\mathbf{M}$Y MOOD IS FAR DIFFERENT ON THIS TRIP TO see Sandra than it was on the first. No fancy dress, no sexual fantasies buzzing around my head like wasps around water. I want two things this time—free Sandra and send Avery to hell where he belongs. Every day I learn more about what it means to be a creature who is not human, and every day I find another reason to hate what I've become. If the alternative were not so bleak, if I didn't have my family and David to counterbalance the evil, it might be an unbearable burden.

What I'm going to do when they are no longer part of my life, I refuse to consider.

My eyes keep straying to the rearview mirror. It's been two days since Williams' watchdog and I had that unintentional run-in at Mister A's. During that time, I've yet to spot Tom's Escalade. Either he's changed vehicles or he's been pulled off the case by Williams and I have a new shadow.

Or Williams called off the surveillance altogether. Maybe he thinks it's no longer necessary to tail me since I won't be around much longer to cause him grief. One bite from a werewolf, and it's good-bye, Anna. Something he's wanted since the beginning. In spite of his lofty rhetoric, I've felt his resentment grow. He hasn't been able to fashion me in his own image any more than Avery could. And like Avery, allowing me to live as I wish is something he can't seem to accept.

Fuck him.

CHAPTER 60

A VERY'S GATE IS OPEN, AND I PULL THE MUSTANG up to the front door. It's easier to be here during the day. I pocket the car keys and start toward the door. It opens and Tamara steps out to meet me. She's dressed in jeans and a tight red jersey knit top. She's had a haircut since I saw her last. A fresh, feathery style that makes her look more feminine.

Too bad David is never going to get a chance to appreciate the effort.

"Cool car," she says. "What happened to the Jag?"

"Oh, you didn't hear? Somebody vandalized it. Looked like it was attacked by a pack of wild dogs. Imagine, in the middle of the day on a crowded street. Shocked the hell out of David and me."

Her lips form an O of surprise, but her eyes reflect only cold amusement.

"If the stunt was meant to get my attention," I say, "it worked. Here I am."

Tamara's look is cool, appraising. "David doesn't know what you are, does he?"

"No more than he knows what you are. It doesn't matter anyway. I'm here to help Sandra. Then I expect you and the rest of the pack to be on your way. No dinner date. No good-bye kiss. David is not going to become your mate or fuck buddy or whatever the hell you call males pressed into stud service. It's not going to happen, Tamara."

I didn't plan that speech. The words erupted when I saw the new, improved Tamara and guessed her game plan. As soon as they did, though, I had the stomach-clenching feeling that I'd said too much. Nothing like tipping your hand. Not too smart.

Tamara doesn't react the way I expect. No heated rebuttal. No threats. No hands-on-hips declaration that I can't stop her from doing whatever she wants. Her eyes and mouth tighten a bit at the corners. Then the shadow passes and she smiles. "You been practicing that speech?"

"Where's Sandra?"

She stands aside and points up the stairs. "Waiting for you. She isn't feeling well. Avery is preventing her from making the change. Do you know what that means?"

I gesture for her to go ahead of me—now that I know the consequences of a bite, I'm not about to turn my back on her. Then, I answer her question. "Yes. He's hidden her talisman. She'll die without it."

She nods. All I see in her eyes now is concern. "I've turned this place inside out. I'm hoping since you lived here for a while, you'd know if he had a hiding place. Something I've overlooked."

I do know, and Avery did have a hiding place. Before I share, I want to set one thing straight. "I didn't live here. Not really. Avery treated me in the hospital after I was attacked. He said he would help me through the transition.

He never mentioned a wife. I can't seem to make anyone understand that I have no interest in his estate. If Sandra wants it, she can have it. I haven't touched anything, nor had I been in the house before Saturday. Not once since he tried to kill me. Do you understand?"

Tamara listens with her head tilted, her hand on the doorknob to the front door. "There's only one thing wrong with your story," she says. "The part about not having any interest in the estate. Not exactly true, is it?"

"What are you talking about? I said I haven't been in the house. If something is missing, I didn't take it. Williams said there was a caretaker. Maybe—"

Tamara holds up a hand and laughs. "I don't think a caretaker arranged this."

"Arranged what?"

She turns her back on me and opens the door. "Arranged to have Avery's vineyard in France transferred to your parents," she says. "Avery is very angry about that."

CHAPTER 61

TAMARA IS WALKING AHEAD OF ME, INTO THE house. My own feet are rooted to the spot. It never occurred to me that the vineyard my parents "inherited" was Avery's. I didn't even remember before this moment that he owned one. How the hell was it possible that his winery ended up with my parents? Who could have made such a thing happen?

As soon as I ask myself that, the answer is there.

Williams.

It has to be. He'd been Avery's friend for hundreds of years. He knew everything about him. He was overseeing the estate because I wanted no part of it.

He wanted me free of human influence. He must have set this in motion months ago, before he knew about Sandra. It would take time to come up with a phony family tree and lay the foundation for the "inheritance."

Tamara stops when she realizes I'm not behind her and turns around. She studies me for a moment. "You didn't know? For real?"

I'm too dazed to do more than shake my head.

"Then who?" She pauses and a sharp flash of surprise widens her eyes. "Williams."

My turn to reflect surprise. "You know Williams?"

"Yes."

It's all she says. Then, "We should go to Sandra."

She moves off and I rouse myself to follow. My brain is still trying to process the implications of Williams' treachery. No wonder he came to see me at Glory's. He said nothing that prepared me for this, but he knew Sandra was about to discover what he'd done. Did he find out that Avery had come back in her body? I doubt it. Otherwise, he would not have been so calm. He'd know once Avery took care of me, he was likely to be next.

He almost got away with it, didn't he? My family may be packing right now for a future that can never happen. A future that's a lie. And I played right into it. I was suspicious, but I never connected the legacy to Avery.

Sandra coming here must have really upset Williams' plans. Did he decide to cut his losses? Feed me to the wolves and hope his part in the deception would go undiscovered?

Tamara has moved through the foyer and, instead of going to the living room, starts upstairs. I realize I have to pay attention to what's happening now or risk the consequences of being caught off guard by a werewolf who suspects me of deceit. Sandra (or Avery) knew all along what I've just found out. I doubt they'll believe it, though. I wouldn't.

Another shock wave hits when I realize where Tamara is taking me. Avery's bedroom. Shit. It was bad enough being in his living room. A tumble of emotions, all negative and too strong to deal with rationally, causes a predictable reaction.

The vampire surfaces.

Tamara is still walking ahead of me. Her own animal instinct causes her to falter, turn around. She senses the change. "We appreciate that this is hard for you. Being here. We wish you no harm. We need your help."

She stands at the door to the bedroom. His bedroom. My body trembles. If I enter that room, if I face Sandra knowing she is a vessel for Avery, I can't be sure how I will react.

Tamara watches. She sees the trembling, reads the conflict in my eyes. "Avery is asleep," she says. "You will be speaking only to Sandra."

How can she know this? The only sound I'm capable of making at this moment is a growl. It comes from a dark place, the pit of my soul. It is meant as a question and a warning.

Once again, she seems to understand. "When you called," Tamara says, "Sandra took a sedative. She knew Avery was sensitive to certain drugs. Since he has inhabited her body, we use the knowledge to allow Sandra respite from his control. It doesn't last long, and when it wears off, he exacts terrible retribution. It is Sandra who awaits you now. Not Avery."

She pushes open the door and waits.

I wait, too. For the blood to cool, for the fight reflex to dissipate, for reason to take back control.

I close my eyes, and when I reopen them, I'm ready.

CHAPTER 62

THE ROOM IS EXACTLY AS I REMEMBERED IT.
Heavy, dark furniture that looks like it belonged in a
castle and probably did at one time. Bookcases lining two
walls; a huge stone fireplace facing the bed. Arched windows send slanting rays of sunshine and shadow skittering
along the walls.

But something is different. It takes me a moment to identify what it is. The light. The light in the room is different.
It's December now, not July. The shift in the angle of a sun
moving in a low winter arc paints the walls in pewter instead
of gold. Even the fire blazing out from the massive hearth
can't remove the chill.

Tamara makes a sound in her throat. It brings me back,
and when I turn, I see Sandra for the first time.

She's lying propped up by pillows in Avery's bed. Avery's bed. At first my senses are overcome by his smell:
male, vampire, musk. Then I recognize with sickening clar-
ity that I'm there, too. A hint of perfume, of sweat. Those
silken sheets are permeated with the essence of our mingled

passion. Pheromones, testosterone, lust. How many times did we have sex in that bed? How can Sandra stand to lie there?

I realize that she's watching me. I center my thoughts and study her. She is pale, without makeup, her hair combed back from her face. She's wearing a nightgown, blue chiffon, translucent against the swell of her breasts. The blankets are gathered around her waist. Her hands are clasped on top. She exudes none of the strength, none of the sexuality, that captivated me before. The woman before me is a child, frightened, lost. It sickens me to realize that the same way he controlled me in life, Avery was able to control me through Sandra. I don't know how long I have before Avery resurfaces. I don't know that I could confront him in this room.

"Why did you wait so long to come here?" I ask her.

"Avery needed time to gather strength," she whispers. Her voice is strained, husky. Then, as if the act of speaking is painful, she raises a hand to her throat. "He tries to keep me from communicating. Even now."

Tamara steps to the bed and strokes Sandra's hair. Sandra turns grateful eyes to her, and Tamara takes up the story.

"Avery and Sandra met many years ago. She was a girl newly turned, and he a powerful vampire who was curious about the werewolf. In all his years, she was the first that didn't exhibit hostility to the vampire. In turn, he took her under his protection and allowed her to choose those of our kind willing to bind with her in a pack."

She looks away from Sandra and to me. "Do you know much about the werewolf pack?"

I shake my head. "Only what I learned recently from an old text. An alpha male dominates the pack. There are more male than female weres and that the female is always subjugated to the male. I remember in Culebra's bar, the proportion of male to female in your pack was reversed. Your pack is different."

Tamara smiles. "The text you read called it subjugation? I suppose that's as good a word as any. In reality, it's rape and often murder. The old laws are seldom followed. The alpha male takes what he wants. If a female survives, as I did, life becomes a nightmare. She is forced to live with the pack, forced to mate in human or animal form at the whim of any male, forced to work to provide money to sustain the pack. I was one of the lucky ones who escaped. I ran to Mexico. Where I met Sandra."

Sandra reaches up to clasp her hand. Tamara takes it, brushes a bit of hair from Sandra's forehead with a gentle touch, and continues.

"Sandra was a survivor, like me. She was with Avery at that time, and when he heard my story, he purchased a compound for us in the jungles of Mexico. Gradually other females found us. Our pack thrives because we are content to live in harmony with the nature of our beast. We live naturally, we do not propagate, we do no harm. The males that are with us are there for exactly the same reason. Freedom."

"The marriage—Sandra and Avery—when did that happen?"

For the first time, she looks uneasy. "There is no marriage. Avery forced that story on us as a way to regain his estate through Sandra. He thinks he can keep her here. He has become the thing he saved her from all those years ago. He has made her his prisoner."

"How did it happen? How did Avery take possession of Sandra?"

"I don't know. It was at the time of change. We were in the jungle, and suddenly Sandra fell ill. She was as the wolf, then her human body took over. It can't happen that quickly. The change must be gradual and when it's not, the pain is unbearable. She screamed and thrashed about, and when the wolf came back, Avery was there as well."

She draws a breath. "In the beginning, Avery was content to allow Sandra to live as we always have. He never prevented her from making the change. Instead, he seemed to revel in the transformation, the freedom of the animal hunt, the freedom from vampire bloodlust. None of us understood what was happening. Not really. He would talk to us sometimes, the way he did with you, but there was no hint of what was to come."

Sandra makes a mewling noise. When we look at her, she is frowning, her hand again at her throat.

"He is struggling to come back," Tamara says. "When he does, he'll punish her. We have to hurry."

"But how is it possible he could have hidden the talisman without Sandra knowing?"

Tamara is watching Sandra, looking for signs that Avery is back in control. "There are hours when Sandra awakens as if from a dream and remembers nothing of what has happened. It was during one of those periods that she discovered her talisman had gone missing. She thinks he did it because she was fighting him. Coming here, for instance, she refused as long as she was able. He has become too strong."

"If we get the talisman back, do you know what will happen to Avery?"

"If Sandra regains possession of the talisman, she can fight Avery as a wolf. He cannot sustain himself indefinitely in the animal body. He cannot escape. She will remain wolf until she feels him die. Only then will she turn back."

"How long will it take?"

Once more, Tamara strokes Sandra's hair, lovingly, like a mother with a sick child. "It could take days. A week. During that time, Sandra will not eat or drink. In ridding herself of Avery, she risks her own death." She raises her eyes to mine. "I believe you understand that though, don't you, Anna?"

Do I understand being willing to die to rid oneself of a monster? Yes. The same monster Sandra battles now.

"If it's here, in the house, I know the place Avery may have hidden the talisman."

I step to the fireplace. It has one of those massive stone fireboxes that is big enough to walk into with storage areas for wood on each side. The mantel is a solid slab of heavy, dark wood. There are two sconces anchored above it to the wall.

The fire scorches my skin as I get closer. I reach up, grab the sconce to the right and pull. There is a grinding sound and the left side of the fireplace moves in on itself. The storage area becomes a door and it opens into a long, dark staircase.

I hear Tamara's breath catch. Then she's beside me, peering into the void. "What's down there?"

"Treasure," I reply. "And pain."

CHAPTER 63

THE STAIRCASE IS WOODEN, AND THE PASSAGE plunges straight down. It is clammy inside, dark, steep, and, at first glance, without end. It is so narrow, Tamara must walk behind me. She crowds close. I don't like having her behind me. My senses are on high alert, the vampire ready to spring forth if it detects anything but the strange emanation of fear she's giving off.

Fear of what? The dark?

But we're nearing the bottom, and the smell of dirt and decay chases the question out of my head. I'm plunged into the nightmare of finding David at the bottom of these stairs, bound and near death.

At last our feet touch soil. Ahead of us is a doorway and it yields to my touch. I find the light switch to the right of the door and stand aside for Tamara to experience what I did that first time six months ago.

The room is large, a storage area with wooden crates stacked along one wall, rugs rolled and stored on another, rows of shelving occupying the center. The overhead light catches and reflects off the hundreds of items displayed helter-skelter on the shelves like the chattel of a deranged collector: piles of gold and silver jewelry, vases of bronze and silver, bejeweled ceremonial daggers, gold-leaf dinnerware that might have served a king. Chinese porcelain, Egyptian antiquities, Mayan pottery. The source of Avery's wealth.

Tamara picks up a small golden chariot and hefts it in her hand. "I know how Howard Carter must have felt when he found King Tut's tomb," she says in a hushed voice.

I point to what she holds. "For all we know, that could be from the tomb. Avery may have been there, too."

She returns the chariot to the shelf and looks around. "Do you know what's in the crates?"

I shake my head.

"You aren't curious?"

"No. This place holds bad memories for me. Avery holds bad memories for me. When this is over, Sandra can have it all."

I let my eyes sweep the contents of the shelves. "What does the talisman look like?" I ask. "The book said it was a belt of fur. Does that mean literally a belt of fur? Or is it something symbolic?"

Tamara joins me in the search, taking one side of a shelf while I, the other. "It's both," she says. "It's a locket that contains a bit of fur. At one time, it actually was a belt fashioned from the fur of a totem animal. Wearing a belt of fur marked us, made us easy prey for human hunters. Now we wear something a bit more discreet. Like this."

She pulls a small gold locket from inside the collar of her jersey top and lets the chain drop between her breasts. "We always keep it with us. It's our lifeline. Our most prized possession."

I've finished my side of the shelf, finding nothing that resembles what Tamara described. I wonder if I've made a mistake thinking it would be here. Yet, this is the repository for Avery's treasure. Where else would he hide it?

Tamara finishes, too, and comes around to join me. She's looking toward the far wall, the place where I found David. "What's over there?" she asks.

From our vantage point, what we see are rugs, rolled up and piled against the wall.

"Should we check it out?" she asks.

I have no intention of reliving the horror. "Go ahead. I'll keep looking here. Maybe we missed something."

She moves off and I make another pass at the shelves. I'm aware that she's now standing on the rug that once held David's body. I think I can still smell his blood, and it sends a tremor of horror through me.

In a moment, she's back beside me. "Nothing. You don't think it's in one of those crates, do you? Jesus. There are a hundred of them. We don't have time to open them all to check."

She starts toward the jumble of wooden crates stacked nearly ceiling high. I follow her, letting my eyes scan the pile. "The dust on these crates is undisturbed. I don't think anyone has been down here—" I start to add since the last time I was. I don't want to have to explain the circumstances of that visit, though, so I drop it.

Tamara frowns. "So what do we do now? Finding that locket is the only way to free Sandra and rid ourselves of Avery once and for all."

There's a flash of movement from the doorway. It catches my eye like the glint of sun on a mirror. Sandra appears at the bottom of the stairs as if conjured up by Tamara's words.

Gone is the vague emptiness that blighted her face, the helpless look of a lost child. She looks at me with the calm detachment of a predator. The neckline of her nightgown has been pulled lower, the outline of her body glows as if light were shining through.

I can't look away. Instantly, my senses spin out of control. She dares me to resist and I know I can't. I'm shivering. She is not close enough to touch me, not physically, and yet I feel her fingers trace a path over my skin, slide down my belly, skim between my thighs. Her fingertips brush against my sex, and I'm shuddering with excitement. She's there, tormenting me with a butterfly's touch. I want more. I want her to finish it. A moan escapes my lips, a plea for release.

A laugh, cold, bitter, breaks the spell.

"Ah, Anna." Her voice. His voice. "You haven't changed at all, have you?"

CHAPTER 64

FOR AN INSTANT, THE ROOM TILTS.
Tamara's voice: "It took you long enough."

I'm yanked back to the present as if from a dream, disoriented and confused. Then my head clears, and I remember.

Sandra's eyes shine with a light that isn't her own and she smiles at me with an expression that holds no warmth, no pleasure.

"What's wrong, Anna? What did I do?" she asks. Her lips move, but it is Avery speaking. "Nothing but respond to your desire. It was the same before. I never forced you to do anything you didn't want to do. You can't dispute it. Your body betrays you."

At once, warmth surges through me. A familiar spark of passion.

"Don't." I turn anger against the rising heat until arousal dissipates into ash. "I won't let you manipulate me again."

"You think you can stop me?"

"Sandra will stop you. We'll find the talisman."

"You mean that talisman? The one around Tamara's neck?"

I'm given no time to respond. A blur of something comes at me with tremendous speed. I pivot toward it, hands instinctively outstretched to bat it away. It's lupine, huge. My blow catches it at the shoulder and it falls back.

But how? Tamara's clothes are in a heap on the floor. She must have made the change while Avery was toying with me.

The wolf leaps to its feet and comes at me again, but this time I'm ready.

We circle each other, the vampire and the wolf. She is as big as a mastiff, gold in color, black lips curled back in a snarl. Her eyes are yellow with slit pupils that reflect more than animal intelligence. She is *aware*. Acting not instinctively as a beast, but deliberately. Is she under Avery's control? Until this moment, I wouldn't have thought it. Tamara sought me out to help Sandra.

Didn't she?

In the distance, Sandra begins to croon in a soft, low voice. The wolf pauses, listening.

"Sweet Tamara. I should have chosen you, but you and I will be one soon. We will be rid of this irksome body. Of Sandra." She steps closer. "You need only to kill Anna. It's the one thing I ask of you. The one thing Sandra denied me. She could not do it. You are stronger. You have the power. You know what you must do."

The crooning stops, and the wolf gathers herself to attack. I remember the words of the book.

Silver.

Silver is lethal to wolves.

I remember Frey's warning.

I must assume a werewolf bite is fatal. My back is against one of the shelves, and my hands grope behind me for something—anything—to use as a weapon. I can't take my eyes off her long enough to search. I can only feel and there is nothing that passes under my fingertips to offer protection.

For the first time, I realize that vampire strength and cunning is not going to be enough. I can't fight her because I can't let her get close enough to bite me.

I'm afraid. It twists around my heart and knots my stomach.

It's unfamiliar and disturbing.

Worse, Tamara senses it. She's in no hurry to attack. She creeps toward me, slowly, fangs bared. Does she know she need only to bite me once? Death may not be instantaneous, but it will be certain.

The muscles along her shoulders tense. She gathers her hind legs under her and snarls her intention. When she leaps, I grab the first thing my fingers close around from the shelf behind me, hurl it, and jump away.

The ceramic vase catches her under her left eye. It shatters, a shard settling deep into the eye socket. She tumbles back, yelps, shakes her head furiously until the shard falls away. Blood spurts from the cut. When I breathe it in, I realize it's human blood. It causes my own to quicken but I can't give in to the bloodlust. It's human blood, but it's not a human I'm facing.

I have to keep distance between us.

She's recovered. She looks for me, sniffing the air for my scent. I've moved to the middle of the room, between the rows of shelves. She catches my scent, howls in pain and anger, and comes after me.

The shelf facing me offers nothing I can use against her. She lowers her head and watches as I back up. Every instinct I have screams to meet her head on, snap her neck, drink her blood. Could I do it before she sank her teeth into my arm or hand?

I can't take the chance.

Think.

There were hundreds of silver objects scattered here among Avery's possessions. I know there has to be something I can use as a weapon. My eyes sweep the shelves.

Jewelry.

Goblets.

Bowls.

The wolf's ears flatten. Blood drips from a ruined eye socket.

There. On one of the top shelves. A dagger.

We move at the same time.

The wolf springs.

I leap straight up, grab the dagger.

The wolf touches down first, landing where I'd been standing, landing on nothing. She skids on the dirt. Clouds of dust rise under her scrabbling feet.

She whirls to face me, howling her frustration. Blood and spit spew out with her rage.

The dagger's blade is ten inches long. The hilt is heavy in my hand. Could I throw it at her? No, I couldn't be sure of a kill shot. The only chance I have is to get behind her, seize her behind the neck and plunge it into her before she can sink fangs into my hand.

How to do it?

The muscles under her pelt bunch; her hind legs draw into each other like a spring being tightened. She is taking her time, gauging the distance, waiting for me to make the first move.

I feint to the left. She hurls herself at me. I wait until I feel her breath on my face before stepping back and around. I dig my fingers into her mane and straddle her. She bucks against me, snapping at air and howling. I work an arm around her neck, yank her backward against me. Her smell, lupine, musk, human.

I plunge the dagger into what I can most easily reach, her

exposed belly. She screams in anger and pain, but the wound is not fatal. Blood, hot, fragrant, flows over my hand. She's pawing at the air, trying to shake me loose. I hold on, fighting her, fighting the vampire lust that thirsts for the blood. If I loosened my grip, a tiny bit, I could turn her to face me, reach her neck, drink.

Her jaws open wide, fangs seeking a target. Seeking skin to ravage, bone to crush. Mine.

I tighten my arm around her neck. Tighten my grip on the dagger. This time, when I plunge the dagger, I find the mark.

Find the heart of the beast.

For a moment the earth stills. Only the wolf moves. She thrashes, whimpers. I jump back and away. She does not come after me. She twists into herself, shuddering, jaws working in a desperate attempt to reach the dagger. Her clumsy, frantic efforts succeed only in driving it deeper.

Another heartbeat and the thrashing stops. The wolf's head falls to the floor. Then there's only the blood. It pumps still, seeping around the dagger, turning the fur crimson. The blood of the wolf/human calling to me. I command myself not to respond, not to move. My nails dig into the palms of my hands until it's the smell of my own blood that fills my head. My eyes remain riveted on the wolf. As if in slow motion, the transformation from beast to human begins.

I feel Sandra watching, too.

The fur retracts into the skin, the head reshapes, followed by the limbs. The vertebrae realign with a crack like the withered branches of a dead tree. The knife in the naked human chest looks much more deadly than in the wolf's. Tamara's face is contorted in death, her mouth open, teeth bared. Around her neck, two gold chains.

She had Sandra's locket all along.

CHAPTER 65

SANDRA HASN'T MOVED. WHEN I TURN TO HER, there is a spark of relief in her eyes. In the next instant it's replaced by fear and pain. She falls to her knees, doubled over, and a cry escapes her lips.

"What is it, Avery?" I say. "Your plans disrupted? You were clever, though; I never suspected Tamara."

I kneel beside Tamara's body and pull both chains over her head. The lockets are almost identical. "Which is yours, Sandra? Tell me and we can end this."

All she can do is clutch at her chest and throat. Avery prevents her from answering. He's exerting some kind of internal pressure that's choking her.

"Okay. We'll do it another way."

I approach Sandra, help her straighten enough to slip the chains over her head and let both lockets fall between her breasts.

There is an immediate howl of rage as Avery feels the talisman's power begin to usurp his own.

Sandra's strength is returning. She grabs my arm. "Go

now. I'm going to make the change. Lock us down here when you go. Don't come back. If I survive, I'll contact you."

"I can't leave you. Avery is my enemy, too. There must be something I can do."

She shakes her head. "This is my battle. Once I change, Avery will try to make me attack you. I may not be able to prevent it."

Still, I can't bring myself to go.

Sandra's eyes become hard. "You are not helping. Every moment you remain, Avery exerts himself more. You must go. One of us must survive in case . . ."

She doesn't finish it. She doesn't have to. If Avery survives, if he comes after me again in her body, I'll know what to do.

"What about the rest of the pack? Can they help you?"

She shakes her head again. "I sent them back to Mexico. Only Tamara remained. I now know why. She and Avery had plans of their own."

"But why? What did she hope to gain?"

Sandra sweeps a hand in a wide arc. "This. Now go."

CHAPTER 66

THE DOOR AT THE BOTTOM OF THE STAIRWAY HAS no lock. Before I leave the cellar, I heave one of the crates against the wall. A cascade of gold and silver coins tumbles out. It's not the contents of the crate I'm interested in, though, but the heavy wood that held it. I choose two boards.

The last image I see of Sandra is a half-wolf, half-human form curled in a fetal position on the floor. Her face is distorted by pain; she is whimpering in anguish. Avery is fighting her.

She clutches the talisman in a hand that's more beast than human. Her eyes are clear. Her resolve strong.

She'll win.

I pull the door shut and jam the boards against the handle. A physically strong, determined human might be able to break out. I doubt a wolf could.

It's not until I'm back upstairs, in Avery's bedroom, that my own rage takes over. I rip the bedclothes off the bed and throw them into the fire. I use my hands to tear apart the mattress and feed it piece by piece into the fire. If I could, I'd dismantle the bed. It's too heavy, too well constructed to yield to bare-handed vampire strength. I have to content myself with destroying anything that my skin comes in contact with, anything that touched Avery's body. When I'm finished, the only smell left is ash and smoke.

I sink into a chair, watch the smoldering remains of the dying fire. Wonder what is happening in the secret room deep beneath my feet.

Tamara wanted what?

Wealth?

A life in this mausoleum of a house?

All she had to do was kill me, and let Sandra die. Avery would jump to her body and the union would be complete. One beast inhabiting the body of another. Was immortality part of the bargain?

With me gone, there would be no obstacle to claiming Avery's estate. What she, what no one, seems to understand is that I would have gladly given it away. I will give it away. To Sandra when Avery is dead. Theirs may not have been a civil marriage, but the hellish union they experienced makes her more an heir than I will ever be.

The vineyard. What about the vineyard? Images of my parents and Trish, excited, exuberant, thrilled beyond words by the unexpected gift of a new life. How can I tell them the truth?

And Williams. What do I do about him?

I have no answers. Not yet.

The fire's last sputtering gasp is my signal to leave. A bedside clock reads 3:00 p.m. I look once more around a room I hope never to see again.

As I turn to leave, a muffled sound drifts up from the bowels of the earth.

The howl of a wolf.

CHAPTER 67

DAVID GREETS ME AT THE DOOR OF HIS CONDO, an impatient frown pulling at the corners of his mouth. He's wearing jeans and a polo shirt, and he has a leather jacket slung over one arm. "I thought you'd never get here. I'm going to be late. Tammy expects me at four."

Tammy isn't expecting anyone.

Ever again.

I furrow my brow in a puzzled expression of surprise. "She didn't call you?"

He crosses his arms over his chest, and the frown deepens. "What do you mean?"

"I mean she told me she would call you before leaving town. She didn't?"

"No. She didn't call me. What do you mean leaving town?"

I push past him and move from the door into the living room. Gloria reclines against sofa cushions on the couch. She's dressed in a silk sweat suit, her hair swept back from her face in a ponytail. Her face, though pale and devoid of makeup, brightens as she catches our conversation.

I want to warn her not to get her hopes up, that this does not change our bargain, but first, I continue the farce with David. "She had a family emergency. Back in Pennsylvania. I can't believe she didn't call."

David pulls his cell phone out of a pocket and lets his jacket fall to the back of the couch. He finds her number, punches the "send" button and puts the phone to his ear.

I have an image of the phone ringing in some inner circle of hell. I don't expect it to be picked up. It isn't. David leaves a message, a rather snarky message, and snaps the phone closed.

"Shit. I bought all this food." He gestures vaguely toward a couple of grocery bags sitting in a corner near the front door.

"Well, I'm sure Gloria is getting hungry. Aren't you, Gloria?"

She nods and David heaves a disgruntled sigh, but he gathers up the bags and takes a step toward the kitchen. "I can't imagine why she'd call you instead of me," he grumbles.

"I told you she was a flake."

He stops and turns around. "No. You told me you didn't know her very well. That she *might* be a flake. Thanks for nothing, Anna."

So once again, I'm the bad guy. First with Gloria, now with Tamara. I can't win.

David bangs things around in the kitchen while Gloria and I cool our heels in the living room. The silence between us is uneasy. I have nothing to say to her.

The sun is low over the water, casting an orange red glow that bathes the room. In a few minutes, the moon will rise. I wonder if Sandra can feel it. If Avery realizes that he is doomed.

I hope he does.

I'm restless and anxious to get out of here. I'd be gone already if I didn't think David would kill me. I have a feeling one of the reasons he made the date with Tamara was to avoid spending this first night alone with Gloria. I need to stay at least until she's in bed—her own bed—and asleep.

"Anna?"

Gloria's breathy whisper pulls me back.

"I want to thank you for what you've done. Jamie was here this afternoon. She told me Jason spoke to the police. DNA tests came back, too. They found something on Rory's clothes. It's not my DNA. Now they'll have to widen the investigation. They're issuing search warrants for the homes of Benton's board of directors. And Rory's corporate offices. He has to have a copy of the contract with the French company somewhere. Laura had to retract most of her story. She had to admit that Jason was telling the truth about what Rory said that morning."

That, at least, is good news. "Did Jamie find out why O'Sullivan would sell the formula instead of going ahead with its production on his own?"

She shrugs. "Your father offered one possible reason. He told Jamie pharmaceutical companies operate like any private industry—for profit. Foreign countries often don't require the same kind of expensive, time-consuming clinical trials our FDA does to approve a new drug. They may have offered to buy the formula and proceed on their own. Rory saw a way to make a lot of money right away. Cash in now and not have to wait. Or share. He took it."

O'Sullivan got greedy and impatient. Look what it cost him.

Gloria adds, "Jamie thinks it won't be too long before charges against me are dropped."

"Unless, of course, they nail you for that stupid fake suicide."

Without missing a beat, she says, "It was stupid, I know. I got so sick. I thought I'd get woozy, maybe, since I didn't really take that much. Flushed most of the pills down the john. I really didn't expect—"

She's telling the story like the worst part was getting caught with puke all over her nightgown. "God, Gloria. You are truly the most self-centered bitch I've ever met. Do you know the trouble Jason could get into if his part in your asinine scheme comes to light? He's a kid. Do you care?"

My voice shakes with the effort to keep from screaming at her. "Protecting him is the only reason I don't turn you in myself. You are a menace and should be locked up."

She looks so shocked at my tirade that if I weren't so angry, I'd laugh. The bitch really thinks she did nothing wrong.

David walks in then, and although he didn't catch the words that passed between Gloria and me, he does catch the tension.

"Jesus Christ. I can't leave you alone for five minutes. If you think I want to sit through dinner with the two of you, you're crazy. Anna, why don't you leave? I think you've done enough damage for one day."

"Damage? What damage? What did I do?"

He glares down at me, hands on hips. He's snorting like a bull ready to charge.

He works his jaw a few times and says, "You really expect me to believe Tamara called you to break our date? Just like that. A woman you claim not to know very well. I think you were the one who broke the date. I don't know why. Yet. I'll find out. She can't avoid my calls forever. I'll get to the bottom of this. Trust me."

He starts back into the kitchen, pausing once at the door to add, "Did you hear me? You can leave, Anna. Now would be good."

Gloria remains wisely silent, doesn't so much as raise her head to watch me leave. So much for making sure those two don't revert to the old ways. If they end up fucking, David has no one to blame but himself.

I close the door quietly behind me.

Well, I got my wish, I'm going home.

Thrown out of two houses in two hours. A new record.

CHAPTER 68

O N THE DRIVE BACK TO THE COTTAGE, REALITY hits. It's over.

I've done everything I can for Gloria. How her legal mess gets resolved is up to her lawyer and the police. As soon as she's strong enough, though, I'll make sure she moves back to the hotel. I wonder if I can sue for breach of promise if she tries to snake her way back into David's affections? One thing for sure, if she tries to renege on that, I'll make her life a living hell.

As for my relationship with David, he's mad at me now. He's been mad at me before. We'll work through it.

And Sandra? I wasn't able to help her the way I had hoped. It's a battle she has to fight alone. At least with Tamara gone, the odds are even. I'd go back to fight right along beside her if I thought it would do any good. Sandra was right, though, one of us has to survive. I hope this time, Avery is gone forever and that there are no other supernatural loopholes he can jump through.

That leaves only one thing unresolved. I grab my cell phone and hit Williams' number on speed dial.

He picks up on the second ring. I don't waste time with niceties. "The vineyard my parents *inherited*, is it legitimate?"

There's a hesitation, then, "Anna. Do you want to talk about it?"

"No. I want you to answer my question."

"If you mean would it stand up in court if challenged, yes."

He sounds neither surprised nor relieved to hear my voice. He asks no questions of his own. It's possible he already knows what happened in Avery's house. He seems to know everything else.

"You'd better be right."

I disconnect and toss the phone onto the seat. The message indicator chimes that there are messages waiting to be picked up. I'll get to them later.

Frey reminded me that as long as my family is here, they could become targets. I may not always be around to protect them.

The decision is made.

As for Williams, there will be time to deal with him later. There's something much more important I need to do first.

CHAPTER 69

ALL THE LIGHTS ARE ON IN MY PARENTS' HOME when I pull up. I run up the porch steps and let myself in. Trish, Mom and Dad are in the living room, taking ornaments *off* the Christmas tree.

"Hey. Did I miss something? Isn't it December seventeenth?"

The three turn at the sound of my voice and greet me with smiles all around.

Trish speaks first. "Grandma left about a million messages for you. We decided to spend Christmas in France." She dances up to me, trailing icicles in her wake. "You can come, can't you?"

I don't know what to say. I never expected this—that they'd be leaving so soon. I can't go with them. In the car, I was prepared to let them go. But not now. Not this soon. I wanted time to get used to the idea. Time to make them understand that my life is here.

Then a wonderful thing happens. My mother takes Trish's arm in one hand and mine in the other. She turns us toward the tree. "It's all right if Anna can't come this trip," she says, squeezing my arm gently. "We really haven't given her much notice. She has a business to run as well as a partner who depends on her. There will be plenty of opportunities for Anna to visit when we're settled."

I glance over at my dad, realize as he does what her words mean. Somehow he did it. He made her understand that my life is here. We grin at each other.

Trish hands me a small, rectangular box from underneath the tree. "Then you have to open your present now," she says. "Go on."

I take a seat on the couch and tear away the paper. I recognize the symbol on the green box before I even open it. "Whoa," I say at first sight of the stainless-steel and gold Rolex. "This is too much, Trish. I can't accept this. You shouldn't have spent this much money."

"It's from all of us, honey," Dad says, joining us on the couch. "It's to remind you of your family. Each time you look at it, you'll know we're a plane ride away. This is just one Christmas. There will be others. We have all the time in the world."

I look from one wonderful face to the other. Time. I'm hit with a surge of such powerful love it leaves me breathless. They can't understand what time means to a vampire. I don't fully understand it myself. Nor do I understand what lies ahead for me. What I do understand is the sacrifice my mother is making. For me. She's letting me go. The fissure between us is gone, healed with a single selfless act.

I slip the watch on my wrist. "I'll never take it off," I tell them, feeling the tears roll down my cheeks, not bothering to try to stop them or to wipe them away.

Soon we're all crying.

Crying.

What a magnificent, liberating, *human* thing to do.